W9-ARI-147

DISCARD

Date: 5/26/11

LP MYS RICHARDS
Richards, Emilie,
A truth for a truth

A TRUTH FOR A TRUTH

This Large Print Book carries the
Seal of Approval of N.A.V.H.

A Truth for a Truth

Emilie Richards

THORNDIKE PRESS
A part of Gale, Cengage Learning

GALE
CENGAGE Learning

Detroit • New York • San Francisco • New Haven, Conn • Waterville, Maine • London

GALE
CENGAGE Learning™

Copyright © 2010 by Emilie McGee.
Thorndike Press, a part of Gale, Cengage Learning.

LIBRARY OF CONGRESS CATALOGING-IN-PUBLICATION DATA

Richards, Emilie, 1948–
    A truth for a truth / by Emilie Richards.
      p. cm. — (Thorndike Press large print core)
    ISBN-13: 978-1-4104-3625-2 (hardcover)
    ISBN-10: 1-4104-3625-X (hardcover)
    1. Sloan-Wilcox, Aggie (Fictitious character)—Fiction. 2. Spouses of clergy—Fiction. 3. Murder—Investigation—Fiction. 4. Ohio—Fiction. 5. Large type books. I. Title.
PS3568.I31526T78 2011
813'.54—dc22   2010050886

Published in 2011 by arrangement with The Berkley Publishing Group, a member of Penguin Group (USA) Inc.

Printed in the United States of America
1 2 3 4 5 6 7 15 14 13 12 11

For Michael, who isn't Ed,
but still understands both
Aggie and me perfectly.

ACKNOWLEDGMENTS

My thanks to Bill Peters, whose knowledge of the inner workings of churches and his willingness to share what he knows was invaluable for this novel.

1

The Reverend Godwin Dorchester always claimed that he wanted to die in the pulpit, hands lifted toward the heavens, gaze riveted on whatever parishioner needed his message the most. Godwin, better known as "Win" to his congregations, thought his last breath ought to be put to good use, seeing as none would follow, and his chance to change the world would be over with one dramatic flourish.

Personally I'm hoping to use *my* final exhalations to say good-bye to the people who love me, but then I'm not a minister. I'm only married to one. And my husband Ed, Win's successor to the ministry of the Consolidated Community Church of Emerald Springs, Ohio, is young enough that dying breaths aren't high on his list of things to worry about quite yet.

In fact, right now my husband is worrying about Godwin Dorchester's memorial service. In half an hour Ed will raise his own hands and fasten his gaze on somebody in Win's honor. Because Win did *not* die in the pulpit. He died taking out the garbage. And according to Hildy, his wife of almost fifty years, the last thing Win said was "911," which was neither inspirational nor effective. Win was dead before he did a nosedive into the garbage can and found eternal rest on a biodegradable trash bag.

"Doesn't that strike you as some kind of divine retribution? Dying facedown in a garbage can?" My good friend Lucy Jacobs stopped slathering hummus on slices of whole grain bread at my kitchen table, and pointed her knife toward heaven in emphasis.

Lucy was helping me put together a tray of sandwiches for the reception following Win's memorial service. She slathered, then I covered her handiwork with slices of cucumber, grated carrot, and alfalfa sprouts. Assembly-line cooperation comes naturally to us, because Lucy and I flip houses together. Compared to installing drywall, sandwiches are a cinch.

"First, Unitarians aren't big on divine retribution," I told her, though the fine points of theology are usually not part of our conversational repertoire. "So I'm not

10

reading anything into the way Win died. But if I did believe in a God who points fingers and yells 'Zap,' I'd think he had it in for me. For the last week Hildy has told me every single detail of Win's final moments, over and over, including everything else in the garbage can."

"You have to learn not to listen so well."

"That's not the half of it. When she finishes, and I'm trying to rid my mind of those images, I get these impromptu whispered conferences about how I can become a better minister's wife."

Lucy rolled her eyes. One of the things I love most about Luce is her complete lack of interest in joining our church. She's a nominal member of a Reform synagogue, but she thinks organized religion is an oxymoron. To Lucy, Aggie Sloan-Wilcox is just an unexpected bargain she happened upon one day in a long checkout line at Kroger.

She went back to work, plastering hummus with a vengeance. "*Better* minister's wife? Exactly what are your shortcomings?"

"Too numerous to mention."

"Try me."

I layered and sliced as I weeded the casual indictments — clutter on the kitchen counters and matted leaves in the flowerbeds — from the more serious.

I began as graciously as I could. "First, you have to understand Hildy really does believe she's helping."

"Helping whom?"

"She's hard to dislike."

"I'm having no problem so far."

"You haven't even met her."

"For which I'm properly grateful."

I looked up. "Hildy and Win moved to Emerald Springs a month ago and rented a house for the next year to see if they wanted to spend retirement here. You *might* have met her if you'd been around more, Luce. Not off traveling to who knows where."

Lucy didn't look up. All I could see was a mop of red curls falling over high cheekbones and a long, graceful neck. "I told you *where.* I was in California. San Francisco, then Monterey."

"Where" was really unimportant. Lucy had been missing for almost ten days. I had my suspicions about "whom" she'd been with, but Lucy would tell me in her own good time if she and Kirkor Roussos, Emerald Springs's hottest police detective, were now an item.

And did I ever want to know!

"Well, it seems I'm not doing enough to enhance Ed's career," I said instead. "I've

12

kind of, well, you know, made a name for myself in our fair city."

"I'm guessing she's not worried about you flipping houses." Lucy looked up. "Not that there's much to worry about along those lines."

In theory Lucy and I are still in business, but we recently completed picture-perfect renovations on a house that we haven't been able to sell again. Any profit we've made on our flipping venture is draining away on those mortgage payments, due to a miserable economy. We're more or less in a holding pattern now. I *hold* the want ads looking for new employment opportunities. She *holds* copies of our bank statements and moans.

I shook my head. "Not the houses, no."

"Well, I suppose tracking down murderers is a bit outside the usual wifely duties," she said.

Of course Lucy had nailed the other thing I'm known for in Emerald Springs. For some reason little ol' minister's wife me is a homicide magnet.

I slapped a piece of bread in place with a satisfying squish, then I hacked away mercilessly until I realized I was creating enough bread crumbs to track Hansel and Gretel to India. I stopped, blew a strand of hair off my face, and tried to keep my tone cheerful.

"There *are* no usual duties. I'm married to a man who chose to become a minister. I haven't signed any contracts, pledged any oaths, taken any vows. Nobody's paying me. This is the twenty-first century. Minister's partners come in all genders, sizes, and persuasions. I can do whatever I want, be the person I really am."

"So, you've explained this to her?"

I scrunched up my nose in answer, because she had me there. Okay, I'm a wuss. Despite everything, I can't drum up any animosity for Hildy. How do you tell a well-meaning do-gooder to find another project, without mortally offending her? And now that her husband is lying in a casket, and she's coping with the new reality of widowhood, I'm even less apt to confront her.

I took the next hummus-laden slice. "Hildy thinks she's helping me. She thinks encouraging me to find my inner Hildy is her legacy. She was a minister's wife for more than forty years, five of them here, although that was fifteen years ago. 'Minister's wife' is how she thinks of herself, the first thing on her personal identity list — probably the second and third, too. In all the years of their marriage, she never took a job. She was sure she had a calling to help Win."

"Win what?"

I knew she was being purposely obtuse. "Help her *husband. Win* is her husband."

"With a name like Godwin, settling on Win shows a certain lack of conceit. He could have gone by God."

"Win *was* God to a lot of people." In fact Ed had privately expressed concern that Win might spend his retirement trying to prove he was *still* the only *real* minister of our church. It does happen.

Lucy finished, using up her tub of hummus and loaf of bread in the same instant. She's the only person besides my sister Vel who could pull this off. Under the wild corkscrew curls, behind the gleaming jade eyes, is a realtor who can figure exactly how much money a potential buyer should spend on a house, and a friend who can assess how much advice to give before a friendship starts to wobble.

She pushed her final slice toward me and sat back. "So Hildy doesn't think finding murderers should be your job?"

Unfortunately, there is something to be said for Hildy's concerns. The last time I nailed a killer, I did so in our sanctuary, in the very spot where Win's coffin will lie in state this morning. Some members are just the least bit upset by this.

"My curiosity certainly seems to be uppermost in her mind," I admitted. "Followed closely by my outspoken children, my refusal to chair and cater the annual pledge dinner —"

"Aggie —"

But I was on a roll now. "My lack of interest in the social action committee's petition to turn downtown into a pedestrian mall, and my insistence that the church board honor their promise to put a new floor in this kitchen!"

"Cheer up. Once the memorial service is over —"

How I wished that were true, but I waved away the rest of her sentence. "Hildy's planning to settle in Emerald Springs. She says this is where she was happiest. Even though her daughters and grandkids live in San Diego."

"Maybe she tries to overhaul *their* lives, too."

"I talked to her oldest daughter last night. I pointed out how much Hildy will need her family now. I even reminded her how difficult our winters can be."

"And you didn't mention that your own mother lives in Emerald Springs, difficult winters and all?"

"I felt it was inappropriate to burden her with my family history."

"Right . . . And?"

"She said her father's life insurance and pension are so generous that her mother has plenty of money for airplane tickets and warm clothing, and she and her sister feel Hildy needs to live wherever she'll be happiest."

"Did she also make it clear she will make *certain* her mother won't be happy in southern California?"

"Pretty much." I cut the last sandwich and carefully placed it on my artfully arranged stack, just as Ed staggered in from outside.

The last week has been difficult for my husband. Spring is never his healthiest time of year. Ed has always had seasonal allergies, but they've grown worse as he's grown older. Two years ago we realized it was no coincidence that Easter week was always the apex of the season, no matter when it fell. From there it was simple to track the problem to Easter lilies.

Strong fragrances have always made Ed sneeze, but the spicy scent of pots and pots of lilies in the front of the church was actually triggering asthma attacks. Luckily the flower committee agreed that baskets of tulips and daffodils would serve just as well to herald the coming of spring, and for the past two years, he's made it through his Easter sermon without wheezing and blowing his nose.

Both of which he was doing now. In earnest.

"Ed?" I gestured him to the chair beside Lucy, and he fell into it like David collapsing after his skirmish with Goliath.

"Lilies." He gasped the word.

"Where?" My eyes widened. "No! In the church?"

He nodded, eyes streaming so forcefully he had to grab a paper napkin. Junie, my mother, doesn't cry this hard during reruns of *Terms of Endearment*.

"But they know you're allergic to them."

"Not Hildy."

"What, she's decorating the memorial service with lilies?"

He nodded. "Win's favorite. She said . . . she wanted the flowers to be an Easter . . . gift to the church. Two birds, one stone. Her treat."

Lucy and I looked at each other. Today was Tuesday. Easter was this weekend. Hildy's a practical woman. Whatever flowers she chose for the memorial service would still be in good condition by Easter morning. And in typical Hildy style, she had simply acted on her own, most likely canceling the flower committee's order for the holiday service, and substituting hers as a gift to the congregation. Since she always knows best, she wouldn't have consulted a soul. Hildy would be certain she had done a good deed for everyone.

Not.

Ed was as pale as, well, a lily. "You've never seen . . . so many in one place. It's a . . . lily blizzard."

I could imagine this. An overabundance of flowers fit with the rest of today's event. Despite every caution, Hildy had ignored Ed and planned a service for Win that was worthy of a king.

Ed is a "less is more" kind of minister. His eulogies are powerful. He knows how to draw the essence from a life and talk about the things that mattered most. He doesn't make saints out of sinners, or use the service to tell cautionary tales to the living. He doesn't ramble or tell pointless stories. His readings and music are chosen with the greatest care. He asks the family of the departed to limit speakers to two or three of the most important. His services last an hour, and not a moment is wasted. Best of all, people are both moved *and* conscious when it's over.

Hildy's thoughts on the matter are quite different. Last week when she grew tired of Ed's counsel, she marshaled forces. A committee of the congregation's old guard — those who thought the church should be frozen in time to preserve Win's ministry — arrived at our doorstep. Ed was encouraged to let Hildy have her way in all things. Since he knows when to fight and when to retreat, we now have an interminable service to look forward to, with representatives from every major committee of the church. The choir will sing every anthem they've performed since Christmas. Anybody who has a memory of Win they want to share, will only have to raise a hand to be recognized. Even those who never met him.

Afterwards Hildy may take her show on the road. Win served a total of ten churches during his ministry, and Hildy has been in touch with each of them, discussing memorial services throughout the remainder of this year and into the next.

At least Hildy will be spending time on the road and won't be constantly available to remind me that a good minister's wife never draws attention to herself.

Ed finished his explanation. "She says lilies were Win's favorite . . . flowers!" The last word came with a sneeze like none I'd ever heard. Luckily he'd turned his head away from the sandwiches.

I got up to whisk the platter to a faraway counter. "What are you going to do?"

Ed glanced at his watch and sneezed again. "I have a new prescription. I took one an hour ago. I'm going to take . . . another."

"Do you think that's a good idea?" Lucy asked, before I could. "I doubled up on an antihistamine once and slept for twenty-four hours."

"I . . . don't have a choice."

I considered suggesting that Ed turn the service over to Teddy. Teddy is our eight-year-old daughter, and she's continually fascinated by all things ministerial. I thought she would do a credible job. Both she and her sister look like their father. Same dark blue eyes and pale reddish hair. Maybe nobody would notice.

In the end I decided not to joke. Ed was in a fix, and besides, Teddy was already helping today, chosen as the representative from our religious education program. She was the only child in the whole congregation who actually wanted to attend the service.

"Take the second pill about ten minutes

21

before the service starts," I said. "The drowsiness will probably kick in about the time you're done. I'll drive you to the cemetery and prop you up."

Ed headed upstairs, and Lucy headed home. I headed to the downstairs bathroom to comb my hair and make sure I didn't have anything edible clinging to my green dress.

No one would mistake either of my daughters for me. I'm the only brunette in the family, the only member with hair that's not bone straight, the only one with more or less hazel eyes, and certainly the only one with a curvaceous figure, although our oldest daughter, Deena, will probably give me a run for my money before long. There's nothing remarkable about me, and nothing to pity. I'm just a normal mother of two who happens to be in the wrong place at the right time far too often. I'm sure there are mothers all over the world who find murderers in their spare time.

Still, I was supremely glad that for once the memorial service I was about to attend had nothing to do with me. Win had died a perfectly natural death, which is sad enough. I didn't have to search for clues. I didn't have to defend myself against bad guys. I could just be a member of the congregation and the comforter of the bereaved.

Oh, and the wife of the man sneezing his head off in the pulpit. Surely that was enough of a job for any reasonable woman.

2

Emerald Springs is the largest town in a ru-ralish county. Officially we're a city, but we've retained our small-town feel, despite an excellent liberal arts college and a historic hotel and spa that feeds its reputation on the mineral waters of Emerald Springs. Our church sits on the town oval, a pastoral green space complete with bandstand and a statue of a former mayor, Josiah Sparks, who personally led an Emerald Springs brigade in the Civil War. Our present mayor, Browning Kefauver, is more apt to lead us to rack and ruin. His statue will, in all likelihood, be larger.

The parsonage, a spacious Dutch Colonial, is just across an alley from the church, and our not-so-bustling downtown begins just a few blocks away. Having the church so close is a mixed blessing. Ed can zip home for coffee or something he's forgotten; I can roll out of bed and attend a meeting or a service without a thought to commuting time or parking. On the other hand, some people see the parsonage as an extension of the church. Until I finally summoned the courage to change all the locks, a number of people had keys, some of whom let themselves in regularly to check on things.

Although Ed served two urban churches before accepting the call to this one, I've more or less made my peace with our quieter life. I grew up traveling the craft show circuit, and from Junie, my mother, I learned that home is wherever and whatever I want it to be. In Emerald Springs, with fewer distractions, we learn to know each other intimately, and we take time to breathe. And the fact that I am consumed with intimate details about people who have *stopped* breathing? Well, that seems to fit here, too. At least the locals haven't yet gifted me with a one-way ticket out of town.

When I opened the back door of the parish house with my sandwiches in hand, the kitchen was alive with activity. Although most of the time the spouse of the departed allows our memorial service committee to take charge of the reception, today Hildy Dorchester was in the center of things, arranging a platter of cookies while she told two other women what they should do next. No one was arguing, and despite being a grieving widow, Hildy was energetically dealing cookies to the platter like the winner in a high stakes poker game. This was the center of her comfort zone.

Hildy looked up and beamed. She's a broad woman, shaped a bit like one of the Potato Head family, with short, thin legs and large feet, which add to the resemblance. Her hair is as blonde as it is white, and she wears it parted in the middle and pulled up in a knot at the top of her head, revealing a plain, square face and ocean blue eyes. When Hildy smiles, which is often, it's hard to decide which is more attractive, the eyes, the smile itself, wide and absolutely unforced, or the warmth both of them convey.

"Aggie, what have you brought us?" She stopped dealing cookies and came to peek at my sandwiches. "My goodness, they look so healthy."

"The vegetarians will appreciate a little something just for them."

"I'm so glad you thought of that. I always say it's important to think about everybody's needs." She lowered her voice. "I always say that's part of our job."

I had no job here, but this was no time for

that discussion, and I certainly wasn't going to point out that Hildy's role as the wife of a minister was now well and truly behind her.

Hildy reached for my plate. "I'll just trim off the crusts and arrange them on a tray," she said, looking genuinely delighted. "There's a better chance they'll be eaten if I fancy them up a bit and put them in among the other sandwiches. This was so kind of you."

I could not find my voice. The bread was homemade, the crust shiny golden brown and sprinkled liberally with sesame seeds, which are something of a splurge on our budget. I watched Hildy carry the platter to another counter and instruct one of her "helpers" to slice and dice.

She returned, and spoke in a confidential whisper. "It's so important that everything go exactly right today. Win deserves a perfect service."

I didn't remind her that Win wouldn't really be able to appreciate it, although Hildy, against Ed's advice, *had* insisted that Win's coffin be present in the church. For the most part, our memorial services take place after the cremation or burial service, but Hildy had been adamant that Win's body should be in the service, too, and that everyone go to the cemetery afterwards. Luckily she *had* agreed to a closed coffin, since the body had not been embalmed and had indeed spent the past week in refrigeration. I wondered if his death would finally seem real to her at the graveside. I had yet to see any signs of mourning, and I wondered if Hildy was just good at hiding her feelings.

"I think you need to stop worrying about the reception," I said, putting my hand on her arm. "Where are your daughters?"

She glanced at the clock above the sink. "I'm supposed to meet them in Win's — Ed's office. I guess I better go now."

Hildy's grieving daughters were waiting for her, and she was arranging cookies. I didn't want to think what that said about their family togetherness. On the other hand, maybe the church office was where they'd seen Win most often.

Hildy removed her apron, patted shoulders and said chirpy thank-yous and good-byes to everybody in the room, then she left.

I was immediately flanked by Dolly Purcell and Yvonne McAllister. Yvonne is not quite fifty, and Dolly's in her eighties, but both women had been part of the congregation when Win Dorchester was the minister.

"What did you say to get her out of here?"

Yvonne asked. "What magical incantation?"

I took in Yvonne's expression, a mixture of annoyance and gratitude. I didn't think the annoyance was aimed at me. "I pointed out that her daughters were probably waiting."

"We have a routine," Dolly said. "We do these receptions regularly, and do them well. Hildy has, perhaps, forgotten."

Relief seeped in. I had expected to be chastised for my sesame seeds. I summoned some charity. "We all cope with grief in our own way."

"Let's get everything in the refrigerator or under cover and get over to the service," Yvonne said. "I think we can do that much without guidance."

We cleared the kitchen in record time, nonperishables under plastic wrap, everything else in the refrigerators. From the window over the sink, I saw Ed and Teddy heading for the church, and plenty of other people, too. The service would be well attended.

The last to leave, I got stuck behind the other two women who had been in the kitchen with us. Fern Booth and Ida Bere are not my compatriots, not even my admirers or my husband's. Neither Ed nor I are as devoted to every passing cause as Ida thinks we should be, and Fern is simply ornery. I am fairly certain no minister and family in the parsonage have ever pleased her. But Fern cured me of that delusion as I turned off the kitchen light.

"It was a sad day when the world lost Win Dorchester," she said to Ida. "He and Hildy were models for the next generation . . . although from what I can tell, few are following in their footsteps."

She'd had the grace to lower her voice for the last part, but I caught her words anyway. I wondered if Fern really approved wholeheartedly of the Dorchesters, or if this was nostalgia. She had been fifteen years younger and fifteen years less disappointed when Win was minister here. But she had always been Fern.

I followed everyone through the social hall, which was decorated with flowers and photos of Win and his family, as well as Win in our pulpit and others. In the reception area I passed our secretary's desk. I was three steps past when I turned and went back. I was right. I'd done too many "what's wrong with this picture" activity books with my daughters. The object on the left corner really did *not* belong there.

I picked up the iPhone and turned it over in my hand. A label with Ed's name and our address peered back at me from the case.

"Yikes!" I slipped the phone in my purse. The iPhone was Ed's most prized possession. The girls and I had saved for six months to buy it for his fortieth birthday last month. It did everything except preach his sermons. If I ever climb into a lifeboat with Ed's iPhone in my hand, he'll grab the phone first, maybe even check to see if it's working, before he helps me inside.

The fact that the phone had been lying forlornly on Norma Beet's desk was a bad sign. Ed was feeling terrible, but that terrible? I shuddered and hoped he remembered where the pulpit was and the name of the man he was about to eulogize.

As I made my way toward the church, people stopped to talk, and by the time I got inside, there were only a few seats left, all at the front. Hildy and her daughters, as well as almost a dozen out-of-town relatives, were standing by the entrance to one aisle, with Ed and two ministers from our area behind them in robes. I recognized the introduction to a hymn often used at the ordinations and installations of our clergy, and knew the procession was about to begin.

I scooted up the aisle. The available seats

were one behind the other, smack dab in the middle section on the first and second rows. I reached the second row and inched my way in front of people, apologizing in whispers as I stepped on feet and knocked an old man's cane to the ground. Finally I reached the empty space. Someone harrumphed and told me to move over so she could see the coffin, which had already been placed at the front. I had landed right in front of Fern and her husband, Samuel, a rotund little man who functions as the enforcer of Fern's edicts.

We stood for the processional. The coffin had been placed in front of the pulpit, rimmed by at least a dozen pots of lilies wrapped in gold foil. There were lilies everywhere, along with fragrant hyacinths and narcissus, but none on top of the coffin, as if the florist had wanted to make sure Win could pop out on cue and preach his own eulogy. The image made me shiver. Or maybe that was Fern staring at my neck. No matter, the mood was set. Good Aggie hoped the service went well. Bad Aggie wished it were over.

Things started well enough. The processional was stirring, and best of all, Win did not rise and join the other ministers. The Dorchester family took up one long pew at the front, and whatever they were feeling, they looked stoic and resigned. The choir's first selection was blessedly short. Then the readings began, and Ed announced that Teddy would be first.

"Oh, for heaven's sake, what was Ed thinking?" I heard from behind me. The remark had been addressed to her husband, but Fern's whispers eat through silence like battery acid.

I wanted to turn and assure Fern that this had not been our idea, but that, of course, was pointless. I watched my daughter, dressed in a dark skirt and pale gold blouse, climb to the pulpit. Ed turned the microphone to accommodate her, then he sneezed into the arm of his dark robe, cleared his throat, and sneezed again.

So much for extra-strength antihistamine times two.

Teddy looked adorable, at least what we could see of her. She's small for her age, although athletic and wiry. Deena had fixed her shoulder-length hair, pulling it back from her face with two barrettes that matched her glasses. From what I could tell, Teddy felt right at home where her father so often stood. She read a wonderful poem — and wonderfully short, too — that equated the soul of the departed with birds in flight, winds that blow, stars that shine. I had practiced it with her for two days, but even I was surprised at the sweet resonance of her voice.

I wanted to turn and smile slyly at Fern, but I'm just one hair too evolved. Teddy came down to sit in the row with the other participants. Ed announced the next one, but his voice cracked, and he had to clear his throat before he tried again. He ended with a sneeze.

I felt a hand on my shoulder and fingers like steel.

"If Ed is sick, should he be spreading his germs?"

I have some training in martial arts. I pictured grabbing the hand digging into my flesh, and flipping Fern over the pew. Maybe the lilies were getting to *me,* as well.

Instead I turned my head. "Allergies," I said firmly. "They're not contagious."

"Perhaps he should have taken some medication." She sat back.

Fern is not my favorite person in the congregation. Okay, Fern's tied for last place with the divorced mother of two who tries to maneuver Ed into corners and tosses her blonde hair over her shoulder at least three times in every conversation. But this was a new low. I wondered if she was fighting grief. Perhaps Win had been a particular comfort to her at a difficult time in her life, or his sermons had inspired her to be a better person.

Okay, that last possibility was a stretch, unless she had started life as Godzilla.

I turned back to the service in progress. By now the third reading was under way. My Fern musings had taken me to this point, at least. Trying to be kind, trying to pay attention and listen to the rest of the inspirational readings, the prayers, the anthems, took me a little further. Worrying about Ed, who was sneezing ever more violently, carried me even closer to the moment when we would follow the coffin to the cemetery. Poor Ed sounded worse each time he spoke, croaking now and fumbling, which is completely out of character. I winced so frequently anyone watching probably thought I'd developed a tic.

Finally the minister of another church, who was representing the local clergy association, got up to give his remarks. We were on the homestretch. Only the open mic, the eulogy, and the final anthem and prayer were left. The minister finished and left the pulpit, and Ed sneezed twice. Then Ed simply sat there, his eyes half closed, and not, I was afraid, in prayer.

Agonizing seconds went by. At last my husband seemed to realize the room was silent, and he was supposed to say or do something. He got to his feet. I think he swayed. I wanted to run to the front and catch him if he fell, but I was completely blocked in by knees and feet, as well as a cane. I could only hold my breath.

Ed made it to the pulpit, which he gripped with both hands, knuckles a sickly lily-white. For a moment I thought he might apologize or explain, then I remembered his gender. Besides, even if he had been capable of mastering his own biology, his desire not to focus attention on himself would squash the impulse.

With what appeared to be superhuman effort, he outlined the procedure for the next part. Two microphones had been set up, and people were asked to come forward and speak. I wondered if Easter week would be over before they finished, but I was wrong. The remarks were brief and few. Fifteen years had passed since Win was minister here. Twenty minutes later, when no one else came forward, Ed got to his feet once more, again unsteadily. For a moment he looked like a man who didn't know where he was or why. His eyes were unfocused. He looked like he was going to pitch himself on the coffin for a twofer.

Then he began to speak. Although Ed always makes a copy of his eulogy for the family, normally he only peeks at the text to ground himself. Not this time. Clearly my husband realized he was not himself. Sneezing and wheezing, he began to read, word for word. Considering how awful he felt, he was masterful, awe-inspiring.

Without considering that? Not so much.

Halfway through, Ed turned a page, and stared at the next one, as if he wasn't sure why it was there or what he was supposed to do with it. His eyes began to close. Before I could catch myself I moaned softly.

He straightened, forced his eyes open, and continued in a monotone.

We were so close. So close! I sat rigid, as if the energy my effort took would somehow transmit itself to my husband.

Hours passed. Okay, maybe not, but at last the eulogy ended. We had learned about Win's early years, his call to ministry, his family, the many churches he had served. I had heard very little, but I was practically moved to tears, just because the service was nearly finished.

The choir sang their final selection, a musical setting of the Twenty-third Psalm. Since this anthem is not their best effort,

Esther, our organist, was trying to drown them out on the old tracker organ. As she got louder, so did they. If the building collapsed, I was willing to claw my way out.

I was counting down the minutes. Ed had only to do the final prayer, and give instructions to the mourners about what was to follow. The plan was for all of us to rise as one after the coffin was removed and the family made its exit. We should file respectfully out of the church and load ourselves into cars for the short trip to the graveside service. Luckily — oh, so luckily — Hildy had asked a friend of Win's to do that one. Then we would all come back to the church for the reception, and after a brief appearance, Ed could go home and sleep off the antihistamines.

The anthem ended. Ed stepped up to do the closing prayer, and in that moment of silence, as he struggled to keep his eyes open and his body upright, "Rocky Raccoon" began to play. Like everyone else, I looked around trying to figure out where the sound was coming from. Ed didn't appear to notice. I guess his Eustachian tubes were blocked, as well as the blood flow to his brain.

Understanding came in baby steps. The noise was a cell phone. The cell phone was nearby. The cell phone was in my purse. The cell phone was Ed's.

In college Ed's nickname was "Rocky Raccoon." Something to do with Gideon Bibles, and Ed's desire to enroll at Harvard Divinity School for his graduate work. When the girls and I gave him the iPhone last month, Deena, in charge of all things techie in our household, had been in charge of programming it. Here was proof she'd done it well. Playing away. In my purse.

I froze. Technology is not my friend. Last week I braved YouTube to watch a video made by Teddy's class, and instead I got an ancient Belorussian woman singing Polish folk songs. Now every time anyone turns on our computer, the kerchiefed one picks right up where she left off. No one can make her stop. For some reason, they blame me.

The strains of "Rocky Raccoon" finally ended. By now my cheeks were bright red. I tried to look innocent, but I wasn't fooling anybody. I stared straight ahead.

Ed made his way unsteadily to the pulpit, and I closed my eyes in gratitude and humiliation. "Rocky Raccoon" began again.

This time I knew I couldn't ignore the phone. Fern Booth knew it, too. I felt her fingers on my shoulder again. "Turn it off!" she said, her breath scalding my neck.

I grabbed my purse as Ed began the prayer. I am as unfamiliar with the iPhone as I am with quantum physics. But even I could read the directions on the screen. I slid my finger where it told me to, and held the phone up to my ear.

I don't think Ed knew what was happening, but as if he felt obliged to make up for wobbling his way through the eulogy, he was nearly shouting into the microphone now. Or maybe he couldn't hear himself. Whatever the case, I could barely make out the voice on the other end as the pulpit microphone screeched and bellowed.

I didn't know how to hang up or turn off Ed's phone. I held it out and stared, hoping that if the iPhone was all it was cracked up to be, it would figure out what I didn't know and patiently instruct me, but no luck. I held it up to my ear again.

"Please, is anybody there?" the voice asked again.

I whispered yes.

Then the man began to speak.

Ed was still praying. I put my finger in my ear and listened. I didn't have to do or say anything else except grow more stunned with each word. The voice stopped at last, and although the phone wasn't off, I figured no one else could call now that the man on the other end had disconnected.

I tried to figure out what to do. The prayer was winding down. Next Ed would launch into instructions, and the pallbearers would get to their feet to help wheel the coffin to the back.

I got to my feet to slip out of the pew, but by now, people were slumping badly. On both sides of me legs were sticking straight out as people struggled to make themselves more comfortable. I couldn't even get past the stranger beside me. As I prepared to rise she narrowed her eyes, and I could tell she was as unlikely to move as a crow in a cornfield. On my other side the man with the cane had his eyes closed in respect. Panicked, I saw only one route to the front.

I put one hand on the back of the pew in front of me, and stuck my leg over it until my foot was resting on the cushion. Then I prepared to lift myself over the seat, taking great care to aim carefully so I didn't stomp on the people on either side. There was just enough room to heft myself up and over, but in that brief moment when I was actually standing on the pew, Ed said, "Amen."

I heard the rustling of people opening their eyes, and a few nearby gasps. I leapt off the pew and made a beeline straight for my husband, waving my hands to try to

41

capture his attention. So okay, if the congregation had needed proof their minister was married to a crazy woman, now they had it. If anyone had needed proof Ed was well and truly not himself, the fact that he completely ignored my charge was enough.

He wrestled with the pile of papers littering the pulpit, as if he was searching for his directions. I took the steps leading up to the front platform and reached him just as he began to speak.

He turned, eyes unfocused and red-rimmed. He sneezed in greeting.

I tried not to listen to the gasps from the family row where Hildy and her relatives sat, tried not to notice the whispers that were rapidly turning into a loud buzz.

"Ed, there isn't going to be a graveside service," I said, pulling him toward me so only he could hear my words. "Tell them to go right to the reception."

He looked at me as if I were a stranger. His eyes narrowed, but only because his eyelids were closing again.

"Ed!" I shook him, and this time I spoke louder. "Just tell them there won't be a service at the cemetery. Tell them to go to the social hall for the reception."

He looked confused. "That's not right."

I had no choice. If there was any decorum

left to preserve, I was going to have to step forward myself. The announcement had to be made here, before everybody followed Ed's prompting and got into their cars to go to a service that was not going to take place.

I moved around him and went to the microphone. I stood on tiptoe, afraid that if I grabbed hold to adjust it, I would somehow reroute my message to Beijing or Bora Bora.

"Friends," I said, and that's when I saw a familiar man, wearing a sports jacket and jeans in the back of the church, leaning against the wall.

Detective Kirkor Roussos.

For a moment I was frozen, then I cleared my throat and tried to smile as if this happened every day. "I was just informed by the funeral director that there's been a change of plans. Instead of a service at the cemetery, we'll all go next door for the reception. You may call the church office next week to find out when the graveside service will be scheduled."

The buzzing got louder, but not loud enough to drown out the shriek from Hildy's row. Hildy leapt to her feet.

"Of course there will be a service today," she said in a voice that probably carried as far as the bandstand at the Oval. "There *is* no change of plans."

I hadn't had time to reckon with Hildy. I turned in her direction. "I'm sorry. I can explain the situation later, but for now —"

"There will be no changes! This has been carefully planned."

Only the truth would shut down this conversation. Hildy's daughters were trying to pull her back to her seat, but they had no hope of success. As if we were all involved in some sort of bizarre tug-of-war, now Ed had taken my arm, as if he thought I was the one who needed to sit. I shook him off, not a difficult task under the circumstances, although I was afraid I might send him sprawling.

I leaned closer to the mic. "I'm so sorry, Mrs. Dorchester, but I'm afraid we have to let the funeral director take Reverend Dorchester's body to the coroner's facility."

"That's ridiculous! We already have a death certificate. Everything is all arranged." When she pulled away from her daughters and started toward me, I realized Hildy was not going to let this go. She was heading for the microphone to give directions to the cemetery herself, and she wasn't above arm wrestling.

I looked up and saw Roussos, arms folded,

watching with interest. Roussos is not a fan of churches.

I had no choice. I was forced to add a final phrase.

"For an autopsy." I cleared my throat. "Autopsy. They've decided to do an autopsy. And that's why Reverend Dorchester won't be buried today."

There wasn't a person in the sanctuary, except perhaps Teddy, who didn't understand what that meant. Win wasn't going to be allowed to go to his final resting place in dignity. Somebody might well have propelled Win Dorchester into that garbage can portal to eternity.

"I'm sorry," I said, just one moment before the buzz in the sanctuary turned into a roar.

3

Since there wasn't the usual rush to congratulate my husband on the excellence of his eulogy, I found Ed alone in his office after the final hymn had been sung and mourners had moved to the parish house. Ed was propped against his bookcase, arms folded over his midriff, sound asleep. Had he toppled like a tree in the forest, I doubt the crash would have awakened him.

I propped myself against his desk, several feet away, and held out my arms, prepared for him to fall into them.

"Ed!" Nearly a shout. When it didn't rouse him, I tried again, a few decibels louder.

"Ed!"

His eyelids parted. He shook his head in a courageous attempt to wake himself.

"You have to leave!"

He seemed to consider. I wondered which word he had not understood.

"You're in no shape to go to the reception," I continued. "You were asleep on your feet."

"Just need . . . coffee."

"I'm not sure the entire urn would do it. I'll help you get home."

"People . . . will wonder."

"I'll come back and tell them what's up."

There was a gentle knock on the door, and January Godfrey, our aging hippy sexton, poked his head inside. He had been present in the sanctuary, having worked at the church during Win's years. January's an insightful, funny guy, with a personal cupboard of stories about Ed's predecessors, and I'd heard my share of Win anecdotes. "Need help?" he asked.

I motioned, and once he was all the way in, I explained.

He was nodding before I finished the grisly details. "Yep, a regular lily forest in there today. And you know what? Reverend Dorchester had a lily allergy, too. Always dreaded Easter, but he dreaded telling Mrs. Dorchester more."

I wondered what this said about the Dorchester marriage, but I was too worried about my own to wonder for long. "Can you help me get Ed home?"

"You stay. I'll take care of it. You'll want to talk to people." He looked up. "Maybe I

47

didn't put that quite right."

I didn't *want* to talk to people, but I did *need* to talk to people. Resigned to my lot, I thanked him. I left them together and closed the door behind me.

There was still time. The Greyhound station was within sprinting distance. There was always room for another soldier in the militia at my father's survivalist compound. If I told Ray Sloan and his cohorts that the establishment was out to get me, that was all I'd ever need to say.

Instead I dragged myself toward the social hall. I was still six feet away when I was grabbed.

"Exactly what's going on?" Yvonne McAllister dug her fingers into my arm, in what nobody would mistake as a gesture of admiration. "Making that announcement about the coroner was like throwing a bomb into the sanctuary."

"I was stuck making it. I had Ed's phone." I smiled and nodded as a couple of frowning strangers passed. "Not having a body at the cemetery would have been something of a problem, don't you think?"

Yvonne hasn't been the same since she quit smoking more than a year ago. Underneath I know she's the same affable and compassionate friend she has always been, but these days she cuts to the chase quicker than a foxhound.

"I thought Hildy was going to wrestle you for the microphone."

I lowered my voice. "Damage control. Quick. What do I do?"

"Hildy and her family left with the body."

I pitied the coroner and felt slightly better. "Who's going to give me the most trouble?"

First she asked about Ed, and I explained the situation. Her lips were a tight, thin line — I knew she wished a cigarette was between them. I was proud of her and slightly afraid.

"I'll be your second," she said. "You get the Booths, Ida Bere, Marie Grandower, Geoff Adler . . ." She contemplated for a few seconds more. "Anybody else who gets in your face. I'll take everybody else I can get to."

"Ed's as out of it as I've ever seen him. Those antihistamines really whacked him." I fished for and finally held out Ed's iPhone. "He left this in the social hall in plain sight when he went over to the sanctuary."

Yvonne's eyes widened. The gravity of Ed's condition was finally clear. "Easter Sunday's going to be a nightmare."

She had nothing to worry about. I'd

49

already decided to sneak over and empty all the water from the vases once the church was dark. By morning the lilies would be irrevocably wilted, and the flower committee would have to remove them. I would offer to buy potted hydrangea replacements. Desperate measures. Sneaky measures, too, but I had Hildy's feelings and Ed's allergies to consider.

Hildy, whose husband might have been murdered.

"Showtime," Yvonne said tightly.

The social hall was buzzing when we walked in. Hildy was sure I needed tutoring, but even she would have approved of my courage and determination. I scanned the room and zeroed in on Fern and Samuel Booth. Fern has graying hair, which she wears in an unflattering bob, plus a bulldog face and demeanor. I've never quite figured out if she disapproves of ministers and their families in general, or just the ones with the misfortune to inhabit our parsonage. Samuel served as board president during Win's ministry, and has taken on other positions through the years. But Fern's sole job seems to be judging us and communicating her verdict.

As I went I chatted when I could, explaining quickly that I'd gotten the funeral director's call during the service, and I'd simply done as he instructed. After all, throughout history people have survived enormous catastrophes by claiming they were just following orders.

I took a deep breath before I reached the Booths. I nodded, but didn't smile. From experience I knew Fern was immune to my dimples. "I thought you might have questions," I said. "I know my announcement was a shock."

"Only a little more so than seeing you climb over the pew during the most important memorial service our church has ever held," Fern said in a voice tight enough to choke a chicken.

"I figured I was going to step on enough toes as it was. Believe me when I say I didn't enjoy the trip or the announcement."

"What's going on?" Samuel asked, for once inserting himself into the conversation. "Why did they take Win's body to the coroner's for an autopsy?"

I contemplated my possibilities. Shrugging. Holding out my hands, palms up. Shifting my weight from side to side evasively. Looking sad or resigned. Dashing for the door.

"The funeral director didn't say." I knew that wasn't good enough and plunged on.

51

"But I'd have to guess they want to be sure of the cause of death."

"Everybody knows Win had a heart attack." Fern was glaring at my forehead, as if I'd developed an extra eye.

I looked thoughtful. "Everybody but the coroner."

"What made the authorities decide this at such a late moment?" Samuel asked.

"I honestly don't know. He was calling Ed, and I had his iPhone, so I got the call."

I realized I'd provided my own perfect lead-in. I stepped closer, to establish a little intimacy, which was too much like cozying up to a pair of cobras. "Ed had a horrendous reaction to all the lilies, and he had to take whopper doses of antihistamines to get through the service. He just barely made it, poor guy. He's home resting."

"Lilies?" Fern made a noise like my mother's vacuum cleaner when it's sucking up throw rugs. "Please!"

"The flower committee has standing instructions not to use them. I'm glad he's still breathing."

I had never been happy to see Ida Bere in my entire life, but when I realized she had come up beside me, I wanted to weep with gratitude. Ida looks like a female Arnold Schwarzenegger, only several decades older and a lot more liberal. But next to Fern, Ida is Mother Teresa.

Fern told Ida what I'd just said, giving it her own personal twist. By the end, even I believed that the entire Wilcox family was part of a conspiracy to destroy the good name of Win Dorchester.

"Win was in favor of a pedestrian mall," Ida said, as if Fern hadn't been outlining a possible murder. "*He* supported any and all social justice causes."

Both Ed and I think a pedestrian mall in downtown Emerald Springs is, in theory, a lovely idea. The reality is that, like too many Midwestern towns, our little burg is suffering high unemployment and low tax revenues. Our downtown businesses are at best hanging on, and our city government has a freeze on new projects. A pedestrian mall, which would cost a fortune to design and implement, is an idea for a better day, when people have disposable income, and leisurely shopping expeditions aren't limited to a bag of potatoes and a pound of coffee.

"There's definitely something to be said for the pedestrian mall," I said diplomatically. "I know it's important to you."

"That little girl of yours is quite a speaker." Ida looked around, as if to see where Teddy was in the room. Although I'd been sure my daughter had gone home right after the service, I was wrong. There she was in the corner surrounded by admiring women, Dolly Purcell and Esther, our organist, among them.

When Teddy caught my eye, I motioned for her to join us, and she came right over, a plate of hummus sandwiches clutched in one hand and punch in the other. Could even Fern be hateful in front of my eight-year-old cutie? I figured we might be locked into some sort of spiritual Rorschach test.

"Did you like being in front of all those people?" Ida asked Teddy, after I'd made quick introductions and given Teddy a hug.

"Sure," Teddy said, as if she couldn't imagine why anyone would think otherwise.

"I think children need safe places to walk, don't you?" Ida rested her arm around Teddy's shoulders. "Wouldn't it be fun if you could go downtown without worrying about cars?"

I would fiercely protect my daughter from wild animals and hurricanes, but until that moment I'd never been called on to protect her from marauding social justice advocates. Luckily, judging from my daughter's expression, I wouldn't be called on today either. Teddy was clearly interested in the discussion. I wondered if she would ask about the theological implications, or quote her favorite political analysts. I watched them stroll off together, and felt only slightly guilty. I smiled at the Booths and headed off, as if I really had some place to go.

As I moved through the room toward Marie Grandower and Geoff Adler, longtime members who only rarely came to church, I was stopped repeatedly. Each time after I gave my spiel, I was inundated with Win stories. Win had done this, and Win had excelled at that. Apparently Ed's predecessor was even more revered now that his cause of death was up in the air. Those who hadn't gone to the microphone to eulogize him finally had plenty of good things to say.

An older woman I'd never seen in church stopped me, delicate fingers on my bare arm and a tentative smile.

"You're the minister's wife?"

"I'm Aggie Sloan-Wilcox," I said, extending my hand. "My husband is the minister."

"I'm Ellen Hardiger." She shook gently. She was probably in her early seventies, with the kind of tissue paper complexion that ages beautifully. She had thin silver hair lightly permed for body and eyes the color of morning mist.

We exchanged the usual "happy to meet you" formalities. I was considering pushing on, but clearly she wasn't finished.

"I'm not a member of your church," she said. "Catholic from birth."

I nodded and hoped she wasn't going to tick off comparisons. I hated to think she would judge our church by this particular service.

"Did you know the Dorchesters?" I asked.

"I knew Reverend Win. I was director of nursing at Russell House. I moved to Florida after I retired."

I've never been to Russell House, but I did know that once it had been an over-crowded, long-term nursing care facility. In the past years, with the help of grants and creative thinking, they had expanded and added a new building for assisted living. Ed claimed the complex was now well run and cheerful, considering that most of the residents had little more than Medicare and Medicaid to fund their stays. Our Women's Society puts on a special afternoon tea there twice a year, but always at the time my girls are coming home from school.

"Was he visiting a patient?" I asked.

"Oh, not just one. He came weekly. I could set a clock by him. Two o'clock, on Wednesdays, and he stayed as long as he needed to. Some of the other pastors whipped in and out as fast as they could, and my own priest only came right at the end. You know . . ." She looked as if that reminder saddened her. "Father Shea gave a lot of comfort to the dying, of course. But Reverend Win? He gave time, comfort, advice, whatever was needed. Every week."

I tried to imagine the bombastic Win Dorchester holding gnarled hands and nodding gently. The picture wouldn't form because it was a new one for me. There was something else, too. We're a small church, and most of our members were or had been professionals with decent retirement nest eggs and long-term care insurance. There are more expensive and expansive facilities in town, and when care is needed, they usually choose one of them. I couldn't imagine that things had been that different at Russell House in Win's day.

Ellen Hardiger seemed to read my thoughts. "He came, you know, whether he had a church member to see that week or not. People began to depend on him visiting, and even if he didn't have anybody from your congregation, he'd drop by and visit our regulars. They adored him. They made him little gifts during craft classes. They wanted to give back whatever they could, although most of them had next to nothing themselves. They even talked about leaving your church money in their wills."

Saint Godwin the Magnanimous. Sadly, I guess I'm all too human. I was growing annoyed at this praise for Win. Maybe I was just sorry to see that ministers have to expire before they finally get their due.

And if Win had been murdered, who had given him his?

"Did you come all the way here for his funeral?" I asked. I couldn't imagine a retired nurse paying the extraordinary prices for a last-minute ticket.

"No, I came last week to hear him speak. A friend told me ahead of time he would be back in your pulpit. I wanted to come north and visit anyway, and the timing was good. I even got to chat with him after the service. Then, when I heard he'd died . . ." Her eyes misted. "Such a sad thing. Can you tell me . . . why they took his body?"

I gave her what was now a thoroughly rehearsed speech. She nodded sadly. "It's a mistake. No one would hurt Reverend Win. He was good to everybody. He even helped my daughter when she needed counseling, and she was never a member of your church."

"I'm sure you're right." At least I sure hoped so.

"I suppose I'll stay to see him buried. I

hope it will be soon."

She thanked me and shook my hand again, then I started back toward the Grandower-Adler enclave. I thought about the nurse's words. It had been interesting to hear accolades from a person Win hadn't needed to impress. The man was obviously kinder than I'd guessed, and as I neared my target, I tried to put that in perspective.

Marie Grandower was a slender, attractive woman who wore her fifty-something years well. Her dark hair showed no traces of gray, and it curled softly around a face that may or may not have spent time in the hands of a plastic surgeon. I decided that if she'd had work done, it had been minimal. With her oval face and high cheekbones, Marie would always find Mother Nature to be kind. She wore unrelieved black, no jewelry, no tasteful scarf at her neck. Mourning suited her.

Geoff Adler was probably a little younger, thin as well, like someone who runs compulsively. His face was lined and long, and his steel gray hair was cropped short. I could picture him in a blinding white lab coat, since I'd seen him that way in advertisements. He was a pharmacist and businessman, the fourth generation Adler to own and run our local Emerald Eagle drugstore. But Geoff had gone one better than his ancestors. He had taken a small family business and was quickly turning it into a successful Ohio chain.

Now that I'd arrived, I wasn't sure what to say. Their conversation had stopped as I approached. Now they seemed to be waiting for me to speak first, and Marie didn't look happy to see me.

I greeted them both. "I'm just filling in some of the blanks of what's happening," I went on. "Ed would do this, but he's having the worst allergy attack of his life. He's home in bed trying to sleep it off, along with too many antihistamines."

"I thought he looked distressed." Geoff didn't smile, but his expression was benign, even encouraging. "Do you know what he was taking?"

"Something superstrength the doctor gave him, and he doubled up."

"When he wakes up, tell him I said not to do that again."

I smiled my thanks. "I don't have much more information than I gave at the service, but I wondered if either of you had questions?"

"Yes." Marie spoke for the first time since my arrival. "How can something like this happen to somebody like Win Dorchester?"

She had punched the words like a boxer

60

walloping a speed bag. She looked devastated and furious simultaneously. Her dark eyes were bloodshot, and as she twisted her shawl in her hands, I saw they were shaking.

I tried to sound reassuring. "We don't know what happened."

"He died!"

I stared at her. "Marie, Ed will be in his office tomorrow morning. Would you like me to make an appointment for you so the two of you can talk?"

For a moment she looked angry enough to slap me. Then she pulled the pashmina shawl she wore closer around her and leaned in my direction. "I've had enough of *ministers,* thank you. I have no intention of talking to another one. Not ever."

I felt the air stir and realized she had taken off while I was trying to figure out what to say. I fixed my gaze on her and followed her path out the social hall door, hoping she got there without kicking a small child.

"Yikes." I looked back at Geoff once Marie disappeared. "Even I can't put my foot in things that fast."

"Please forgive her. She's taking Win's death very hard. He was a great help after her husband died, and they stayed friends through the years. She was active in the church during his ministry, and she was here last week to hear him speak. I'm afraid she's like a lot of people. She expects her minister to have superpowers, and superheroes aren't supposed to die."

"The autopsy may find traces of kryptonite."

He smiled a piano keyboard smile, but it lightened his face and made him more attractive. "Don't take it personally. Death brings out the best and the worst in people."

"Win's death seems to have ripened him for canonization."

"Never that, but he was a good man and a good minister. I was on his board, and Marie was on committees. We could both tell you he had his hand on everything that happened here. He had more energy than any two people combined. He was a smart administrator and a powerful preacher. He was too big for us, you know. That's why he moved on."

I thought about that. Unfortunately, the ministry isn't too different from other professions. In our denomination and in others, if a minister does well, he moves up to a larger church with a larger salary. The Consolidated Community Church of Emerald Springs is what's known as a stepping-stone church. With the exception of Ed, who wants to stay in our quiet little burg, so he has plenty of time to study and write, Tri-C's ministers probably hadn't planned to stay in Emerald Springs any longer than they needed to make the next step.

With all his talents, Win should have moved up quickly, ending in one of the denomination's larger and more prestigious churches. But from what I could tell, he hadn't stayed anywhere long, and his moves had been mostly lateral ones. His final church before retirement hadn't been much larger than ours.

"I'll let Ed know he should call Marie, but to give her some time to heal first," I said.

"That will be perfect." He raised a long-fingered hand in farewell and headed off after her. Marie was older than Geoff by at least five years, but I wondered if the two had more in common than admiration for their former minister. I filed that question for my husband, although Ed's nose for gossip is as clogged as his real one was today.

By the time I finished my rounds, Teddy was gone and people were drifting away, so I could escape as well. I found Yvonne in the reception area, holding a light jacket with tiny gold buttons down the front. She followed me to the corner outside Ed's office for privacy.

"Mission accomplished," I told her. "Although I didn't have much I could add."

Yvonne pushed her fists through the sleeves and settled the jacket at her waist before she answered. "You know, Win seemed fine the night he died. A little frail, but energetic and alert. I saw them last year at General Assembly, and he looked tired and old. Since then he changed medications, and Hildy told me he was eating well and exercising regularly. I was surprised when the doctor signed his death certificate so quickly, but apparently he had examined Win the week before and warned him about avoiding stress. Hildy said he told Win he was just one heart attack away from forever."

Unitarian-Universalists have an annual convention, something Ed tries hard not to attend every year. But some of our members, like Yvonne, wouldn't miss our General Assembly for the world. I suppose that's one way congregants had stayed so closely in touch with the Dorchesters.

"You were at the Dorchesters' party that night?" I asked.

"Right. I heard you were invited, too."

Win and Hildy had thrown a small dinner party for old friends at their rental house the night Win died. In fact, they'd been in the midst of finishing the cleanup when he collapsed. Ed and I *had* been invited. A former minister socializing with former congregants is tricky. Protocol demanded that Win first clear the party with Ed, and he had, out of duty, invited us at the same time. But issuing the invitation had been good enough, and I was sure everyone was delighted when Ed explained we had a spring play of Teddy's to attend instead.

So what if Teddy had only been a chipmunk with no lines except "chee, chee, chee"?

I couldn't help myself. I tried to look innocent. "Who else came?"

She saw through me right away. "Do you think one of us murdered him?"

I held up my hands. "We don't know he was murdered."

Yvonne knew I would never suspect her of anything more dire than sneaking a cigarette, and she took her time buttoning up. "Esther and Dolly. Sally was there. Marie Grandower came with Geoff Adler —"

"Are they a couple?"

She shook her head. "Oh, I don't think so. There's an age difference, of course. Six or seven years. Besides, Geoff's so driven, I doubt he has time for a woman. His wife left him years ago because she never saw him. She said he came home late one night and she nearly shot him because he looked unfamiliar. Marie's husband died almost twenty years ago, I guess, and when she's in town she shows up here and there with different men, but I think she enjoys the single life. No hint of anything serious."

"When she's in town?"

"Oh yes, she spends most of her time in Hilton Head. She's usually only here in the summers, and I've heard she's moving south permanently. Her house is up for sale."

I prodded a little. "What about the Booths?"

"They were there, too. Ida was there." She licked her lips in thought. "I think that might be it. Hildy had the entire party catered, and the food was wonderful. At the time I wondered what kind of investments Win must have made for their retirement. It has to have cost a pretty penny."

"It was Win's last meal. I guess he deserved the best."

Yvonne looked sad. "I guess."

"And no-nobody else was there?" The moment Yvonne walked out I was hoping to sneak into Ed's study and write down the guest list, so I was mentally repeating it to myself and stuttering from the effort.

"Well, I did leave early. That always seems

so rude, but I'd warned Hildy. I had a ticket to a concert at the college and couldn't find anybody else to take it. I hate waste, so I went late."

"I wonder if anybody else came along after you left. Maybe they just stopped by to say hello."

She shrugged. "Sally could tell you, but that reminds me. When she called me the next morning to tell me Win was dead, Sally *did* say there'd been some kind of unpleasantness at the party's end."

If ears can really perk, mine were now thrust forward and as wide as a clamshell. "Unpleasantness?"

"That's all she said. Let me see . . . She said something like 'the whole thing is so awful, particularly after the unpleasantness at the party's end.' I asked her what she meant, and she said she had to leave for the airport, but she'd tell me when she got back."

I had noticed that Sally Berrigan, one of the town and church's driving forces, had not been present today. Now I knew why.

"Where'd she go?" I asked.

"Washington. She's visiting our congressmen and senators to keep them on their toes."

If anybody could do that, Sally Berrigan

would be the one. There was talk she was planning to run for mayor again in the next election, after a sound defeat last time. Our little city would be a very different place if she won.

"She's coming back soon?" I tried not to sound hopeful.

"This evening. You can ask her about it yourself." Yvonne had long since finished with her buttons. She put her hand on my arm. "Aggie, this could be a very serious matter. Just because Win was one of Ed's predecessors, you don't have to get involved. You've already done enough, making that announcement —"

"Climbing over the bench, knocking my own husband out of the pulpit, halting the graveside service, practically arm wrestling Hildy," I finished.

"Yes, well, some things are best left to the police, right?"

I drew a blank, but I nodded like a team player. Yes, I had a reputation as an amateur sleuth, but Yvonne was right. This time I really needed to stay away. Win was my husband's colleague, and his wife was, for lack of a better way to put it, mine. My role now was to offer comfort, not to dig for clues. In all fairness to the police, they usually did come to the right conclusion, if later in the game. For once I needed to do only what was expected. Casseroles. Hand-holding. Prayer.

So what if I wanted to call Detective Roussos right this minute and mine our odd little friendship for every bit of information he was willing to part with?

"I'm planning to stay out of this," I told Yvonne.

She looked at me strangely, eyes narrowed, head tilted.

"What?" I demanded.

"Are you capable?" she asked.

It was a question I hoped to find an answer to in the next few days. But I wasn't sure if I wanted to hear a yes or a no.

4

Either Ed had borrowed a chain saw and was busily carving up our bedroom furniture, or my husband was snoring with terrifying gusto. I chose not to discover which and left our bedroom door closed.

Teddy was downstairs in the play corner of our dining room, giving her two American Girl dolls and Moonpie, our silver tabby, Spanish lessons. Teddy's fourth grade teacher is a native speaker, and Teddy shares all new vocabulary with Molly and Josefina — although if Josefina could actually talk, she would certainly add some of her own. Moonpie is a recent addition to the classroom, and not a willing one judging from the number of times Teddy steered him back to higher education.

Teddy, having gotten home a few minutes before I did, had warned me about Ed. Her money was on the chain saw.

"Do you and the girls want to help me

make pizza dough?" I asked, as I walked past the classroom on my way to the kitchen. "You'll have to change clothes if you do."

"We're very busy," Teddy said. "When we finish our lesson, we're going to write letters to the mayor."

I didn't ask about what. I could see the pedestrian mall would be providing my daughter and her huggable friends with hours of entertainment.

I would have been happy to skip dinner entirely. Teddy had eaten sandwiches at the reception, and after everything that had happened, I had no appetite. But I still had a teenage daughter and a husband who might regain consciousness at some point in the evening. Pizza seemed sensible.

I proofed my yeast in warmish water while I assembled ingredients. I had turned on the stand mixer and was adding whole wheat flour to a rapidly forming dough when Deena walked in. Like Teddy's, Deena's coloring is her father's. Her hair is strawberry blonde and Teddy's is a bit redder, but they clearly swim in the same gene pool. Same dark blue eyes and peachy complexions to go with the hair. Had I not been awake and aware at both births, I would wonder if we were related.

71

Today Deena was dressed in a long turquoise hoodie over leopard print leggings. The outfit was a present from my younger sister Sid, who also gave Teddy Josefina. I'm ashamed to say I'm hopeful Sid doesn't marry and have children of her own until my girls no longer need clothing or toys. Vel, my older sister, is in the same unmarried, childless, gotta-shop state and she, too, will delight me by remaining that way a few more years.

"Pizza?" Deena asked, peering in the mixer bowl.

"Want to help me put one together?"

"I'm not hungry. Tara's mother made sugar cookies, and we decorated them like Easter eggs. We ate all the broken pieces."

I'm always encouraged when my fourteen-year-old daughter takes part in childhood rituals. These days Deena's a confusing blend of adult and child, and I'm never sure which Deena I'm talking to.

"Think you might be hungry in about an hour?"

Deena shrugged, which I took for a yes. I added more flour.

"Where's Dad?" she asked when I turned off the mixer and the kitchen was quiet again.

I told her the basics of our afternoon,

including Ed's double dose of antihistamines. She's my daughter, so she's used to
drama and took all this in stride.

"Do you think he'll sleep through dinner?" she asked.

"I think it's possible he'll sleep through
tomorrow, too."

"Then I guess this is a good time to tell
you something."

Warning bells sounded. They were so loud
I was afraid Deena could hear them ringing
in my head. "Can't be good if you don't
want your father to hear it."

"It's not like that." She rolled her eyes.

"What's it like, then?"

"It's just, he might be hurt."

"Uh-huh." Now that I have children those
are my two favorite words. Someday I'll
write a parenting manual called *Uh-huh*. I'll
make bestseller lists.

"You always say that!"

"Uh-huh."

"I quit the debate team."

The kitchen fell silent again as I considered this. Deena joined the middle school
debate team last year, after listening to Ed
talk endlessly and enthusiastically about his
own years as a debater. A delighted Ed has
been with Deena every step of the way. He

even chaperoned trips to debates in nearby towns.

I kept my voice neutral. "Isn't there a tournament scheduled here in early May?"

"Yeah, I guess."

"Wasn't your dad helping you prepare?"

"He's been trying." Moonpie had escaped, and now Deena grabbed him as he walked by and cuddled him against her. "I told him I wanted to prepare by myself."

Warning bells again. "Deena, *when* did you quit?"

A long pause. "A couple of months ago," she said at last, without looking at me.

"And you didn't tell him?"

She finally looked up from Moonpie's fur. "Well, it's not my fault. I just knew he'd make such a big deal out of it. And I didn't want to get into a fight. I didn't want him to feel bad, either."

I understood. Deena and Ed had gone through a bad patch this past summer, and I could see that inviting another would be way down on her list of things to do.

"Your dad would have been just fine with your decision," I said, because it was true. "Disappointed yes, but certainly not angry. All you had to do was tell him why you quit." I paused. "Why did you?"

She looked away again, setting the cat

back on the floor. "Because."

"That's an explanation?"

"I just wanted to, that's all."

"And your reason would be?"

"Why are you making a big deal out of it? I just don't want to be on the team anymore."

This time my warning bells were playing a concert. Something had happened, something Deena didn't want to talk about. From experience I know that the things kids don't want to talk about are the very things they should.

"Did you have a fight with Mr. Collins?" Stephen Collins was the middle school debate coach, an English teacher in his late twenties with wild dark curls and a grin for everybody. He was exuberant, funny, and passionate about debate. I'd never heard a bad word about him.

She hesitated. "No."

That hesitation said a lot. "Deena, I know Mr. Collins can be kind of out there. Did he say something that hurt your feelings?"

"No." She didn't sigh. She exhaled forcefully enough to scatter the traces of flour I'd spilled on the counter. "I just wanted to quit, that's all. And I didn't want an inquisition. That's why I didn't say anything right away."

75

Stay out of my life. I heard that loud and clear. Of course the problem is that for parents, these are fighting words. Most of the time we are actually quite thrilled to stay out of our children's lives, since hopefully we have lives of our own. Deena's hair is Deena's hair. The color of her nail polish, whether she wears pants or a skirt any given morning, chooses *Twilight* or *The Book Thief* at bedtime, sleeps over at Tara's or Shannon's? These are pieces of Deena's life, not mine. But possible problems at school? Problems she might not be able to handle on her own at fourteen?

Whose problems were those?

"It just seems odd," I said. "You're not involved in that many other things. It can't be time."

"Give up, okay? My decision, not yours. And I'm happy about it. What kind of sauce are you putting on the pizza?"

Mothers regroup, they don't quit, and I know my role. I dropped the subject for the moment, but I knew we weren't finished.

"Garlic and oil?" I asked. "Tomato? Pesto? I think I still have some in the freezer."

"Let's do garlic and oil with mushrooms. We have mushrooms?"

"Gorgeous mushrooms. And red peppers."

"Maybe I am hungry." She wandered off

to see what Teddy was doing.

I had just set the dough in my gas oven to rise when Lucy came barreling into the kitchen. Lucy knows she's always welcome, and she does knock, more or less. But this time she surprised me.

"Murdered?" she shrieked.

I hadn't had time to call and tell her the events of my afternoon, although it had been the next thing on my agenda. I went to the sink to wash my hands, and she followed me.

"I promise I was going to call," I said. "We don't know anything for sure. We just know the funeral director had to take Win's body to the coroner for an autopsy. Maybe they want to study the effects of heart disease on retired ministers."

"Aggie, the police got a phone call! Somebody claimed Win Dorchester was murdered, somebody they took seriously enough to interrupt your service."

I grabbed a towel to dry my hands, but I was facing her by then. "How do you know all that?"

"I keep my ear to the ground."

Two evasive females in short succession. What was it about my kitchen?

I struggled to sound casual. "What ground exactly?"

"The police got a call. I think it was a woman, but that part's up in the air. I overhead some of this."

"Where?" When she didn't answer, I smiled reassuringly. "Lucy, I can tell you're involved with somebody, and now it's pretty clear it's a cop. Is Roussos the mystery? You don't have to hide that from me. I promise if you tell me that much, I'll never mention it again."

It's a sad day when a friend snorts at you.

I wrinkled my nose after the noise died away. "Okay, I'll *try* not to mention it again."

"It's not even important where I heard it."

"Well, if it *was* Roussos, you and he have something really special going on, because that man doesn't give out information to anybody."

"You mean to *you*. And why? He knows you're practically a professional snoop."

"And you're not?"

She threw her hands in the air. "Did I say that?"

My head was whirling. "Okay, what else did you overhear?"

"Nothing else, darn it. But I wanted you to know that much."

I filled her in on the scene at the service, plus my attempts to make peace with Win's admirers afterwards. "I hate to think about my next meeting with Hildy," I finished. "I ruined the service for her. Not that I had any choice, but will she see it that way?"

"I have to meet this woman." Lucy glanced at her watch. "Gotta run."

"You could stay for pizza."

"Gotta run." She smiled a little. "I'll keep you in the loop if I hear anything else."

"Good friends tell each other everything."

"Everything they want to." She winked. In a moment she was gone.

By seven o'clock the pizza was gone except for two slices I managed to save for my slumbering husband. If Ed didn't wake up by ten, I planned to eat them myself. I was cleaning the kitchen again, Deena was upstairs on a marathon phone call, and Teddy was taking a shower when our doorbell rang — which immediately ruled out a second visit from Lucy. I was still drying my hands on the same dishtowel when I opened the door to find Sally Berrigan on our threshold. If I'd ever had doubts about a benevolent creator, they were now put to rest.

I locked arms with her and pulled her inside. This was not the easiest of tasks, since Sally is tall, with wide, almost masculine shoulders, not to mention Sally is a woman who will not be pulled where she doesn't want to go.

Luckily she wanted to come inside, and did. I let go of her once I was sure and closed the door with a resounding thud.

"Sally, do you know what's going on here?"

She looked puzzled, which is not an expression one often sees on her no-nonsense face. In her sixty-plus years, Sally has rarely been puzzled. She's almost always sure of herself and her opinions and never hesitant to express them. That's why Emerald Springs is chafing under the mayoral leadership of Brownie Kefauver, who will say anything anybody wants to hear. Sally, the forthright candidate, scared the town to death.

"I know Win Dorchester's memorial service was this afternoon," she said. "I feel so bad I had to be away. Did it go all right?"

That was such a loaded question, I wasn't sure how to answer it. "Would you like a cup of tea?"

"Not really. I just got back into town, and I'm looking forward to some dinner."

"I have homemade pizza. Mushroom." I saw her eyes light up. "Red pepper and whole wheat crust." I tried not to feel guilty about poor, snoozing Ed.

"Would it be any trouble?"

"Not one bit. Come in the kitchen. Would you like wine to go with it? I'll have a glass with you."

Sally looked pathetically grateful. "My plane was held up at Reagan National. We were on the tarmac for two hours. Then we circled the Columbus airport for half an hour before we landed."

I nodded as she continued her litany of travel woes, all of which sounded too familiar these days.

She was seated with the pizza and a glass of cheap cabernet before I dared interrupt.

"I'm just glad you stopped by."

"I'm really here to see Ed. I have some papers for him." She gestured to the large leather satchel at her feet. "He's interested in health care legislation, so I brought home everything I found on my stops."

"He'll be thrilled. But he's sleeping off some powerful antihistamines." I segued into the story of the lilies as Sally nodded and chewed.

"That wasn't the worst problem, though," I said, and filled her in on the phone call and all the trouble afterwards. "I think the police might suspect more than a heart attack."

For a moment she went perfectly still, then her eyes widened. "Murder?"

I couldn't add what Lucy had told me, even though it was a confirmation. "Why else would they stop the burial?" I asked instead.

"Unbelievable."

"I'd have said so if I hadn't seen it with my own eyes."

"This is terrible."

It was, which made me feel even worse about pumping Sally for information. But I was a pump that was primed and ready. I gushed forth.

"I spoke to Yvonne after the service. She told me about the party that Win and Hildy had the night he died. She mentioned that you said there was some unpleasantness after she left? Do you think this is something the police might be asking about?"

This was a pretty direct request for information, but I was talking to a direct woman. If Sally didn't want me to know, pussyfooting around wouldn't get me anywhere, either.

"You really think it's relevant?"

"I don't know. I'm trying to put all these pieces together, but there are a lot of holes."

"Are you going to get involved in this, Aggie?"

I tried to smile. "I really hope not. But I guess I'd like to know enough to make a decision."

Sally was quiet through half of her second piece of pizza. Then she put down her fork and picked up her wineglass.

"Win was always a big proponent of the United Nations, and you know I am, too. I'd read two interesting articles I'd promised to share with him, only I left them in the car that evening. I remembered when I was halfway home, so I turned around and went back. I had to park a block away, so it was maybe twenty minutes after I'd left? Maybe even half an hour? I walked up the block toward the house and as I did, I heard two women arguing. For the first moment or two, I was sure it had to be at somebody else's house because it was so heated, but as I got closer to Win and Hildy's rental, I realized the argument was coming from there. Then I saw Marie Grandower rushing down their front walk. I don't think she saw me. I'm almost sure she didn't. She turned in the other direction and disappeared down the block. She was really moving. I realized one of the voices I'd heard must have been hers."

"And the other?"

"Hildy's. At that point I stopped, trying to

decide if I ought to just turn around and leave and give Win the articles another day. A part of me wondered if I ought to check on things, you know. I wasn't sure what had happened, and maybe I was needed. Then I heard Hildy, inside, I think, arguing with Win." She shook her head. "That was the last time I'll ever hear his voice."

I didn't like the sound of any of this, and I almost wished I hadn't asked — *almost* being the key word. If Win had been murdered, this argument between Hildy and Win just before he died might come out, would, in fact, if Sally was questioned or decided to go to the police on her own. I might not like this, but the facts couldn't be changed.

I leaned forward. "Did you hear anything that was said?"

Sally was clearly mulling over whether to tell me. She finished the last of the pizza and the wine before she did. I wondered if she was afraid I'd snatch it away if she chose to keep the rest of her thoughts to herself.

"I didn't hear much." She held my gaze with her pale blue eyes. "But I did hear Marie's name. Hildy was shouting. And she called Win . . . a bastard."

I winced.

"The rest was garbled. But you've seen

enough of Hildy to know how out of character that kind of anger would be, particularly anger at Win. They'd been married practically forever. She adored him."

"Maybe they survived that long by yelling and forgiving. It works well for some people."

"Maybe. But I've known them a lot of years. I've never seen or heard any reason to think that's the way they operated. Hildy never raises her voice."

I wondered at all the interactions I'd had with Hildy since Win's death. She'd been so focused on the memorial and graveside services, the reception afterwards, the flowers, the music, the photographs. I'd been surprised that she'd been so serene through it all, and I'd waited for her to crash, as people sometimes do days, or even weeks after a death, when the reality of the loss finally penetrates.

But maybe the loss had been welcome.

I shuddered.

"Now I do have to get home." Sally stood, thanking me for the pizza and pressing papers from her purse in my hand on the way to the door.

"I'll keep this to myself," I told her. "Of course I'll have to tell Ed, but he'll be discreet."

"I know." She patted my hand and left. I stood at the door and watched as she walked to her car, but the entire time, Sally's story was taking on a life of its own. Why would a wife be shouting another woman's name in anger after a party for old friends? Especially after a fight with that woman just moments before? A fight that had ended with the other woman fleeing?

Just how angry had Hildy been at her husband?

I was afraid it was a question that other people might be asking very soon.

People in uniform.

5

Ed finally woke up at one and found me sleeping peacefully on the sofa downstairs. *I* woke up when he banged his shin on our coffee table and said a few unministerial words. We had scrambled eggs and toast at the kitchen table, and I recapped the entire day, since even the parts when his eyes had seemed open were hazy to him.

I finished with advice. "And Geoff Adler says you're never to take two antihistamines at the same time, even if you have to do a memorial service in a lily field."

"I had that part figured out. Thanks." Ed rested his head in his hands. "How will I get through Sunday?"

"Not to worry."

He looked up. "Do I want to know what you've done?"

"Just start planning where to put a dozen potted hydrangeas when Easter services are over. And how we'll pay for them."

He smiled, which is all he ever has to do to make my nerve endings jitterbug.

I watched the smile fade as the events of the day began to make more sense, and I nodded. "I know. It's a pretty terrible thing to wonder if a colleague was murdered. I hope the autopsy doesn't turn up anything more than a heart that got tired of beating."

"Who would want to kill Win Dorchester?"

I told him about Sally's visit, since he seemed able to comprehend almost anything now. He looked more and more unhappy as I spoke.

"Do you know much about Marie Grandower?" I finished. "She's not in town very often, is she?"

"Almost never. She's one of our wealthier members, but her pledge to the church is minimal."

I'd hoped for more than a financial report, but I sensed there *was* no more. Apparently Marie had been present and active during Win's ministry, though. How active and in what ways? I hated to speculate.

We finished our meal and stacked dishes in the sink. Ed promised he wouldn't snore, and like a fool, I believed him.

The next morning I slept in. Ed was up at first light, and promised he would get the girls off to school while I tried to make up sleep after his chain-saw nocturne. The next thing I knew, Hildy's voice was bellowing up our stairwell.

"Aggie! Aggie, it's Hildy."

There was no point in pulling a pillow over my head and ignoring her. Hildy would be up the stairs tugging me out of bed before I could get back to sleep. I pictured a brisk round of jumping jacks and a jog around the block as she instructed me on the proper way to fold napkins for church potlucks. I sat up, pulled on a robe, and went to the head of the stairs, peering down through slitted eyes.

"What . . . time's it?"

"It's late. It's almost eight. I just thought you'd be awake by now —"

"Why?"

She looked puzzled. "In case somebody needs you."

I pondered this. Who would need me badly enough to come knocking before breakfast? And even so, was it my duty to be up and dressed, just in case? I wondered if I'd missed that course in seminary.

Oh, wait! *I* didn't go to seminary. *Ed* went to seminary. I just married him, in spite of it.

"Be back," I said, with a vague wave of

my hand. "I bet there's coffee . . . in the kitchen." I turned and felt my way back down the hall to our room.

One quick shower plus jeans and a sweatshirt later, I made my way downstairs. Hildy had not only found the coffeemaker and brewed a fresh pot, she'd found the dirty dishes from our late-night breakfast, washed them, cleaned my counters, and sliced bread for my breakfast.

Hildy's husband had just died, and she was taking care of *me.*

"You didn't have to do this," I said, glancing out the window at heavy rain. I hoped that meant the aerobics were on hold. "I just had a rough night, and I was catching some extra sleep. I guess Ed drove the girls to school."

"When we lived here, people were always dropping by, at all hours. I used to tell Win it was Grand Central Station, but I never minded. It was part of my job."

I knew better than to correct her. Hildy felt a calling to this life. She had embraced it with enthusiasm, even, for the most part, excelled. My own take was different. I tried to view myself as another member of our congregation. I was even putting together a book on Tri-C's history, using a scrapbook I'd done a few years ago for the Women's

Society and material from our archives to celebrate the church's 150th anniversary. But the moment I began to feel obligated, to rise early in case I might be needed by some commuting congregant, to micromanage every social event and reception, to view my marriage as a "job," I planned to resign from the church and take long walks on Sunday mornings. Ed needed a wife. The church could live without one.

"We don't have a lot of droppers by," I said. "I hope you're making some toast for yourself, too."

"I'm too upset to eat."

I examined her more thoroughly. Hildy did look frazzled. Her hair wasn't as neatly pinned as usual. Her white blouse was rumpled, as if she'd pulled it out of the laundry hamper this morning. And she wasn't bustling pleasantly. She was bustling like somebody who was afraid to stop.

Of course why wouldn't she be upset? Yesterday her husband's body had been spirited away to the morgue instead of our local cemetery. Win Dorchester had not received the dignified burial he'd deserved.

"I'm so sorry about yesterday," I started. "I hate that I was the one who —"

She waved me to silence. "What choice did you have? I just didn't understand. I

91

didn't know! I thought . . ." She shrugged. "I don't know what I thought. If I'd thought, I'd have known you would never cause a problem in church, if you didn't have to. You would know how badly it might reflect on Ed."

I didn't wince, but that took a great deal of self-control. "I was more worried about you than Ed, Hildy. I knew my announcement would be a shock."

"The police called this morning. They want me to come down to the station. They were asking so many questions. Whether Win and I were happy together. Who might have wanted him dead. Why I didn't call an ambulance sooner."

That last part was new to me. "I just assumed you called the ambulance right away."

"I called them the moment I found him! But I didn't follow him outside, so that took a while. Who follows somebody outside while they're emptying the garbage? Do they think I checked up on everything he did?"

Her voice was rising, and I tried to soothe her. "I'm sure they're just making certain everything's okay, Hildy. If this is a mur—" I changed course. "A suspicious death, they'll be asking lots of other people questions. See if they don't."

"They want a full accounting of any problems in my marriage! They want to know if I killed Win. That's what they want to know."

"Did they ask you that?"

"Not in so many words. I think they'll wait until I get to the station."

"Hildy, if they really were suspicious of you, they would have sent an officer to get you."

"They offered."

I was sorry to hear that, but it might mean nothing. The authorities knew Hildy's husband had just died — who would know better? Quite possibly they figured she wasn't up to driving herself. Cops are always thoughtful, right?

"Um, I know more about this kind of thing than I should," I said. "I can tell you it's way too early to worry. The, um, autopsy will probably show he died of natural causes. He had a heart condition. His doctor even certified the death without an examination. Another heart attack wasn't unexpected."

"I don't know if it was a heart attack. His heartbeat was irregular, and in Westbury, where we were living, they'd had problems getting his medications adjusted. Win had always trusted our family doctor here, Dr. Jake Gordon, do you know him?" She didn't wait for an answer. "Jake was part of the reason we moved back. At least that's what Win said . . ."

That last part was so loaded, I was afraid to touch it now, while Hildy was obviously upset. "So what happened with Dr. Gordon?"

"We thought he'd worked wonders in the month we'd been here. Win wasn't a well man, I'll grant you. But he trusted Jake, and for once he listened and did what he was told. I thought . . . I thought he was going to get better. I was trying to keep our life on an even plane. I was trying to help him avoid stress. Then that night —"

She stopped abruptly and shook her head.

I wished I knew what to say and do. I wasn't about to interrogate Hildy. But I wondered if she wanted me to ask leading questions, if she had things she needed to say to somebody. Hildy viewed me as Ed's appendage. Could that be why I was the chosen one? Or was it because I had a certain reputation for sticking my nose where it wasn't wanted?

"I need a lawyer," she said, before I could decide.

"You do?"

94

"I do. I'm not going to the station without one. The man on the phone, Detective Rousseau?"

"Roussos. He's blunt but fair." I didn't add that I counted Kirkor Roussos as a friend, even though we'd never discussed anything as intimate as friendship.

"I can't believe anybody would think I might do something as horrible as murder my husband!"

I crossed the room and grabbed her hand. "You don't know anybody does, Hildy. Don't blow this out of proportion."

"Do you know a good lawyer?"

"I know exactly the right man for the job. You sit. Drink some of that coffee you made. Eat my toast so you'll have something in your stomach. I'll call him."

Hildy was used to giving orders, but she sniffed and nodded. I figured she had to be upset to give in so gracefully. She sat, and I poured coffee and brought her the toast. She cut off the crusts before she ate it. But what's a crust or two when murder's on the menu?

Yvonne's son Jack was an attorney in his late twenties at one of our town's better law firms, but Jack McAllister was still young enough to enjoy his job and greet the day with enthusiasm. He'd been lured back to Emerald Springs after law school with the promise he could work in criminal law when cases appeared. Of course, despite the number of bodies I'd personally witnessed, our fair city was not a teeming hotbed of murder and mayhem, which was why Hildy was able to get an immediate appointment. I was afraid Jack was planning to wander elsewhere before long, somewhere darker and grittier. Possibly somewhere closer to my sister Sid, who lived in Atlanta and admitted that she and Jack had a hot e-mail correspondence.

Hildy, of course, remembered Jack as a gap-toothed towhead who'd played the part of Joseph in our religious education department's nativity pageant. She had to tell him so, but without her usual enthusiasm.

I noted Jack's office had been upgraded. He now had a window of sorts looking over the Oval. He was working his way up the lawyerly chain. I calculated and decided he must be a fourth-year associate, probably still working under the careful eye of a partner but able to proceed a certain distance on his own.

He gestured to chairs and asked if we wanted coffee.

I turned to Hildy. "I wasn't expecting to

stay. I'm sure you need some privacy —"

Her outstretched hand implored me to stay. "Please, don't go. You might as well hear this straight from me and know what's up."

I gratefully accepted the coffee to help steel myself, but I was glad to be present. Sadly, I'm always glad to be anywhere when secrets are told. Jack went to get the coffee himself, which said a lot, I supposed, about his status.

"He was probably thirteen when we left town," she said, after Jack disappeared.

"He's all grown up now," I assured her. Wide-shouldered, athletic, handsome enough to turn heads. I imagined someday, like Hildy, I'd be awed by the changes the passage of time had made in children I knew.

"I didn't want to tell this to a stranger."

"He's very bright. He would be my pick if I needed somebody."

Hildy was twisting the handle of her purse. For some reason it reminded me of Marie Grandower twisting her shawl at the reception. I wondered if I'd be thinking of her again, once Hildy started her story.

Jack returned with coffee for everybody and muffins. I was too hungry not to dig in. Besides, I didn't have to worry about talking with my mouth full. My job was to stay silent, and the muffins would remind me.

Jack began. "Aggie told me on the phone that the police want to talk to you about Reverend Dorchester's death. She said you were concerned about being questioned and wanted an attorney present."

Hildy twisted and nodded.

"To me, that says you may have things you're worried about telling the police," Jack said. "Is that right?"

"I didn't kill him."

"I'm sure you didn't."

"It's just that . . ." Hildy twisted the handle around her fingers. I was beginning to worry about her circulation, maybe even amputation.

"Take all the time you need," he assured her.

"Win and I had words that night," she said tightly. "After the party."

"Would you like to tell me about what?"

Hildy glanced at me. I chewed and nodded, afraid to smile reassuringly because of muffin crumbs on my teeth.

"I found out that night . . ." Hildy's nostrils were narrowed, but she was breathing quickly anyway. "I found out that after all these years, Win was still having an affair with Marie Grandower." Now she stopped breathing altogether. I wasn't sure which was worse.

"Still?" Jack asked. "Exactly what did you find out and when?"

At last Hildy sighed, for which I was supremely grateful.

"I found out about his affair with Marie when we lived in Emerald Springs, right at the end of his ministry here. I told Win I would leave him if he didn't resign and get away from her. I suppose he believed me, because he did find another church and quickly."

She glanced at me. "I guess you already knew this?"

"No." I swallowed my crumbs. "I really didn't."

"I always wondered if the affair became common knowledge after we left. Maybe it didn't. Or maybe your husband knows and just didn't tell you."

It would be like Ed not to tell me, but often in those situations when he's keeping secrets, I suspect. I was betting he didn't know about this affair, that perhaps those who did know had kept it private.

Hildy continued. "He was a good man. I want you to believe that, but that affair was his great weakness. I asked myself if I should put up with him afterwards, if I should just

99

leave. But . . ." She shook her head. "I loved our life, and I loved him. And I knew I was doing good as his wife, that I had a talent for helping people in our churches. I didn't want to give that up."

I had felt sorry for Hildy after Win's death, but not as sorry as I felt for her now. We never really know the burdens other people carry, particularly when they are so good at hiding them.

"Of course we had children, too," she added. "They loved their father."

I was trying not to judge Hildy's decision, but I couldn't help wondering what I would do in her situation.

She went on, speaking a little faster. "Anyway, of course I thought about Marie when Win and I discussed coming back to Emerald Springs. But fifteen years had passed. Win was not a well man, and I doubted an affair was on his mind. I knew Marie spent most of her time in South Carolina, and that her house here had gone up for sale. So I thought there was nothing to worry about. I always hated the way we left, because this was one of my favorite churches. Maybe I thought if we came back, we could put a better spin on things. End happily? I don't know. There were enough good reasons that coming back seemed to make sense."

Jack was leaning on his forearms, as if to move closer to Hildy. "And the night he died? How did you find out about the affair?"

"I didn't invite Marie to the party, of course, but she came with Geoff Adler. I gather they often attend parties together. I was upset, but I decided to ignore her. I did, until the party's end when I saw her in the corner of our side yard with my husband. Geoff had already gone home. Marie lives close enough to walk. No one else was out there, and Win and Marie didn't see me. They were as close as Siamese twins." She looked embarrassed. "Oh, I guess that's not the politically correct way to say that."

"Don't worry," Jack said. "So you suspected that the affair was ongoing or about to start up again?"

"I didn't interrupt, but once Win came back inside, I slipped out and challenged her. She told me . . . She told me Win loved her, had always loved her, and that they've been together every chance they could since we left Emerald Springs. She said all those times when I thought he was at meetings out of town? He was with her!"

I was sorry I'd eaten the muffin. My stomach was rolling. I felt awful.

"We had words," Hildy said. "Loud, ugly words, then she left. I found Win, and I told him what Marie had said. We fought. Of course, he said Marie was lying, that she'd waylaid him that night, and he'd told her as gently as he could that they would never have a relationship again. He claimed he hadn't seen her at all through the years, except once when we'd come back here to visit. He said she waylaid him that time, too. He reminded me that moving back to Emerald Springs had been my idea, not his, and he'd been afraid of this."

"Was that true?" I asked, before I could stop myself.

"Does it matter? If he was having a secret affair with her, we could have lived anywhere and it would have continued. Moving here just made it more convenient. And at this point, I can't even remember who talked about moving back first." Hildy reached for a tissue box on the corner of the desk.

"Whether he was or wasn't having an affair doesn't seem to make much of a difference now," Jack pointed out. "The fact that you'd been told about one *is* important, unfortunately."

"I didn't kill him!" Hildy sniffed. "At least not outright. If I'd been the murdering type,

I'd have wrung his neck. But I was furious. I did shout at him when he was supposed to be avoiding stress, and I left him to finish the cleanup alone, when maybe he should have been off his feet and resting."

"Getting angry at somebody and telling them what you think isn't murder," I said.

Hildy didn't look convinced. "I went for a walk. When I got back, I didn't see Win, but the kitchen trash can didn't have a bag inside, and it had been pulled out toward the center of the room. I assumed he was emptying it, and I was glad I didn't have to face him just then. But when time passed and he didn't come back inside, I opened the back door to see where he was. I even wondered if Marie had come back and they were outside together. And that's when I found him clutching his chest by the garbage cans. He gasped my name and 911, then he fell forward and died."

"Okay." Jack waited, and when she didn't speak, he added, "Anything else before I call Detective Sergeant Roussos and find out what's going on with the investigation? Because I don't see any point in having a conversation with the police unless the autopsy shows something we hope it won't. Until then, this was just an unfortunate heart condition."

"Win had so much to offer as a minister." Now Hildy was speaking to me, not to Jack. "I knew that. Everybody knew that. But he was flawed. I just felt he had so many good things to offer anyway, I could cover up for him a little. It was my job, and I did it, even when I hated to."

I reached over and took her hand. "I know you were doing what you thought was right." Whether I thought it was right or not didn't really matter now.

"Everybody's going to know," Hildy said glumly. "I wanted to preserve the illusion Win was almost perfect. I didn't want this to come out."

"I'm sorry." I rubbed her hand in mine. It was as cold as Marie Grandower's heart.

Finally I dropped it and stood. "I'm going to leave now. I think you and Jack should have a heart-to-heart about strategy. You don't need me for that."

Hildy gave a short nod. "I wanted you to hear this from me rather than from somebody in the congregation. You'll tell your husband?"

Minister's wife to minister's wife. You and me against the world. And now I knew I was supposed to cushion the news when I told Ed, to make Win sound better than he had been. But I nodded anyway. "You know we'll both stand by you, Hildy. We'll do whatever you need."

I was halfway to my car when I wondered what I'd gotten myself into.

I stopped by the church on the way home from Jack's office, both to see if Ed was asleep at his desk and to get papers to bring home. When we first arrived, I volunteered to be the church historian, because communing with members from the past is less risky than communing with those in the present. No long-gone parishioner withholds a pledge to the church because I inadvertently step on somebody's toes in a committee meeting. No pledges, no toes, plus I'm a self-congratulatory committee of one. You can't beat it.

A few years ago I had put together a scrapbook of church history, then I'd figured that since I'd worked hard to clean up our deteriorating archives, putting more bits and pieces into an anniversary book would be simple. The First Commandment for Clergy Families? Nothing ever is.

Since the moment I volunteered, I've been advised, chastised, and neutralized. My original plan, a simple paperback volume filled with photographs, has now been upgraded into a hardcover tome with fine print to be locally published late this summer. Why did I continue? Because if there were proceeds from the sale, all profits would go toward a new storage room, and that was the major reason I'd agreed to the project.

Good cause or not, after all the fuss, last month I put my foot down and made the church board my final offer. We would use previously written histories for the first one hundred years of Tri-C, then for the past fifty I would organize years by ministries, publishing one sermon per minister, a recap of important events during his or her tenure, and interviews and photographs if possible. We struck a deal.

Now, with my deadline approaching, I still have several ministries to complete. These days, with no houses to flip, I sift through old photographs and page through board minutes from the 1950s and 1960s. This week I hoped to complete all the documentation from the speed-dial ministry of one Frederick Yarberry, a perfectly nice man who only served two years. So far the minutes show no hint of discord. I'm assuming two particularly difficult winters led to his move. The Yarberry sermon I'll include is entitled "Palm Trees at Christmas Time." Maybe it *is* about the climate and terrain of Bethlehem at the birth of Jesus, but I think the title speaks for itself. Particularly since his next church was in South Florida.

I parked in front of the parish house and sprinted inside to get more records. Our secretary, Norma Beet, greeted me from her desk in the reception area. Norma has undergone a change recently. She's joined an aerobics class and lost weight. I'm hoping that soon, she'll trade in the cat's-eye glasses and the dark hair dye for something less startling. Norma is blossoming.

Blossom or not, I had hoped to avoid her. Not because I don't like her — I do — but because Norma notices and remembers every little thing. Unfortunately, she's never afraid to share.

I greeted her and didn't pause for a response, knowing what a pause can bring. "Is Ed in his office?"

"He's making a parish call, or several. Yes, several, I think. People are upset about yesterday. They've been calling all morning."

This didn't surprise me, and if Ed felt chipper enough to zip around town, then I had nothing to worry about. I listened as Norma ticked off names of callers and the exact length of their calls.

She switched gears. "The lilies in the sanctuary look so terrible, we can't use them for the Easter service —"

I cut her off before I could hear details of every wilting petal. "I was afraid of that. I stopped by the sanctuary last night. They were looking pretty droopy then." Particularly after I'd finished with them. I did feel badly about the subterfuge, but I would have felt worse if Ed stopped breathing during his Easter sermon.

"I took the liberty of calling in an order for potted hydrangeas," I added. "Our family will donate them."

"I'll tell the flower committee."

"Let's not. Let's make it a surprise." I didn't want supplements.

"It must have been a terrible day, with the police taking the body and all."

Norma had been absent from the service. She hadn't lived in town when Win Dorchester was our minister, and on Wednesday afternoons she tutors at Teddy's school, an event she hates to miss. I imagined she had already heard every detail from everybody who called, so I didn't expand.

"It was terrible," I agreed. "Although there was only one detective, and he was probably just there to escort the body to the coroner's office." Or more likely because he was interested in seeing what happened when the announcement was made.

Norma looked worried. "Now it's going to be even harder for you to get one of Reverend Dorchester's sermons for the anniversary book, isn't it? I mean, he's gone, and I'm sure his wife is too upset to be helpful."

For a moment I drew a blank. Then I remembered that two weeks ago, I had mentioned I still needed one of Win's sermons for the chapter devoted to his ministry. But this was Norma, and nothing remains buried in Norma's gray matter.

I nodded vigorously. "That's right. In the hoopla after Win's death, I forgot all about the sermon."

"You do have the one he preached two Sundays ago."

"But I want something he preached during the years of his ministry here." I'd found sermons in our archives from every other minister since the turn of the twentieth century, but nothing from Win. The lack seemed odd.

"Maybe one of the older members still has a copy," Norma said, her brain audibly whirling. "We could ask in the newsletter."

"Good idea. Will you put that in? He told me he had a print version of every sermon he'd ever preached, but they were all packed in storage back at their last home. He even checked his computer, but he didn't have anything that old with him . . ."

"You've looked through the archives?"

The archives were on the third floor, in what was nothing more than a commandeered attic, hot in the summer and cold in the winter. I'd insisted on archival quality envelopes and cases plus a dehumidifier, which January emptied every day, but even that was a stretch for our antiquated wiring. With profits from the sale of our history, we hoped to renovate and divide a small room in the second-floor religious education wing. Half for teaching supplies, half for church history.

"I'm headed up there now," I said. "Got my car out front."

"Looking for more sermons?"

I was already on my way, but I turned and smiled without stopping. "Among other things."

I didn't add that the "other" things were mentions of Marie Grandower, and anybody else who had been at the Dorchesters' party. I'm the historian, right? I wasn't snooping.

I was just doing my job.

6

There's nothing about Emerald Springs Middle School that a tax levy and two years of construction can't fix. The tired brick building is three stories capped by a perpetually leaky roof. Unfortunately, neither the levy nor new construction are in sight. We have a strong contingent of citizens whose motto is: "We sent our children to that middle school, why can't you?" The fact that the school is now many decades older and out of date is immaterial.

Buildings are important, but staff is more so. Luckily the middle school is filled with devoted teachers and administrators with innovative ideas. Schools are a huge part of community life in a town like ours, and volunteerism flourishes. All in all, Ed and I are satisfied with Deena's education.

On the Tuesday after Easter, I parked in the strip designated for visitors and started toward the front office, where I signed the visitor's book, picked up a badge, and asked where to find Stephen Collins, Deena's former debate coach. I knew this was his free period, because I had called ahead. Neither Ed nor I had been able to get another word out of Deena about why she quit the team. Ed's inclined to let this go, but I'm not. Deena has a strong sense of duty and a tenacity that serves her well. I couldn't remember her dropping out of any activity this way, not midyear, and certainly not without telling us.

So here I was, being nosy again.

I followed the office volunteer's directions up a set of well-trod stairs to the end of a hallway lined by classrooms. I passed laboratories and a multimedia room the PTA had raised money to provide in the fall. I found Mr. Collins in the last room on the left, perched on the edge of his desk surrounded by a group of four chattering girls, none of them familiar.

This was a man I had liked on sight. Stephen Collins is tall and thin, inclined toward turtlenecks or polo shirts and khakis with hiking boots. His hair is longish and curly, and when he moves — which is often — curls bounce around his face exuberantly. His smile is always welcoming, and he radiates charm. I suspect most of the girls in his classes are madly in love with him.

As I watched, one of the girls said something that made him laugh, and he slung his arm around her shoulders for a moment. Not a hug, exactly, more of an affirmation. Then he shooed them away with long-fingered hands.

"Scat now," he said. "I've got papers to grade. Trust me, you don't want me to be tired tonight when I'm grading your essays."

In a moment the girls were pushing past me, a giggling gaggle with braces and flat chests, on the brink of greater beauty.

"Do you have a moment?" I asked from the doorway.

He tilted his head and tried to place me. I know that feeling well. I often experience it at church social hours.

I helped. "Aggie Sloan-Wilcox, Deena's mother."

His eyes lit up, and he nodded. "Come in. What brings you up here? Deena's not in my class this year."

"Or on your debate team."

He looked surprised. "That's old news."

"Not to us. She just told us."

He didn't respond. His smile didn't fade, but I detected a new wariness. My antenna was well and truly raised.

"We were surprised she didn't tell us

sooner," I added. "But not as surprised as we were that she'd quit."

"Kids this age change their minds a lot."

"Not Deena. She's loyal to a fault."

He moved behind his desk and started stacking papers. "It's not disloyal to leave the team. Middle school's a time to experiment."

"I would agree if she was doing something else instead. But that's not the case."

He didn't look up. "Deena's a smart girl. She'll figure out how to spend her time."

"Can you tell me any reason why she might have quit? Was she having problems with some of the other debaters? Was it too time-consuming?"

"We work hard, but nobody complains. I try to make the process fun for the kids. It's not a big team, so I'd know if the others were hassling her. Nobody was."

I was increasingly mystified. Something was up here. Stephen Collins had gone from being openly friendly to evasive. I couldn't imagine that he had no idea why Deena, who had been so involved, had quit.

I told him as much. "I've watched you with the kids. You're very involved. You're a friend and a coach. It's hard to believe you don't have a clue about this."

He stopped stacking papers, and smiled

disarmingly, but there was something about that smile I didn't believe.

"It's a fine line between friend and coach, friend and teacher. I walk it carefully. One of the things I don't do is pry."

"So one of your debaters comes to you and says she's quitting, and you just say fine?"

"No. I ask enough questions to be sure there's not something going on that I ought to know about. Then I stop."

"So you did ask questions."

"I'm satisfied Deena knows what she's doing."

I wasn't satisfied *he* did. I moved a little closer. "Can you tell me what her reasons were?"

He considered a moment, then he shook his head. "I'm going to have to consider that conversation confidential."

"What? First you say you don't know why —"

"I didn't say that. I said it wasn't because she was being hassled by the other debaters. And I said it wasn't a time issue."

"You can't say more than that? You won't?"

"Here's what I think. Let this drop. She's good with her decision. I'm good with her decision. So we're both fine. You're the only

115

one who isn't."

I wasn't, and not because I don't let my children keep secrets or change their minds. Because this time, I sensed there was something going on that Deena couldn't handle alone.

We said polite good-byes, but it was likely Stephen Collins would see me again. And the next time I would know enough to ask the right questions.

I hadn't seen Hildy since Thursday morning at Jack's office. She'd written a formal thank-you instead of calling, which seemed strange to me. As convinced as Hildy is that I need training, I even wondered if this was meant to set an example. Was I supposed to write a note every time someone did a good deed or said a kind word in my presence? I was going to need a secretary.

More likely, I guessed she hadn't wanted to face me. Her revelations had been painful. I had passed the story on to Ed, as I knew Hildy wanted, but he hadn't been surprised. Seems Win wasn't the only minister out there who'd fallen into an affair with someone in his congregation. It was a problem in every denomination, and ministers do talk among themselves.

Now, on my way home from the middle

school, I decided to stop at Hildy's little rental with a plate of homemade brownies Teddy and I had made. Hildy and Win had chosen a colonial on Robin Road, in an older residential neighborhood, not far from much pricier digs in Emerald Estates where Marie Grandower had an appropriately grand house.

Hildy's new home might not be grand, but it suited her. It was tidy and cozy, brick and stone, old enough to have character and new enough to have en suite bathrooms. I couldn't see Hildy mowing the expansive lawn on her own and hoped she didn't try when there were plenty of teenagers in town who would be grateful for the job.

I took back streets, just because I haven't gotten out of the habit of looking for run-down houses to flip. Maybe if I had gone a quicker way, I would have seen the police cars sooner. Instead I turned onto Robin near her house and saw several parked just in front. I was not pleasantly surprised.

Never one to drive on when I could be poking into somebody else's business, I parked just beyond Hildy's and took my keys — but not the brownies. I could see Hildy offering them to her uniformed visitors, and decided to avoid that scene.

An officer who didn't look much older

than Deena approached and barred my progress. "Nothing to see here, ma'am."

I didn't back away. "I'm a friend of the woman who lives here, and I want to be sure she's okay."

We were saved from a showdown by Hildy's appearance in the doorway. I saw my chance and shouted her name. "Hildy! Over here."

She saw me at once and started down the steps. I resisted saying "See!" like one of my daughters. I just smiled at the young cop, who sighed as he walked away.

While I waited for Hildy, I noted that the cops were taking boxes out of the house and loading them into a van. This did not bode well.

Hildy smiled a greeting, but nothing about the smile was genuine. In fact, she looked like somebody who'd just faced a hundred flashing cameras. Eyes wide and startled, smile frozen in time.

"Are you okay?" I rested my hand on her shoulder.

"They're looking for evidence."

"I guessed as much. Do you know why? Do you know what they're looking for?"

She gave one shake of her head. "I called Jack. He's trying to find out."

"Do they have a warrant?"

"Well, no, I let them in. I don't have anything to hide."

"Hildy!"

"Jack said my name just like that."

"If you hadn't agreed, then they would have gone to a judge for a warrant. And maybe they wouldn't have gotten one."

"I hate to put them to all that trouble. And I have nothing —"

"To hide. You said that. The problem is they might find something completely innocent you can't explain to their satisfaction." I was watching the latest trip to the van. The boxes made it impossible for me to take stock. "What kind of things are they taking away?"

"I don't know. They asked me to stay out of their way. They've been in the kitchen, and upstairs in our bedroom and bathroom."

I had a bad feeling about that. "Have they completed the autopsy?"

She gave a short nod. "They told me to go ahead and make arrangements for the burial. I have to call Ed. I'd like to do it Thursday morning."

"Did they say anything about their findings?"

She looked away. "They said they still had more tests to complete, that it wasn't

119

conclusive. I — I didn't ask more. It's just all so terrible."

I put my arm around her for a quick hug. "Look, why don't you come home with me? There's no point in standing around in there. We'll ask the police to lock the door when they're done. I'll make lunch, then we'll see if Ed's in his office. If he is, you can go over and work out details."

She looked grateful and fractionally less stunned. "What could they be looking for?"

I, too, was afraid to ask.

I made grilled cheese sandwiches and tomato soup, the most comforting meal I know. Hildy was appropriately grateful, but she shredded more sandwich than she ate and probably never realized it.

I tried to make useless conversation. I told her about funny things I'd learned researching church history. I told her about the plans for a new storage room, and my hopes that volunteers could be cajoled to scan important documents that were fast deteriorating. I didn't explain that I needed volunteers because my grasp of technology extends as far as the click-and-close ballpoint pen, and anything more advanced will forever remain a mystery. Every time I mention this out loud, our home computer

120

laughs maniacally, but no one else seems to hear it.

She responded when spoken to, and even started a story that drifted into silence without her seeming to be aware of it. I made coffee and served some of the brownies, and she took both, but I swear she didn't taste a thing.

"Maybe we ought to go see Ed now," I told her, when lunch was obviously over. I had called him as soon as we'd gotten home, and he'd told me to bring Hildy as soon as she was done eating. He promised he'd drive her back home when they had finished and make sure all was well at the house before leaving her. I figured if the police were still on the premises, Ed might have a better chance of getting information.

Hildy took her dishes to the sink, but she didn't even try to wash them. Instead she gazed out the window.

"I used to like this view," she said. "I could see just enough of the church to know it was there. I felt like I was right in the center of things."

I subscribed to the other school of thought. I insisted the shrubs be allowed to grow between the parsonage and the church proper, so that I wasn't constantly reminded of Ed's job.

"I bet our kitchen still feels like home," I said in another conversational foray. "It's hardly been touched in the past decades."

She faced me. "You've asked for renovations?"

I wasn't sure whether I was being criticized, but Hildy went on. "You should ask, you know. Congregations can forget so easily. You have the right to a comfortable, attractive house."

I figured my grilled cheese had done her some good after all. She must feel better if she was advising me again. "The board promised a new kitchen floor, but that was a couple of years ago. Unfortunately, these old asphalt tiles may have asbestos in them, which makes them harder to replace. So the board says they'll get to it eventually. In the meantime I mop and wax a lot."

Her gaze drifted floorward to the big black and white tiles. "I always liked this floor. Too bad it's beyond saving."

I had never liked the floor, which reminded me of a 1950s soda parlor, but I didn't quibble. "I'm hoping they'll install laminate right over it. Someday."

"I guess I need to talk to Ed."

"I'll walk you over."

She looked as if she knew she ought to protest, but I shooed that away. "Besides, I could use the exercise after that brownie."

She smiled back. If she knew I was just coming up with an excuse to walk with her, she didn't call my bluff.

Although the sun was shining now, an early-morning rain had gifted the parsonage with a muddy path from our side door. I steered Hildy to the front porch, and didn't bother to lock up, since I'd be home soon. Outside along our sidewalk, grape hyacinths bloomed and daffodils prepared to launch. Spring was in the air, and as we started down the steps, the sun warmed my hair and shoulders. I stretched a little, and hoped the weather was a sign that better times were ahead.

Hope lasted about three seconds, until I realized that Marie Grandower was walking toward a dark Mercedes parked just down from our house. The last thing we needed was a catfight in front of the parsonage.

Sometimes the last thing you need is the first thing you get.

Marie saw Hildy before Hildy saw her. Of course, it was too late to haul Hildy back inside the house. Even if she'd wanted to go — unlikely — she would not have sacrificed her pride. She continued down the steps, but I heard her draw a breath. Like a bull before he charges the cape.

I grabbed her arm. "You know what? Let's cut across here."

Hildy shook off my hand. "I have no reason to avoid anyone."

By now Marie had stopped, as if she, too, was preparing. All we needed was a crowd of onlookers shouting "Olé!"

I grew up with sisters, and a mother who dislikes conflict. Junie — the only thing I've ever called my mother — was adept at heading off trouble before it began. But even though Junie's on speed dial on my cell phone, that wouldn't help a lot right now. She was teaching at a quilt show on the West Coast, and unlikely to answer.

I struggled to remember how she'd handled trouble, but I was still struggling when Marie strode up the sidewalk and stopped just inches from Hildy's reddening face.

"You thought you could get away with it, didn't you?" She pointed a finger at Hildy. "You thought you were so clever!"

"I'm not the one who carried on an affair with my minister behind his wife's back."

"Don't blame that on me. I'd have been happy to tell you right after the affair began! Your husband was the one who stopped me. He said there were children to consider."

"Really? My girls grew up years ago. And

if I'm not mistaken, Win remained with *me*."

"Well, he had his career to consider, too. He knew you'd try to ruin it if he left you!"

Hildy's cheeks were the color of ripe tomatoes, but she still hadn't raised her voice. "He was retired, remember? He stayed with me to the end."

Marie made a noise of dismissal. "He felt sorry for you."

"Really, now that I think about it, I don't know why I didn't just hand him over to you."

"Maybe you should have, instead of murdering him!"

I had to step in. I moved closer, so I'd be harder to ignore. "I think enough's been said here. I'd like you both to back off."

This was like stepping into the middle of Pickett's Charge and asking the North and the South to go back to their camps and avoid the Gettysburg slaughter. Neither woman budged.

Marie leaned toward Hildy, as if I hadn't spoken, and she picked up speed. "I bet you're wondering why the coroner asked for an autopsy. Do you want to know why? Because I called him myself! I told him Win didn't die a natural death. I told him that the night Win died, you had just discovered us together and were furious enough to kill him. I told him Win died not more than an hour after my little revelation, although he'd been perfectly well that evening. The coroner was a friend of my husband's. He knows me. He *knows* I don't make accusations lightly!"

I remembered that Marie's husband had been a surgeon, hence the house in Emerald Estates and the expensive jewelry beautifully accenting what looked like an Armani or maybe a Versace pantsuit.

"I did not kill my husband!" Hildy roared.

Now I inserted myself between the two women. Junie might be a lot heftier than I am, but I'd finally remembered that acting as a physical barrier had always worked for her when things got tough. And thanks to my father, I do a mean karate chop.

"Done," I said, remembering that repetition was also good. "Done, done, and more done. No more, either of you. This isn't going to help anybody or anything. And you will not come to blows in my front yard. Please don't make me demonstrate how I know."

Marie gasped and stepped back. "Of course you would side with her! You're two of a kind."

Now that hurt, but I didn't let on. I was suddenly glad the Grandower pledge was so small. Call me practical, but when I re-counted this scene to Ed, I didn't want to do it with smelling salts at the ready.

"I think you need to leave, Marie." I took Hildy's arm. "And we need to get to the church, Hildy."

"If you try to come to the graveside service," Hildy told Marie, "I will tell the funeral director to eject you."

Marie gave a nasty laugh. "I have my memories."

"We are so leaving." I tugged, and Hildy gave ground. In a moment we were moving over the damp grass toward the alley that separates the church and our house. I didn't look back to see what Marie was doing, but I was fairly confident with Hildy gone, she wouldn't stand there. She would head back to her lavish home and pull out her mental scrapbook, with its many empty pages. Despite what she'd said, Marie's memories wouldn't be much comfort.

"I didn't murder Win," Hildy said, when we were finally off the lawn and nearing the church. "I didn't."

"I believe you."

"You're just saying that to make me feel better. Nobody's going to believe me!"

"I do believe you." I took a moment to figure out why. We were nearly to the door

127

before I stopped, and she did, too.

"You may have been mad enough to kill him," I said, "but I know you didn't. One, you would have confessed by now. Hildy, if you'd killed him, you'd be riddled with guilt. You couldn't keep it to yourself. You're the most open person I've ever met." That was not particularly a compliment, but I didn't elaborate. Instead I continued.

"And two? You value who you are and what you do too much to jeopardize either. Not only is it hard to be a minister's wife when the minister is dead, it's really hard to take the moral high ground when you've just murdered your husband."

She sniffed. "I don't know what I'm going to do."

I'd already hugged her more today than I ever, ever guessed I might. But I hugged her again, for good measure. "We'll see you through this. Just take it a step at a time. Go talk to Ed. Get through the cemetery service. Let Jack handle everything else."

"How can I be a good example with something like this hanging over my head?"

In her place, that certainly wasn't the first question I would have asked, but I nodded as if I understood. "You have many friends here, Hildy. It's going to be fine."

She walked into the parish house through

the kitchen, and I walked home. When I rounded the house, I was delighted to see Marie was nowhere in sight. I let myself in and stared down the front hallway. It was way too early for a glass of wine. I don't take tranquilizers. I settled for another brownie, a glass of warm milk, and Bruce Springsteen at top volume on our stereo.

When The Boss is belting, it's blessedly hard to think about anything else.

7

Because of the uproar centering around Hildy, I didn't have a lot of time to think about my encounter with Stephen Collins until late afternoon. The more I considered our meeting, the less comfortable I felt. He had been evasive, even disingenuous. But something else nagged at me, and it wasn't until I thought about the girls who had surrounded him when I stood in his doorway, and the way he had so easily slung an arm over the shoulders of one in an "almost" hug, that I realized what it was.

Stephen Collins and my daughter had spent a lot of time together before she quit the debate team. Exactly what had transpired in those hours of practice? Had she been alone with him often? Had he overstepped boundaries? And if so, would she talk about it with me?

From experience, I've learned that the best way to help Deena open up is to face her over a table. With that in mind, I picked her up from a friend's house late in the afternoon, and since Teddy was at soccer practice, I drove Deena to our favorite deli. The standard American favorites here are fine, but the Middle Eastern food is divine.

We greeted the owner, Ahmed Bahram, a gentle, scholarly man who loves to discuss theology with my husband, and I bought the falafel that was my excuse for coming. Then I asked Deena if she would like to sit at one of the tables with a plate of Ahmed's splendid hummus and freshly baked pita bread.

"I feel like I've been running all day," I said. "It would be nice to sit before we head home and make dinner."

She looked faintly suspicious, but the hummus was too great a lure. We added steaming peppermint tea to our order and took one of the tables in the back. The deli decor is uncluttered and functional, with an emphasis on plain, hard surfaces that are easy to clean. This strongly discourages lingering on the molded plastic chairs. We had the back to ourselves.

I told her about Hildy and the police search. She was as interested as any fourteen-year-old can be when her mother introduces a subject. I examined her covertly as I talked. In the doldrums of winter she had gone to a sleepover at a friend's house and come back with poorly cut bangs. A quick visit to a better stylist had resulted in a new cut that angled away from her face and fell just above her shoulders. She looks older, and even though she's not as graceful or sure of her developing body as she will be in a few years, she is still lovely enough that I'm glad our summer visits to my father have resulted in self-defense training.

"I thought you didn't like Mrs. Dorchester," Deena said after my recital.

"What made you think that?"

"She's so . . . I don't know. She's so pushy, like she knows everything. Kind of like a mother."

I smiled. "Yeah, kind of like that. But she's good-hearted. She genuinely wants to be helpful. It's hard to dislike her."

"That's not the same as liking her, though. It's like in between."

I considered a moment, because this was an interesting observation. "It's just hard to feel close to somebody who's trying to tell you how to live your life."

"Tell me about it." Deena reached for a second piece of pita bread. Her first had disappeared under a mound of hummus.

"There is a difference between Mrs.

Dorchester and me, and you and me."

"She's less annoying?"

"She's not responsible for me. I *am* responsible for you."

"That stops at some point, right? You aren't going to be running my life when I'm married with kids of my own?"

"Sure I am, are you kidding? I plan to follow you everywhere."

She smiled a little, because despite the adolescent jabs, Deena still has a warm spot in her heart for her mother.

I was pleased I could easily segue into the real reason for our afternoon snack. "I know you think we interfere too much, and I know you think we ought to trust you at all times."

"I goofed up last summer, and ever since, I feel like you're looking over my shoulder."

Last summer Deena had gone to a party without our permission and unknowingly imbibed several cups of strongly spiked punch. She had spent a lot of the summer doing chores as penance.

"That was one episode, Deena. And we know you were sorry."

"Then stop hovering."

I took more bread and tore off a hunk. "You're my first child, so there's some practice involved here, but I honestly want you to live your own life and do things your way, unless I see you making a mistake you might have to pay for big-time." I hesitated. "Or if I think something's going on that's just too big for you to handle on your own."

"You don't think I'll come to you if that's true?"

"I think sometimes you might not know you can't handle it, until it's too late."

"Nothing's going on. This is all because I quit the debate team, isn't it?"

"I just wonder . . ." I really didn't want to ask her outright. I was almost sure if I did, she would close up completely. Right now, at least, I felt there was still a little wiggle room.

"I just wonder," I started again, "if something happened that upset you or humiliated you, would you be embarrassed to tell me, or maybe worried I might think it was your fault?"

"Nothing happened."

I wished I had more training in this. I needed a graduate degree in mothering. Instinct was telling me not to push harder, but I wondered about my reasons. Maybe I just didn't want to hear the worst.

Or maybe my instincts were right and I had to sit back and trust my daughter to come to me when she was ready. I could still keep my eyes open and my ear to the ground. If Stephen Collins was acting inappropriately with students, I needed to blow the whistle, and loudly.

"Okay," I said, although it wasn't. "I just worry. I'm sorry."

"You have a problem leaving things alone. You always have to have answers. You need to know everything."

"It's not easy being me." I smiled. "Is it easy being you?"

"It is when nobody's looking over my shoulder all the time."

I was in no mood to cook, so I was glad I'd bought the precooked falafel and added taboulleh and a bag of pita bread before we left Ahmed's Deli. I was particularly glad when I drove up and saw Jack McAllister, tie loosened and shirt collar unbuttoned, knocking on the parsonage door.

Deena got out of the car and went inside through our side door, and I walked around front to greet him. The afternoon was almost warm enough to sit on our porch, but I had a feeling we weren't simply going to pass the time. I led him into the kitchen for a warmer chat. Ed wasn't home, and Deena had disappeared upstairs.

I put dinner in the refrigerator and offered

Jack tea. All this took seconds. He refused the tea and launched into his reason for being there.

"You know Hildy Dorchester better than I do. I need advice on breaking bad news."

"It might be easier if you tell me what it is."

He ripped off his suit jacket and slung it over a chair, like somebody who does this first thing, the moment he's out of the office. "It's not confidential, so I can. Everybody will know soon enough."

I made my best guess. "Win *was* murdered."

"Poisoned with his own medication."

"Medication?"

"He was taking digoxin to regulate his heartbeat. They found large amounts in his fluids and tissue, but since the autopsy was performed so late, and the drug becomes concentrated after the blood stops circulating, it wasn't conclusive. Anyway, that and some other factors make it hard to tell if an overdose really occurred. So they had to do more extensive testing."

"They're sure now?"

"The amount was *so* high." As I sat down at the table he looked straight at me. "And the lethal dose present in the shrimp dip in Hildy's garbage was something of a clue."

136

"What?" I slapped my hand on the table. "You have to be kidding me!"

"I wish I were. I've done some research in the past hour, and if Hildy goes to jail and this goes to court, I can argue the autopsy results. Win was on varying amounts of the drug for several years, and patients develop something of a tolerance. So what looks like a lethal amount after death might have been tolerated well during life, and not be the cause of death at all. But the shrimp dip kind of renders that point moot."

"Shrimp dip? Did other people eat it? Why didn't they die?"

"That's the other thing. According to the police, plenty of people sampled the dip with no bad results. So the digoxin probably went into the dip after the guests left. And guess who was the most likely person to add it?"

I sat back in my chair. I had been suspicious when I saw the police carrying boxes from the house, but at no point had I expected this.

"How could they prove that?" I asked. "Maybe some maniac at the party slipped it in close to the end, and it was just good luck nobody else ate more, or enough for symptoms."

"We can come up with other possibilities,

but of course, the police suspect Hildy. She had means, motive, and opportunity."

"Everybody at the party had opportunity. Probably means, as well, if Win's medication was anywhere it could easily be seen."

"He kept it beside his bed, but Hildy had one heck of a motive, Aggie."

"Maybe somebody else had a better one."

Jack glanced at his watch. "She wasn't home when I called a little while ago. Would you happen to know where she is?"

"They're burying Win Thursday morning. She might be at the florist or the funeral home making the final arrangements. I'm sure she'll call when she gets your message. Tell her what you know so far, but be sure to tell her you know she's not guilty, and talking to the police will help clear this up. If she goes in thinking everybody's sure she murdered Win, she'll be a basket case."

"I left my cell number. I told the police I'd bring her to the station for an interview as soon as I get hold of her." He got to his feet. "She might need a friend afterwards."

Hildy and Win came back to Emerald Springs because this was where they felt most at home. But for somebody who claimed to feel at home here, Hildy seemed to have nobody to share trouble with. The families of ministers have a special burden.

We have so much tied up in being helpers, that asking for help ourselves is almost impossible. We can't be seen as weak or needy, so most of the time we can't confess problems to members of our congregations. I understood this, and understood that for Hildy, whose self-image was tied so closely to Win's job, asking old friends to support her, to listen and advise, wouldn't even occur to her.

Enter one Aggie Sloan-Wilcox, who by circumstance, if nothing else, understood her plight. Hildy and I were like in-laws. We hadn't chosen each other, but our husbands' jobs at Tri-C had bound us together, whether we wanted it that way or not.

"I'll make sure she's all right," I promised Jack. "Call me when you're finished?"

"Will do." He gave a wan smile. "This was the part of the job nobody warned me about. I never thought I'd be defending the woman who used to read us Bible stories in Sunday School. I've never forgotten our discussion about inheritance laws in the Old Testament. The whole story about Ruth and Naomi and Boaz? That's what got me interested in the law in the first place."

Jack had only been gone for a few minutes when I realized we didn't have enough food for dinner after all. Okay, we had plenty, but buying some stuffed grape leaves to add to our Middle Eastern feast seemed like a convenient excuse to get in my minivan. And if I stopped by the police station first, what was the problem?

I knew I had little chance of discovering anything new. Jack had probably told me more than I was supposed to know. But Jack knew my history, and he was hoping I could help Hildy. Hildy had towed me along to his office and revealed Win's affair in front of me, so he knew I was in that loop.

Detective Roussos wouldn't know that, of course. But I could tell him, then he could tell me to go home and make dinner. Roussos and I have a system.

I drove out to the Emerald Springs Service Center, which houses the new police station. I'll confess I sometimes miss the old one downtown. So much personality. So many memories. I pulled into a neatly sectioned lot. I had an abundance of legal choices for parking. No more scrounging for quarters to feed meters. No more parking tickets. I was getting misty-eyed.

Inside I tried to look businesslike, since "friendly" quickly raises suspicions. The haggard-looking woman behind the Plexiglas partition scrutinized me as if completing a mental assessment. I asked for Roussos, and she asked why.

I wanted to tell her I had come to make a murder confession. I *wanted* to tell her Roussos and I had been brother and sister a long time ago in a galaxy far, far away. The temptation to shoot those overly plucked eyebrows right through her hairline was enormous. But my better self won out, and I told her I wanted to talk to him about one of his cases.

She got up and disappeared into the back. I figured just picking up the phone and giving my name wasn't nearly good enough. She wanted to outline all my identifying characteristics and her opinion about the risks inherent in speaking with me.

I checked the pamphlet rack for reading material, but nobody had refreshed them since flu season, and I am already pretty good at covering my mouth when I cough.

Roussos came out before I could dig into my purse and balance my checkbook. I've never been more grateful.

"I wondered how long it would take you," he said.

Kirkor Roussos is by all feminine standards gorgeous, dark-haired, olive-skinned, with a smile that, though rare, is enough to throw any woman, even the happily married, into first gear. "Kirk" seems immune to his effect. He's prone to faded jeans worn, in a pinch, with a casual sportcoat. I'm not sure I've ever seen him in a tie. Roussos is the only man I could fall in love with, if I wasn't already in love with the man I married. Still, there's a tingle that zips back and forth when we're together. I felt it now. Harmless but enticing.

I wondered how I was going to feel if Roussos and Lucy were serious about their relationship — if there is a relationship. It was an interesting question.

"I guess you know which case I'm here about," I said.

"Let's take a walk."

Walks were Roussos's favorite excuse for keeping me away from the station. If he invited me back to his cubbyhole, he would have to explain me. Explaining me couldn't possibly be easy.

"I'm in trouble if I ever want to talk to you in February, aren't I? I'll need snowshoes."

"You need a jacket?"

"I'm okay." I figured I could turn up the heater in my van on the way home to thaw.

He lifted a brow, left me standing there, and came back a minute later with a navy sweater, handing it to me without a word.

"Are we going steady?" I asked as I slipped it on.

"Would I invite that kind of trouble? Even if you weren't married?"

"I guess we'll just have to remain the top two detectives in Emerald Springs history."

"Dream on."

We were outside, strolling toward one of the short paths that wind through the service center property, before I spoke. "Hildy Dorchester didn't kill her husband."

"You were there? Nobody told me."

I ignored that. "I know you found digoxin in the shrimp dip."

"You are a woman with mysterious resources."

I ignored that, too. "Kirk, why would anybody keep shrimp dip around that long if they'd loaded it with a lethal drug? Hildy's not stupid."

"Stupid? I don't know. Cocky? Apparently. She nearly got away with it."

"And the minute Hildy realized an autopsy was about to take place, she would have marched home, removed the dip from her fridge, and taken it to a public Dumpster. Or somebody else's garbage can. She certainly wouldn't have left it there for days, finally tossing it out in the same garbage can where Win expired."

"That's what you would have done, because you're the local expert on these things. Suspects aren't always as crafty as you are."

"Come on! That's darned elementary, Watson."

"It's not enough evidence to give the nice lady a pass. Murderers behave in strange ways. If they didn't, we might never catch them."

"I know this won't impress you, but this is not a woman who would commit murder."

"No kidding? Call her lawyer and tell him Mrs. Dorchester's off the hook."

I pretended he hadn't spoken. "Hildy's entire life was tied up in Win's position in the community. She wouldn't jeopardize that. And yes, I know he had an affair, maybe even an ongoing one, although we only have Marie Grandower's word about that. But Hildy knew about it, and she stayed with him because she liked her position too much."

"He retired recently. What position?"

"Win was still a respected minister. They were probably going to stay here, because retiring where he'd had a church would guarantee he'd keep that respect and some authority with it."

No sarcasm this time. "So what kind of

144

respect would he have if word got out he was slipping between the sheets with a member of his former church?"

"We don't know word would have gotten out."

"We can be pretty sure — witness the scene at that party. Maybe your Mrs. Dorchester realized she wasn't going to have respect after all, so she settled for revenge."

He knew a lot, and I could tell he had been questioning people at the party. Sally, or Marie herself.

"That's the other part of this," I said. "Hildy's the kind of person who would confess to stepping on an ant, or yanking a weed. Her life is so entwined with moral principle, she might pull off a murder, but never lying about it. And lacing shrimp dip with digoxin, when somebody else might eat it? That's premeditated, dangerous, and completely outside the realm of possibility."

He didn't laugh, which was a nice change.

"I want you to find the real murderer," I said.

"You mean *you* want to find the real murderer. That's why you're pumping me for information."

"No, I don't mean that. But let's say I did. What else should I know?"

This time he did laugh.

"Okay," I said, "I'll ask a few questions. Maybe I can get an answer from your grunts."

"We could just enjoy the spring air."

"Have you checked Win's prescription bottle? Do you know for sure some of his pills are missing?"

"Yes to both."

I nearly tripped. An answer? I figured this must be something they weren't keeping secret, and he knew I'd hear it from Jack or Hildy.

"So his own meds were used to murder him?" I asked.

He shrugged. "Looks likely."

"Who else was around at the party's end who might have put those pills in the dip?"

"Your friend Hildy can tell you that."

I knew she would. I moved on. "Who are your other suspects?"

"Nice try."

I knew this was all I was going to get out of him. "How did you like San Francisco?"

"What?" He looked surprised.

"Your vacation to San Francisco."

He looked wary. "I thought we were talking about the Dorchesters."

Darn. This time I shrugged. "Are you going to interview Hildy today or tomorrow?"

It was a short stroll. We had circled around

and were heading back toward the station. As I asked the question, I saw Jack's Camry pulling in beside my minivan. I had my answer.

"Don't bother with that one," I said. "But I'm going to stay until Hildy's finished. She's going to need a friend. Just remember, she's not a bit stupid. If she poisoned him, she wouldn't have left that dip where it could be found."

"No? By your own description, she's the kind of person who would confess if she murdered somebody. Strikes me, leaving the dip where it could be found was as good as a confession."

I hated that I'd given him ammunition. I was angry at myself for not thinking that through. I tried to regroup. "No, Hildy would be right up front. She wouldn't trust something like that to luck."

"We'll see. And now, a word of advice. Watch yourself this time, okay? And no half-baked theories. You figure out something important, you come to me, and maybe I'll listen. But I don't want to chase down your shadows. I see enough of my own."

At the door I stripped off the sweater and handed it back to him. "Hildy just lost her husband. Please remember she's fragile."

"That's the way we like it." He didn't

smile, and neither did I. He went inside, and I waited outside for Hildy and Jack.

I greeted them and told Hildy — pale as a ghost — I would be in the waiting area for as long as the interview took. She nodded, and I knew she was grateful. Then I settled myself in a chair, and pulled out my checkbook.

At some point in the past three months, I lost forty-two cents. I still, after an hour of calculating, counting on my fingers, and calculating again, hadn't accounted for it when Hildy and Jack came out.

The fact that she came out sans handcuffs was a fine thing indeed. I threw my recalcitrant checkbook in my purse and got to my feet.

Hildy looked as if she'd been standing in high winds, and they'd blown everything out of her. I wanted to grab her hand and chafe it in my own to make sure blood was still flowing. Jack looked a little better, but nothing like happy.

We didn't speak until we got outside.

"I can take Hildy home," I told Jack. "I'd be happy to."

"I'd like that," Hildy said, before Jack could speak. "I want to talk to Aggie."

Her voice sounded windblown, too. Jack looked grateful. He clasped a hand on

Hildy's shoulder and reminded her that if the police had been absolutely convinced they had a case, she would not be a free woman. Then he said good-bye to both of us and started toward his car.

"He grew up to be a fine young man." Hildy turned to me. "Thank you for recommending him."

"Let's get you home." I put my hand on her arm, and her skin felt clammy. I wished I'd kept Roussos's sweater to drape over her shoulders.

The drive was almost silent. She said something about my missing dinner, and I told her I'd called home and they were eating without me. I assured her I wasn't hungry, which was true until the moment I said it.

I parked in front of her house and followed her inside. There was no sign the police had conducted a search. She had probably spent hours cleaning up afterwards. It was a huge burden to add to sudden widowhood.

"Let me make you some dinner," I said.

"There's nothing in the refrigerator. They took it all. I haven't felt like shopping for replacements."

I wondered what she had been eating and vowed to make casseroles and bring them to her tomorrow, along with a bag of groceries. Maybe some of the women in the Women's Society would help, as well.

"Let me run out and get something then," I offered.

"I think they left canned goods. Too difficult to poison, I suppose. I'll heat up some soup in a while, but thank you anyway."

"What can I do for you, then?" I asked.

"Come sit a moment. I need to tell you something."

For a moment, just a moment, I flashed on "confession." Then I put it out of my mind. I really did not believe this woman was guilty. Even if she confessed, I still wouldn't believe it. That was something of a revelation.

I joined her in the tastefully furnished living room. Hildy had once instructed me that when choosing furniture, a minister's family needed to be sure their choices were both reasonably priced — or parishioners would think the minister was paid too much — and comfortable — so that anybody who dropped by would feel welcome. I might be welcome this evening, but I sure felt uncomfortable.

"This could wait," I said, after Hildy pulled a pillow behind her back, and rested her head against the sofa. "That must have

150

been draining."

"No, I thought about this before that terrible interview with the detective. And I've come to a conclusion. I know you've been involved in several murder cases, and you seem to have a talent for finding murderers. But Aggie, I'm going to ask you to stay out of this one. You've dealt so kindly with me, and with Win's memory, as well, and you'll be blessed for that. But I can't ask more of you. You can't be tainted by what's happening to me."

I should have expected this. Hildy was still taking care of others. Even though her entire future was in jeopardy, she wanted to be sure that I would be all right. I felt my first real surge of affection for her. Yes, she could be overbearing, too certain she was right, too willing to instruct when it wasn't wanted or needed. But saying she had a good heart was a terrible understatement. This was a woman who genuinely cared about the welfare of others.

So how could I, the wife of her husband's successor, be any different?

I took her hand and rubbed it, the way I'd wanted to at the station. "Don't ask me to stay out of this and leave you to face everything alone, Hildy. Whatever you have to go through in the coming weeks, I'll go through

151

it with you. Don't forget, your church is my church. Your friends are my friends. The religion that tells you to take care of others is my religion, too."

She was silent, but her eyes filled with tears. I squeezed her hand. "Tomorrow we'll talk about what to do next. Have some soup and get some sleep. Or come back to the parsonage and let us take care of you."

"I'll be fine here." Hildy enclosed my hand in hers. "Thank you, Aggie."

I told her everything was going to be okay, but on the way home I didn't have a clue how to make sure I was right.

8

Last year the *Flow,* our local newspaper, put the story of a local farmer who grew a potato that resembled the Virgin Mary on page one, and the Minnesota bridge collapse on page two. The *Flow* will never replace the *Washington Post* or the *Boston Globe* in my heart.

Nevertheless, on the morning after I'd assured Hildy I was on her side, I sat alone and bleary-eyed at the breakfast table, drinking a second cup of coffee while I tried to focus on our local headlines. I had slept poorly, thoughts of Hildy in an orange jumpsuit whizzing through my head. By the time the rest of the family got up, I had baked a blueberry coffee cake, cleaned the kitchen again, and made the day's grocery list. Now they were gone, and I pondered going back to bed.

With no enthusiasm, I scanned stories about a summit meeting and a local debate by representatives of our two major political parties on U.S. policy in the Middle East. Debate made me think about Deena and wonder, again, if I was doing the right thing by not confronting the issue of Stephen Collins head-on.

At the bottom of the page I zipped through an article about a hit-and-run that had resulted in the death of a former Emerald Springs resident. I had nearly turned to the comics, when the woman's name jumped off the page at me.

"Ellen Hardiger."

The name seemed familiar, although I couldn't remember why. I got the church directory out of the drawer by the telephone and flipped to the *H*s on my way back to the table. No Hardiger. I was relieved, although not very. Some poor woman named Ellen Hardiger had died, whether she was a member of our congregation or not.

I went back to read the article more carefully. I was finishing my last swallow when I realized why the name had grabbed my attention. According to the article, Ellen Hardiger had been the director of nursing at Russell House.

Ellen Hardiger had spoken to me after Win's memorial service. Hadn't she even said she planned to stick around to see him buried?

I read the article one more time, then I set the paper down. Ellen Hardiger was a runner. Yesterday morning she had gone for a run on a rural road outside of town, and somebody had hit and killed her instantly. The police had no leads, and were asking anybody with information to come forward immediately. The *Flow* reported that Ellen had been wearing headphones connected to an MP3 player, and the police thought she might have strayed into the car's path without hearing it approach.

According to the article, Ellen was seventy-three. She had run for more than forty years, although a former colleague and friend, Florence Everett, reported that these days, she hadn't run far or fast.

I wondered how the police could seriously believe that a woman who had been running on the side of the road for as many years as Ellen would make the mistake of turning up the volume on her headphones so she couldn't hear a car approach. Granted, some of the new hybrids were nearly silent, but on a deserted road, wouldn't anybody who saw a woman along the edge swerve into the next lane to avoid her? Since nobody else had come forward, most likely the road *had* been deserted and the lanes wide open.

Was there a connection here to Win's death?

I'd had one brief conversation with Ellen, and I'd nearly forgotten it. Just because she had come to town to hear Win preach, then stayed on for his memorial service and lengthened her stay to make certain he was properly buried didn't mean there was any link between Win's murder and her fatal accident.

Of course hit-and-runs aren't always accidents, are they? Vehicular homicide is a convenient way to kill. Particularly in the early morning on a deserted rural road.

I wasn't going to let this go. I could no more ignore this development than I could serve a steak dinner to my vegetarian family. And I could start with her former colleague. This time when I got up, I pulled out our local white pages and looked for *Everett.* There were four listed, all preceded by initials or men's names. The first two didn't turn up a Florence, but the third one did, although she told me she preferred Flo. I told her who I was and asked if we could talk in person. She gave me directions to her house, and told me to come soon, since she was working the night shift this week and needed to get to bed.

Crime is an amazing motivator. The previously groggy me was showered, dressed, and out my door in ten minutes.

Flo lived with her husband about eight blocks from the Dorchesters' house. Theirs was a salmon-colored brick bungalow, with neatly laid out flowerbeds showing signs of bulb activity. An old apple tree was center stage in the yard, which imparted a charming, country feel.

Flo greeted me at her front door in a green cotton housecoat that trailed to the floor. She was younger than Ellen, but still approaching retirement, her hair a mix of pale brown and gray, her green eyes red-rimmed and swollen.

"I'm so sorry," I said, and meant it.

She nodded and swallowed hard, as if tears were still close to the surface. "Coffee?"

I decided that would give her something to do while she pulled herself together. "Black," I said, "and only if it's no trouble."

She bustled needlessly around her green and yellow kitchen, while I complimented her on the collection of bright folk art plates on the wall. By the time she sat down at the table with coffee and a plate of bakery doughnut holes, she seemed calmer.

"I know you're wondering why I'm here," I said, "so I'm going to get straight to the point." I told her about meeting Ellen at Win's funeral, and what I remembered about our conversation. Then I told her that the autopsy suggested Win had been poisoned with his own heart medication.

She sat silently a moment, taking that in. "The two events seem completely separate," she said.

I took a doughnut hole. "They may be, but they may not, too. I'm just hoping you can tell me a little more about her. I remember so little. She mentioned Russell House. She said Win used to visit patients there frequently, even some who weren't members of our church."

"So I was told. I came on staff almost seventeen years ago, but I worked on the Alzheimer's unit at first, so I never met him."

"Ellen thought so highly of him," I said, hoping for more.

"She did. She used to talk about the reverend a lot, about what a difference his presence had made for some of our residents. That's why I called her when I saw the notice in the *Flow* that he'd be speaking at the church. I'd been trying to get her to visit . . ." Her bottom lip trembled, and she swallowed again.

I knew what she was thinking. "You can't blame yourself."

She gave a short nod and had a sip of coffee. I hoped she could sleep after I left.

"I think she mentioned another connection to Win," I said, "although I can't remember what exactly."

"Her daughter. Zoey. Reverend Dorchester did some counseling with her."

I remembered now, although in the seconds we had spoken, that was as much as Ellen had said. I wondered, knowing what I now knew about Win's affair with Marie, if he had been involved with either woman, the mother or the daughter. Had counseling led to something more intimate with Zoey? Had he turned Ellen's gratitude into an affair?

I wished those things weren't even possibilities. They should never *be* possibilities. But his affair with Marie opened that door.

"Can you tell me more about Ellen and Zoey?" I asked. "So I can get to know her a little better?"

Flo was examining me. "I've heard about you, you know. You work with the police."

I was sorry Roussos wasn't around to hear that. "Not exactly. I've just gotten caught up in a couple of situations. And I guess I'm caught up in this one, too."

She seemed to accept that. "Ellen was a wonderful woman, the kind you can always count on. Our staff adored her. She was never angry, never vengeful. She put the residents first, the nursing staff a close second, and everyone else, especially doctors and administrators, a distant third. The years when she was director were the best we had."

"She seemed thoughtful and concerned when I met her."

This encouraged Flo. "You ever ask yourself why some people come out of bad situations as mean as snakes and others just get nicer? She was one of those last kind. Her life was tough. She took care of her own parents, and after they died, she married late. Then right after Zoey was born, her husband left. She was never able to find him long enough for child support. She raised that little girl on her own, and did a great job of it, too, getting a nursing degree by working nights and taking classes during the day when Zoey was in school, but Zoey suffered anyway. She needed a man in her life. When she turned eighteen, she married the first one who asked her. He was a bartender at that awful bar in Weezeltown.

160

You know the place?"

Don't Go There. I did know it. Unfortunately, I'd been there, despite the name.

After I nodded, she went on. "Ellen worried about her something awful."

"Zoey made a bad choice? Or was she just too young?"

"Bad choice. He was an abuser. At first a slap or two, then eventually he got to beating her. Zoey wouldn't press charges, and she always ended up back with him again. That's when your Reverend Dorchester comes in. Ellen begged him to help, so he started doing counseling with Zoey. It took a while, but she finally asked for help getting away from her husband for good. The reverend found a safe house, out of town somewhere, I think. Zoey got her life together and never came back."

"Good for her." I meant it.

"The husband was furious, even threatened Ellen to try and find Zoey, but she divorced him and that was that. She's made a good life for herself, too. Remarried, with two children, and now she's a nurse herself."

"You're in touch with her?"

"Oh, yes, she's going to fly in and make the arrangements to have Ellen's body transported back to Florida for burial. She doesn't want to come back, of course, but

161

she thinks her ex-husband's been gone for some time. She'll slip in and out and be fine."

"Do you happen to know the ex's name?"

"Craig. Craig Brown. I heard it enough, that's for sure. He used to pop up when Ellen least expected him. She'd find him going through her mailbox, looking for a letter from Zoey. The police kept after him, and eventually he just disappeared."

"Did a judge issue a restraining order, by any chance?"

"I don't think it went that far."

"Did you mention Craig? To the police, I mean?"

"Uh-huh, I told them, but they weren't very interested. Zoey's been gone almost sixteen years. If that man wanted revenge, they said he'd have come after Ellen a long time ago. She lived in Emerald Springs for years afterwards."

"Both Win and Ellen helped Zoey escape," I pointed out.

Flo sipped her coffee in thought, but me, I continued to think out loud.

"Win would have been easy to find anytime. He was a public figure. And poisoning him? Right at the end of his party? Then lying in wait until Ellen left the house and running her down with his car?"

162

Said out loud it did seem improbable, although I didn't think the connection between Win and Ellen could be dismissed. I resolved to mention it to Roussos, but only if I got some helpful information. He'd warned me not to bring any half-baked theories his way. This one was still rising on the windowsill.

"The police think Ellen's death was probably an accident," Flo said. "She veered into the road and didn't hear the car approaching. Then, after the driver hit her, he sped off, afraid he'd be arrested. They said they'll notify all the body shops, in case whoever it was brings a car in for repair work, but they aren't optimistic."

I got to my feet and took my cup to the sink. Hildy would have been proud of me, although *she* would have cleaned the house and baked a casserole before she departed. "I'm going to let you get some sleep. But may I leave my number? In case anything else occurs to you?"

Flo stood, too. "I want them to find whoever did this. If you're the one who makes that happen, I'll be glad to help. Please call again if you need to."

I jotted my number on a sheet of paper by her phone, then I thanked her for her hospitality.

Outside in my van I wrestled with what to do next. I didn't know if anything I'd just learned was helpful. I was trying to tie together two separate events, and maybe I was reaching. The link between Ellen and Win was ancient history. For now I decided to concentrate on something more recent.

I called Hildy at home but I didn't get an answer. On a whim I called the church, and sure enough, according to Norma Beet, that's where she was. I headed home, parked, and walked over to the parish house and Ed's office.

Norma was at her desk, but she got up to greet me when I came in. She looked so different, that for a moment, I didn't recognize her.

"Wow," I said, and meant it. "You look great!"

"Do you think so?" Norma patted her new hair, which was new in every way. She had lightened the color to a flattering golden brown, and the slightly shorter cut was layered and flattering, too. She had also ditched her outdated black frames for a less obtrusive gold with chic oval lenses. The improvement was enormous.

"My gosh! Did you have a makeover?" I asked. "I love what you've done."

"Hildy's responsible. She's been nagging

me to change my hair color and glasses. She told me what I should do."

I couldn't believe Hildy had wrought such a miracle. Then I couldn't believe I had never tried.

Here was Norma, looking wonderful, and feeling just as wonderful about herself. And even though I had believed there was a more attractive woman under the dowdy church secretary, I hadn't made any overt attempts to help find her. Hildy'd had no such compunctions.

"Well, good for Hildy," I said, and meant it — for the most part. "Good for you."

Hildy herself appeared at that point, following Ed out of his study. She looked tired, and I imagined she'd gotten very little sleep last night. But she still looked resolute.

"I'll call the funeral director and tell him what we've decided," Ed told her.

Ed looked like he needed a nap, but Hildy can do that to anyone. He smiled at me, said a few consoling words to her, then left her in my care.

"It's all so sudden," Hildy said. "We've decided I'd better call anyone who might want to be there tomorrow when Win's buried. My girls can't come back, and I do want people who knew and cared about Win at the service. And I want to keep it private.

No onlookers."

A moment passed before I realized what she meant. Onlookers. People who'd heard that Win had been murdered and wanted to be there purely as voyeurs.

I nodded. "No onlookers."

"But friends."

I was still nodding, wondering how to move from the burial into the subject of Win's final party.

"So I told Ed I knew you'd help me make those phone calls," Hildy finished. "It's what we do."

What we do. I was afraid "we" meant women who happened to be married to ministers.

"Unless you don't have time?" Hildy added.

I did have time, and I did have an agenda. I wanted to know more about the party, about who might have been able to sneak pills into the shrimp dip. I was guessing the actual transfer had happened in the kitchen, but I wanted a clear picture of events. Besides, I'd promised Hildy I'd stand beside her. I told myself calling people to let them know about the graveside service tomorrow was a small thing.

"We can do it over lunch," I said.

"We'll just go straight through the directory."

My heart sank. We aren't a large church, but that could go on until dinner.

"Just the people who knew Win," Hildy added. "Not everybody."

I was so relieved I didn't even mind that Hildy and Norma chatted another fifteen minutes before I could pull Hildy away.

"Geoff Adler volunteered to do a reception at his lake house after the service," Hildy told me, as we walked back to the parsonage. "The cemetery's in that direction. Wasn't that kind of him? He called last night to see how I was. He was always Win's supporter."

It was more than kind of Geoff Adler, because now, at least *something* was out of Hildy's hands. She could let somebody else take charge and just be the grieving widow.

At home I settled her at my kitchen table with a phone and the church directory while I made lunch. I wanted to feed her well, since her own cupboard was bare. I hadn't had time to call church members about casseroles, but I had a vegetable lasagna in my freezer that was going home with her today.

I steamed rice and thawed black bean chili to go with it, adding a salad on the side, and a hunk of my whole wheat sourdough.

167

Hildy ate everything, a sign she was fighting back. She would need her strength.

Hildy made calls between bites. I served her, ate my portion, and cleaned up. Then I made several calls to give her voice a rest. By then we were halfway through her list, and I hoped we'd finish soon.

For some reason I'd been gifted with calling Fern and Samuel Booth. I hated to explain to Hildy that the Booths despise me, so I made the call. I was delighted when I got a message saying their phone was temporarily out of service.

I hung up and told Hildy.

"Oh . . ." She sounded genuinely saddened. "I won't have time to find their house and tell them in person. And they were both so fond of Win."

"So they were big supporters?" It seemed obvious, but I was in investigation mode, and the Booths *had* been at the party.

"Oh yes, especially at first. They helped us settle in, find doctors and a bank, a veterinarian for our cat. All the things that are so hard when you move to a new community." She nodded as if agreeing with herself. "Samuel was the board president for part of Win's ministry here. That puts a different spin on things, you know, and it's harder to be friends."

That sounded to me like a qualification, as if perhaps Win's relationship with the Booths had worsened further into his ministry. That was common enough when a church leader and minister don't see eye to eye, and usually not permanent, but I made a mental note. Then I heard myself volunteering to drive to the Booths that evening to deliver the news. I couldn't believe it.

"Would you?" she crowed. "That would be so wonderful. I would hate to bury Win without them. And they'll want to be at the reception."

Of course my offer hadn't been completely selfless. If I was going to find out who killed Win Dorchester, then I needed to talk to everybody who had been at the party. An idea had been simmering since Hildy and I sat down at the table. I had the perfect cover. I could interview everyone who had been there, not as potential suspects, but as members who knew Win for the 150th anniversary history. It was perfectly legitimate. I'd saved Win's section for the end, since I'd expected him to be right here, ready and willing to be interviewed himself. Now that this was impossible, I needed to interview his friends.

The friends who had been present when

one of them had succeeded in murdering him.

I surfed Hildy's wave of gratitude right into the subject I needed to broach. "Hildy, I know this is difficult to consider, but mentioning the Booths reminded me. Did anybody at your party" — I had no need to explain which party — "have a private quarrel with Win? Something that might make them angry enough to, you know . . ."

"Certainly not the Booths. We may not have been quite as close at the end, church politics, you know, but they were always supporters."

"Anyone else?"

Her nostrils flared. "Marie Grandower. Even if that affair continued, which I don't believe, Win wasn't about to leave me for her. If he'd wanted to, he would have done it a long time ago."

I had thought of that, of course, as had the police, most likely. But there was one flaw in the theory. A big one.

"Marie was the person who alerted the police that Win might not have died of natural causes," I said. "If she killed him, why would she point it out?"

"Because she was hoping I'd go to jail for it! Or death row. Maybe she killed Win to get even with me."

I winced at the mental picture of Hildy on death row. I could almost hear her asking her jailers how they were feeling, if they'd considered taking vitamins or maybe getting more sleep, as she took her final walk.

"That seems pretty extreme," I said. "Kill a man you claim you love, just to get even with his wife?"

"Not so extreme if he rejected her that night."

I supposed that was possible, but the logistics seemed impossible. "Didn't you chase her away right after Win and she had their private talk in the yard? When would she have had time to get the pills and add them to the shrimp dip? Unless she did it earlier hoping *you* ate it."

"I wouldn't put it past her, but that's doubtful. I never eat shrimp. I'm allergic to it. I only asked the caterer to make it because that recipe was Win's favorite. People teased me about it that night, because I nearly died at a party in the parish house years ago, before I knew I had an allergy."

So Marie would have known, *everybody* would have known, that Hildy wasn't going to eat the dip. It really was likely that Win, whose favorite it was, had been the target.

"How about anybody else?" I asked. "Any

possible grudges?"

"Why would we invite people who carried grudges to a party?"

"Just think back, Hildy. Fifteen years ago. Do you remember anybody who might have had a score they wanted to settle with Win?"

"These people were our church leaders. They worked hand in hand with Win, and they were his cheering section. They were devastated when he said he was moving on."

I could see I wasn't going to get any help from her on this. St. Win again, everybody's favorite guy.

"And can you remember anybody at all going near the kitchen that night at the party's end?"

"I wasn't paying attention, Aggie. I was saying good-bye to guests. Then I saw Marie and Win . . ."

"One more question," I said, changing the subject, to quickly move beyond that. "Let's assume the shrimp dip was doctored late in the evening, after people finished eating. Why would the murderer think it wasn't just going to be tossed in the garbage? It had been sitting out all night, after all. Seems reasonable the caterers would just throw out the leftovers for the sake of safety."

Hildy chewed the inside of her cheek. She really was trying to help, but thinking like a murderer was just so far out of her realm, this wasn't easy.

"Win wouldn't let them," she said after a moment. "I remember now. On her way out the caterer told me she tried to throw out the leftovers, but he said he wanted to keep them. She told him she wouldn't recommend it, that if the dip especially went into the refrigerator, bacteria would breed. And he said . . ." Hildy swallowed. "He said, fine, just leave it out, he'd pack it away himself, so she wouldn't feel responsible."

"Oh." I was sorry I'd asked, but the story certainly seemed to absolve the catering staff, more people I needed to check out.

"Everybody knew how much he loved that recipe," she said sadly. "Somebody knew he would eat it that night or the next day. And what if the dip was thrown away? The murderer would probably have had plenty of other opportunities to kill him. Because these were our friends!" She ended on a wail.

"I'm sorry." I patted her hand ineffectually. "Talking about this is hard. But we have to figure out all the possibilities."

"Maybe somebody will confess." She looked at me. "Most people are good. Maybe whoever did this will realize they can't live with the guilt."

"I don't think we're going to count on that," I said. "Okay?"

For once, Hildy didn't correct or lecture me. She just looked glum.

9

With everything else going on in our lives, I'd hardly seen Ed for a real conversation since the memorial service. So I was delighted when he walked in right between Hildy's departure and the girls' return from school.

"Quick," I said, grabbing him and hauling him into the living room. "Sit. Speak."

"Do I get a doggie treat if I obey your commands?" He settled himself on the sofa and patted the seat beside him. I snuggled close, and he put his arm around me.

"It's just that I haven't seen you for a conversation in such a long time," I said. "It's crazy around here."

"And that's different how?"

I leaned my head against his shoulder. "You have to admit, things haven't been remotely serene since Win died. First the death, then the funeral, and now the investigation."

"That's a pattern that's gotten to be pretty familiar."

"But never with one of your predecessors, Ed."

"Let's make this one an exception and not the rule, okay?"

"You say that like I have control over who dies. I don't have anything to do with that part."

"Just the sleuthing."

"Want me to stay out of this one?"

"If I said yes, would it do any good?"

"Try me."

He was silent a moment, as if he was considering. Then he squeezed my arm. "I'm a fair judge of people, but it doesn't take an ounce of insight to figure out Hildy didn't murder Win. Almost anybody can be provoked to murder in the heat of anger, but whoever killed him planned and executed their part with care. Hildy's incapable."

This was as much of a blessing as I was likely to get, and a lot more than I'd usually gotten in the past.

"But stay out of trouble," he added, before I could ask for confirmation. "And stay out of the sanctuary, okay? Figure out what you can and turn it over to Roussos the minute you're really on to something."

"Good idea. He listens so well, and he's so impressed with my conclusions."

"Build a good case. He'll listen."

I know when to let a subject drop. I told him about my afternoon with Hildy, and all the calls we'd made. "It looks like there'll be a good turnout for the graveside service and reception," I finished. "It's nice of Geoff Adler to do the reception at his house."

"He called me to suggest it. He said Win needed to be sent off with dignity, plus he wanted to show his support for Hildy. He wants her to know she still has friends and supporters. He said rumors are circulating."

"I imagine Marie Grandower is making sure of that."

"Marie won't be at the service or reception. Geoff said he'll make sure of *that*."

"I guess Win's affair with Marie is going to be common knowledge." I remembered my conversation with Flo and related that now, along with the details of Ellen's death and her relationship to Win. "Do you suppose Win was involved with Ellen Hardiger or her daughter, too?"

"That's the problem, isn't it? Once you step over a line, everything else you've done is suspect."

"Hildy stood by Win all those years, even knowing what he was capable of."

177

"She loved him, and love's complicated. Sex, power, control. For some people it's all tangled together. There's never a good excuse to cheat on a spouse, but we've both known other men like Win, powerful men who change the world for the better by their actions and courage, and still have serious problems with fidelity."

"You're not defending him, are you?"

"Of course not. Not at all. But I am saying that along with the bad about Godwin Dorchester, there was good we can't lose sight of. I wouldn't have any trouble believing his relationship with the Hardiger women was completely innocent."

"Or believing it wasn't?"

"That, too, unfortunately."

The front door opened, and Teddy came in. Most children are delighted to come home after a long day at school. Not Teddy. As much as she loves us, she's always a little sorry classes are finished for the day. Today, though, she looked happy. Before she could tell us why, Deena came in, too.

"I'm going to speak at a rally for the pedestrian mall," Teddy announced as Deena closed the door behind her. She was beaming, the way most children might if somebody had just announced a plate of chocolate chip cookies was sitting on the kitchen counter.

I held out my arms, too comfortable to go to her for a hug. "How did that happen?"

She joined us on the sofa, throwing herself across both our laps. "Mrs. Bere asked me. It's okay, isn't it?"

I tried to think of a reason it wasn't okay, and couldn't, although I did wish Ida Bere had asked us before she presented the idea to Teddy.

"We'll have to speak to Mrs. Bere first," Ed told her. He settled Teddy's bottom on his lap and I got the length of her legs. I patted the sofa next to me for Deena, but she raised one eyebrow, as if to question my sanity.

"Why do you have to ask?" Teddy asked.

"Because we have to know what's expected."

"I already told her I would do it. She was waiting for me in front of school. She wants me to represent all the children of Emerald Springs."

"Speaking is a big yawn." Deena deposited her books on the stairs and started into the kitchen. "You do all that work, and in a minute it's over with and nobody remembers a thing you said."

"They'll remember me," Teddy said. She wasn't arguing. She sounded convinced.

179

"I'll make sure they do."

"Whatever," Deena called.

"People are all different," Ed told Teddy. "That's what makes this an interesting world."

Teddy helped me make four-cheese macaroni for dinner, and Deena put together a salad. Since Ed didn't have any meetings tonight, he volunteered to do the cleanup, which left me without any excuses. I had all the time I needed to drive to Fern and Samuel Booth's house to tell them about tomorrow's graveside service and reception.

"Nobody needs help with homework?" I asked after the table had been cleared.

"If they do, I'll help," Ed said. "Quit stalling."

"Easy for you to say." But I went upstairs to get ready, and a few minutes later I was in my van on the way to Emerald Estates.

The Booths' house resembles somebody's fantasy of a French chateau. Blond brick, mansard roof, multipaned windows. The landscaping consists of tortured evergreens and in summer, regimented rows of annuals for color. Every blade of grass stands tall at exactly the same height. A walkway of the same brick leads up to the front door, and I am convinced if I ever stray off it, an alarm will sound.

I knocked, and eventually the heavy wood door swung open, revealing a marble tiled foyer. If the Booths ever need more income, the foyer is large enough to double as a roller rink.

Fern was behind the door, and she stepped into view to glare at me.

"Did you call to let us know you were coming?"

"I'm sorry, but your telephone was out of order when I tried to reach you."

"There was a problem on the line in the afternoon. It's working now."

I hadn't tried a second time, since I wanted a few minutes of face-to-face conversation with both Fern and Samuel, but I certainly wasn't going to tell her that.

"I'm sorry," I said with the smile that has never impressed her, "I must have come at a bad time."

"I suppose it's as good a time as any." She stepped aside to let me in.

From what I've been told, once upon a time minister's wives were expected to make calls on parishioners with their husbands. Church members routinely brought out their best china, tiny tea sandwiches, freshly baked delicacies, and chitchat. Times have definitely changed. These days the significant other of a minister is as apt to be a man as a woman. We are sometimes the same sex as our partners. We often work at time-consuming jobs, and some of us have nothing to do with church or attend a different denomination's.

But even with all the changes, basic hospitality on both sides is still a norm. I was surprised to find so little of it tonight.

"We were watching PBS," Fern said, as if I had purposely gauged my visit to interfere.

"I'll be glad to tell you why I'm here and leave," I offered.

Even Fern has limits to rudeness. "No, come in and say hello to Samuel. Would you like coffee?" She sounded marginally more welcoming, although I knew if I said yes to the coffee, I would regret it.

I thanked her and refused, and after another minute of walking through stultifyingly formal rooms, we ended up in the only one that hinted at real comfort. The family room, where Samuel stood to greet me, was paneled in cherry, with dark plaid furniture and a brick fireplace that took up most of one wall.

I shook Samuel's hand. Like Fern, he was dressed informally, which in her case meant she wasn't wearing pantyhose and in his, no tie.

Samuel gestured me to a place on the sofa. I lowered myself to the edge and folded my hands.

"We're having a lovely spring, aren't we?" Samuel asked.

I'd hardly noticed, considering everything else that had been going on, but I nodded. "On the way over I saw crocus."

"Spring's my favorite time." He nodded seriously, as if he'd been giving this hours of thought. I wondered if he'd been forced to consult Fern, or if he'd made this discovery on his own.

We chatted aimlessly for several minutes. Yes, my family was fine. No, I was no longer actively rehabilitating houses, not until the real estate market perked up again. I asked them about their granddaughter, Shirley, who is the spitting image of her grandmother in every way, including Fern's bad temper. Luckily their daughter-in-law Mabyn is a good influence, and if Shirley is lucky, nurture may thwart nature.

When the conversation lagged, which it did almost immediately, I explained why I had come.

"Hildy and I spent the day calling church members," I concluded. "We didn't want you to be left out. I know you were friends with both Win and Hildy."

"Of course not," Samuel said. "Thank you for making the extra effort."

"Our phone is working now," Fern repeated, as if to hammer home the point.

"As a matter of fact, it's not," Samuel said. "I tried it a moment ago. Dead again."

Fern harrumphed, as if Samuel had stolen all her ammunition. I was glad I wasn't going to be around for pillow talk.

"I know Hildy will appreciate her old friends being there," I said, trying to feel my way into a discussion of the people who were at the party the night Win died. "I hope when Ed and I revisit former churches, we have as many people who remember us as they do."

"Yes, well, Win was an inspirational speaker and an artful administrator," Samuel said.

"His sermons always made the congregation think," Fern said. "No theological gobbledygook. Good rational, logical subjects. Nothing we had to stretch to believe."

Personally I thought people should stretch on Sunday morning, but this was definitely not the time to say so. Discussing Win's sermons did bring something else to mind.

"Do you happen to have any of his old sermons?" I asked. "I'm sure you know I'm putting together the church history? Win didn't have copies with him of any of the sermons he gave during his years here. And there's not one in the archives. At least none I can find."

"I'm not one to keep old papers around," Fern said.

"I don't think we have anything like that," Samuel agreed. "His sermons were excellent, but I kept them here." He touched two fingers to his forehead.

"They must have been memorable." I smiled.

"It was, perhaps, his greatest gift."

I decided to broaden my approach. "I've heard he was an excellent counselor, too."

Samuel's expression changed. One moment he had been affable and smiling. Now he looked almost stricken. The change didn't last. But even when he smiled again, I thought his eyes looked haunted.

Of course, try to measure *that*. It had all happened so quickly, I wasn't sure what I'd seen. I just wondered what nerve I had hit and why.

"Win was good at everything," Fern said. "One had to be in those days. It was expected. Seminaries were much more difficult to get into, and they only graduated the best."

I couldn't imagine how to reply. Ed had

graduated at the top of his class at Harvard, but Fern's message was clear.

Samuel seemed to pull himself together again. "Win did have a brilliant gift for administration. I was board president while he was our minister, you know, and I've only rarely seen someone that capable of organization and management. The church ran like a perfectly calibrated clock."

I thought he was laying this on awfully thick, like too much icing on a crumbling cake to lay on another simile, too. I wondered if he hoped I wouldn't notice that something was out of whack.

"I know this whole thing must be a terrible shock for their friends here," I said. "It's a shock for those of us who hardly knew Win. And right after the party to celebrate their return."

"I, for one, think the police have just made an error," Samuel said. "Nobody could possibly have wanted to murder Win. And Hildy least of all. I hope she demands more tests. It must be a mistake."

"They're certain it was murder," I said. "I'm afraid that's no longer in doubt."

"Well, no matter what happened, we will certainly be there tomorrow." Fern's voice had chilled to arctic temperatures. "Is there anything else we should know?"

186

I know a dismissal when I hear one. I got to my feet, and she was on hers in a nano-second. "Nothing else," I said. "Hildy just wanted to be sure you knew tomorrow's schedule."

Samuel had lumbered to his feet in the meantime, but Fern held out a hand to stop him from walking me to the door. "I'll escort Aggie, Samuel. You finish our show."

I wanted to volunteer to find my own way out so they could both finish it, but I was afraid I might wander the house for days, stumbling from one room of ponderous antiques and reproductions to another, looking for an exit.

I said good-bye to Samuel, then I followed a silent Fern through the house. I was sure she made two wrong turns, but we got to the door in record time.

I wasn't sure what to say. Not thank you for seeing me. That sounded pathetic. After all, I was the one who'd given up a valuable evening with my family to let them know about the service.

"Have a good evening, Fern," I said instead, falling back on a cliché, which is the sole reason for having them available. "We'll see you tomorrow."

"Just a minute." She didn't open the door; in fact, she stood in front of it, barring it with her body. "I hope you don't intend to investigate Win's death, Agate. I know that's something of a hobby of yours."

Scrapbooking is a hobby. Whittling is a hobby. Finding murderers, and putting my own life in danger? That isn't a hobby, that's an unhealthy obsession. I was surprised she couldn't see the difference.

"I think I'm already involved," I said carefully. "Win was Ed's predecessor, and Hildy is being questioned as a suspect in the murder."

"Have you no idea how bad this will look to the residents of Emerald Springs? This murder is already much too close to home. How do you think *your* involvement will look to the community? The entire episode is a blot on our reputation!"

"Um, don't you think it will be a bigger blot if the wife of your former minister is arrested and tried for a murder she didn't commit?"

"What I think is that you should stay out of this. The church needs a lower profile in this sordid affair, not a higher one."

I considered, then I shook my head. "It's strange, Fern. When I got here tonight, I started thinking about all the differences in expectations of minister's wives fifty or maybe even fifteen years ago and now. In those days I would have been expected to agree with you and stay out of everybody's way. But times have changed."

She snorted. "What you're really saying is that dedicated minister's wives like Hildy Dorchester have come and gone. Well, it's too bad, if that's true."

I couldn't believe she'd used Hildy as an example. I waited until she'd opened the door before I answered.

"Hildy Dorchester herself may come and go, if I don't try to find out who murdered Win. She might even go upriver, as they say, for a murder she didn't commit. Surely that's not what you're after?"

She didn't answer, and I didn't push it. I just nodded and walked carefully down the driveway to my van, making certain not to flatten even one blade of grass.

Just in case.

10

On Thursday, after the solemnity of Win's graveside service, Geoff Adler's house on Lake Parsons was a welcome sight. The lake lies about forty-five minutes outside of Emerald Springs, and in high summer looks like a Jet Ski version of a bumper car ride. But in spring, the lake is inviting, particularly the farthest reaches where the depth is too shallow to encourage supercharged activity. Geoff's property takes up a fair amount of shoreline there, and the house, a rambling old structure with brown wood siding and wide porches along every side, was set back from the water with an expansive lawn as buffer. A long dock stretched into the lake anchored by an octagonal gazebo on shore. Two Jet Skis and something like a fourteen-foot powerboat were docked there.

"How do you like that dock? Pretty nice setup," I told Ed.

"He told me about the boat. He built it himself, and it has some kind of low-impact electric motor. Very quiet and environmentally friendly."

"In partnership with the Jet Skis? The yin and yang of water sports." Super detective that I am, I figured this attested to two very different sides to our host. A quiet, meditative side that yearned for peace, and a rip-roaring side that wanted action and adventure.

The house itself was meant to be appreciated by a large family, with jigsaw puzzles on the round porch table and kites on the lawn. Did Geoff have a family side, too? As we drove up to the house I wondered this out loud.

"Geoff's great-grandfather built the place, and it's always belonged to the family," Ed said. "Geoff told me he grew up here, so even though it's too big for one person, he can't make himself sell it."

"Maybe he'll get married again and have a family to fill it."

"Any number of women would volunteer, I'm sure."

I imagined that was true. Geoff wasn't bad to look at. He was smart and thoughtful, and from everything I knew, the Emerald Eagle drugstore chain was thriving, despite an economy unfriendly to small businesses. I wondered if Lucy knew Geoff. I wondered if Lucy no longer needed my matchmaking abilities, and if not, why didn't she just tell me?

A young man with an orange armband and a matching pennant waved us along a grassy path to an open area where we could leave the van. Considering what a short time he'd had to plan, Geoff had gone to a lot of trouble.

The graveside service had been brief and moving. Under the circumstances, brief was particularly good. I think most of us were holding our breaths, afraid something else would happen to postpone Win's final rest. But Ed turned off his iPhone for the duration of the service, and nobody dove into the open grave. I did catch sight of a woman, watching from a distance, who might have been Marie Grandower. But if it was Marie, she didn't disturb the service. Maybe she planned to wait and say her final, private good-byes after everybody else left for the reception.

Most people had carpooled to the lake, and about ten cars had already parked. We were probably the last to arrive, since the moment he turned on his phone again, Ed received an emergency call from Norma

Beet, who couldn't convince the church mimeograph machine to print out Sunday's order of service. Ed's solution sounded like mechanical voodoo to me. Unplug. Wait thirty seconds. Plug. Wait thirty more seconds. Press Start. Then hold down . . . I lost interest before they sacrificed a goat, but whatever they did got it working again, even though the lengthy solution made us late.

We crossed the grass and climbed the steps to the front porch, where several people with plates heaped with fried chicken and other traditional picnic fare were already seating themselves. Esther, the forbearing church organist, greeted us and sent us inside where food was being served.

Most of those in attendance were church members. I recognized a few community leaders and noticed a few strangers, who might have attended when Win was minister and had since gone on to other churches or solitary Sundays with the *New York Times.*

A young woman delivered frosty glasses of lemonade while we stood chatting in what passed for a food line. Ed excused himself to talk to somebody, and I held his place. I noted that Hildy was backed into a corner with the Booths flanking her. I wondered if Fern was insisting that Hildy convince me my real role in life is washing dishes after potlucks. Since Fern kept glancing in my direction, I wasn't being paranoid. Okay, not very.

"You and Ed are vegetarians, aren't you?"

I hadn't noticed Geoff Adler approaching, but now I saw he was standing right beside me.

"Looks like plenty for us to eat anyway," I said.

"I play at it, but I fall off the wagon a lot, hence the fried chicken."

In addition to all the other desirable traits Geoff possessed, he was clearly a good host. The room was large, paneled in dark wood, with a dining area to the left, and a living area to the right. The dining table was huge and pulled far enough from the wall that guests could easily move around both sides. Another table was set under a large pass-through window to the kitchen, and that surface was divided between drinks and dessert. Geoff might be a bachelor, but he understood how to make a room comfortable and his guests comfortable with it. From the old linens covering the tables, to the opalescent serving platters and pitchers, to a coffee urn that looked like an antique Russian samovar, the room radiated quiet, old-fashioned comfort, without a hint of shabbiness.

"I like the house," I told him. "I feel instantly at home."

"I haven't changed it much in the years I've lived alone here. My mother and grandmother didn't have much to work with, but they had good taste. They would buy a piece here and a piece there whenever they found a bargain. I can't imagine what they could have accomplished with more money."

"Then Emerald Eagle hasn't always been the going concern it is now?"

He gave a soft laugh. "Long on service and short on cash."

"All heart and no business sense?"

"My great-grandfather, the first Geoffrey Adler, was a terrific businessman. If I looked closely at family history, I'm pretty sure I'd find snake oil and hootchie cootchie dancers. But he landed in Ohio, saw the need for a hometown drugstore in Emerald Springs, with a smiling, family-friendly druggist, and that's the image he projected while he raked in the dough."

I was trying to wing myself that far back into Emerald Springs history. It was easy to see where Geoff's Jet Ski side had originated. "And he built this house?"

"The core of it, yes. It was just a summer place at first, too far from town to manage a business and live here year-round. He moved full-time to the lake when he and my great-grandmother were in their seventies, after he turned the business over to their son. My grandfather and my father were exactly the kind of pharmacists the original Geoffrey claimed to be. Kindly, homebodies, generous to a fault, hardworking."

The quiet, electric-motor side of Geoff's personality. I had to smile. "But not great businessmen?"

"Short on common sense and long on compassion."

"So, who do you take after?"

He laughed, and I liked the sound. "Some of all, I hope. The store was a shambles by the time it came down to me. Even a sterling reputation can't compete against cheaper prices and the assortment of products from the big chains. Dad was ready to sell and move Mom to Florida, but I convinced them to let me see what I could do. In the end, it turned out well. They're happy in Ft. Lauderdale, and I'm happy growing the family business. Not that it's been easy."

I edged us back to the reason for this gathering. "That must have been just about the time Win was the minister of Tri-C."

"Those were lean years for Emerald Eagle.

Win and I used to have long conversations about old-fashioned values and modern business methods. I learned a lot from watching him run the church. He kept me on the right track."

Geoff lowered his voice. "Win was almost a second father to me. I know he wasn't perfect. But don't let everything that's come out about Marie convince you his years here had no value. I saw him up close, and I know how much good he did for the church and the community."

"Do you think she's exaggerated her role in Win's life?"

He didn't seem to mind the question. "We've talked since the whole story came out. Win was the big love of Marie's life. She told me as much. But was she his? I can't answer for certain, of course, but I think Marie may have been an occasional respite from the demands of living with Hildy. Hildy's expectations were so high for everybody in that family. That's why her daughters seem so aloof. They're still afraid of being swallowed alive. But there was also a lot of love. It was easier for Win to escape the occasional problems than to confront them. Marie was a weakness, but I guess I understand."

Since I was standing in his house about to

partake of his hospitality, I managed not to say so, but I was beginning to think it was easier for men to "understand" than it ought to be. Let the little woman step out of line, and all the guy's buddies winked when the husband went looking for solace. Okay, that wasn't exactly what Geoff had said, nor my own husband either, but for men, forgiveness of infidelity seemed at the ready. Maybe it was attached to the Y chromosome.

"Marie was one of the last people to leave the party," I pointed out.

Geoff didn't try to misunderstand. "She wouldn't have hurt a hair on Win's head."

"Not even if he'd just told her that he had no intention of picking up where they left off? Not even to get even with him and Hildy in one fell swoop?"

"You really look for the worst in people, don't you?"

"Luckily it's *Ed's* job to look for the best. What a team."

"I know Marie well. We've been friends for years. She even house-sits for me when I'm away, if she's in town and needs some peace and quiet. So you can see how much I trust her. After a disappointment she'd be more likely to buy herself a really fabulous piece of jewelry than to poison somebody. I just wish I hadn't brought her with me to the party that night. But I was clueless about their past history. In all the years I've known her, she never mentioned it. Not until he died."

"Why *did* you bring her?"

He lifted a brow, as if he wondered what gave me the right to ask. But after a pause, he answered. "We've discovered if we appear in each other's company often enough, there are fewer attempts to match us up with the recently divorced and widowed. So it's convenient and pleasant when she's in town, and nothing more."

"I'm sorry, Geoff, but I'm worried about Hildy, and if I can find out anything that will help . . ."

He put a hand on my arm in reassurance. "I know. But not everybody's going to be as forthcoming as I've been, so be careful."

"Believe me, I know."

"Anything else I can help with?"

"Do you know about the church history project?" I waited until he nodded. "I was planning to interview Win about his years here, but now, of course, I can't. So I'll be talking to people who knew him best. Will you have time at some point?"

"Of course."

"Great. And would you happen to have

any old sermons that he gave during that time? We've confirmed the church printed them, but there aren't any copies in the archives."

"I'll be happy to look. If I do, they're filed in my office in the next building. Catch me later and we'll go and see."

I thanked him. He squeezed my arm, then he wandered off to talk to other guests.

By the time I had a plate of baked beans, potato and pasta salads, and a square of cornbread, several other church members had agreed to an interview about Win. I knew I was overdoing this, but it was such a perfect way to dig deeper into the man's life and death, I couldn't contain myself. I really would try to use something each of them told me when I wrote up the history, just so I wouldn't feel so guilty about the ruse.

Ed was still chatting, and hadn't gotten back into line for food, so I wandered outside and around the side porch to see what was there. Picnic tables were set up under hardwoods beginning to leaf out in earnest. Half-blooming fountains of forsythia lined the path, and I found a spot at the end of one table.

I wasn't alone long. Hildy arrived carrying a small plate of food, more for show, I guessed, than for nourishment. She looked pale and tired, and black was not her color. I had spent the morning trying to figure out who had killed her husband, and she had spent it saying her final good-bye.

"Come sit with me," I said, patting the place beside me. For once she didn't point out she might be needed elsewhere, that somebody might need a helping hand or a listening ear or any other of the many "ing" imperatives that motivate women. She just sat and sighed.

"It was a beautiful service," I said, "and Win is finally at rest."

"No, not until this matter is settled. Not until we know who killed my husband."

Unfortunately, she was right. I patted her hand, which was not reaching for her fork, as it should have been. "We're going to figure this out. The police are still working on it."

"My daughters will come back if they have to."

She had stressed "have." I was sure her girls were not excited about coming back to the scene of the crime, and fairly sure they weren't excited about trying to help their mother through this crisis. I imagine Hildy had rarely if ever allowed her daughters to assist her. The role would be unfamiliar to them and possibly even distasteful.

201

"Right now let's just see what happens," I said, reaching for my own fork in hopes she would do the same.

"Fern wants you to stay out of the investigation," Hildy said. "She's adamant."

So I hadn't been paranoid. Fern really had been discussing me when she and Samuel had penned poor Hildy in that corner.

When I didn't say more, Hildy went on. "She can be difficult, I know. But you really must try to get along with her."

"Must I?"

Hildy sighed. "It's not an easy life, is it?"

I couldn't help myself. "I think it's easier if you control it yourself and don't let every member of the congregation have a say in who you are and what you do."

"Such a difference a generation makes."

She hadn't said this critically. I wondered if Hildy wished now that she hadn't worked so hard to please everyone and uphold a certain image, perhaps alienating her husband and children as she did. But what did I know? I hadn't been there, and I would never know how any members of the Dorchester family viewed their years together.

"I'm not staying out of the investigation, just because Fern decrees it," I said. "I'll stay out if it looks like I'm making things worse, not better. Right now I'm just putting facts together." I didn't add that the few I had were darned lonely, too.

Others joined us, and just as I thought my luck would hold and the Booths would stay inside to eat, Fern and Samuel came around the side of the house with filled plates. There were two places at the end of our table, and they took them.

Conversation had flowed smoothly enough until they arrived. Now it grew stilted and uncomfortable. I finished eating and got to my feet, thrilled to be able to escape.

"I'm going to look for dessert. Does anybody need something from inside?"

People murmured polite no's, but Samuel Booth stood. "I'll come with you. I need . . ." He paused as if inventing something. "Cornbread."

I repeated that I'd be happy to bring some back with me, but Samuel shook his head. In a moment he was at my side.

Charming. I know an excuse when I see one. I was the mistress of transparent excuses, the queen. We started off and sure enough, the moment we were out of easy earshot, he stopped.

"I want to tell you something."

Reasons and ways to stop him jumbled together in my mind, but none were good

203

enough, and besides, I was too slow.

"You're going to be poking your nose into Win's life, aren't you?" he asked.

I'd been prepared for a lecture, not a question. Since I'm no good at lies, I answered truthfully. "Somebody killed Win Dorchester, and the police are pointing fingers at Hildy. I'd like to see them point their fingers in the right direction, wouldn't you?"

"You won't just leave this alone?"

"I seem incapable." I tried to smile. "Call it a personality flaw."

He didn't reply for so long that I wondered if we were finished. Then he grimaced. "You'll be digging into our lives, too. Everybody who was at that party. You've already started. That's what the other night was about."

I really didn't know what to say to that. I waited, but I didn't have to wait long.

"Win knew something about me that nobody else did," Samuel said. "And he used it against me."

This was the last thing I'd expected to hear. Again, I'd been primed for a lecture. "Used it?" I squeaked.

"If you dig hard enough, you'll discover this yourself. So now you can hear it right from me. In my early twenties, late one night I hit a man with my car and killed him. I'd had too much to drink, and he stepped off a curb and into my lane, and I couldn't avoid him. To this day I still think I'd have hit him, even if I was stone sober. But, I wasn't, so I'll never be sure. Of course the cops thought otherwise. I was arrested and charged with vehicular manslaughter, and I served a little time in jail for it."

Samuel was turning a bright, unhealthy scarlet. I wondered if he would survive his own revelation. He went on without giving me time to stop him. "I wasn't an alcoholic. I was just young and stupid. No day goes by that I don't think about that man and his family. It was terrible."

"It must have been," I said. "But what does it have to do with Win, Samuel? How was he involved?"

"He did some counseling with me. All those years later, and I was still having nightmares. I hadn't told anybody about the conviction, except Fern. It happened in Massachusetts, and I got out of New England as soon as I was released. After I married Fern, we moved here, and nobody ever knew. But the nightmares were horrible. I thought . . . I thought I could trust Win. And talking to him helped. Until . . ."

He was growing redder. I wondered if

anybody at the party had a medical degree. I wanted to grab him and unbutton his shirt collar.

"Until the day I confronted him about Marie," Samuel choked out. "You see, I saw him coming out of her house early one morning when Hildy was out of town. And I realized that couldn't be good. So I went to him that afternoon at the church and confronted him. I was the board president that year, it was my duty. I asked him what was going on. And you know what he said? He said some things need to be kept quiet, that nobody should understand that better than I did. When I asked him to clarify, he said that revelations of bad behavior are almost always harmful for everybody concerned, and again, I should understand."

I let that sink in. "You think he was saying that if you told anybody what you'd seen, he would tell people about your past?"

"He made it crystal clear, even though he never came right out and said it. My silence for his silence."

I wondered if Win really would have exposed Samuel if he had gone to the board about Marie. But even if he hadn't, making the threat had been bad enough.

"I'm so sorry," I said, and meant it. "That's terrible, Samuel. You had every right to expect complete confidentiality from Win. And you were right to confront him about Marie."

He didn't seem to hear me. "So now you know my secret. But let me tell you something, young lady. You go ahead and expose me if you think that will help anybody. I did not kill Win Dorchester, even if I was sorry to see him moving back to Emerald Springs. And I'll tell anybody who asks that I told you all this of my own free will, because maybe I have been trying to hide something that happened more than fifty years ago, but when it comes to Win's death, I have nothing to hide. Nothing!"

I thought the man was one angry word away from a stroke. "Honestly, I have no intention —"

"Samuel!"

I turned and saw Fern bearing down on us. She was nearly as red-faced as her husband. As angry as she looked, I was still glad to see her.

"What's going on?" she demanded.

"There's a bench over there." I pointed to a quiet spot under a small group of trees. "I think Samuel should sit for a while. Will you go with him?"

"What did you say to upset him?"

"Samuel's under a lot of stress. I really

think he needs to sit and calm himself. I'll be glad to go with him if you don't want to."

The look she shot me would have felled a rampaging elephant. "I will take care of my own husband."

"I'll get you both water."

She leaned closer and took Samuel's arm. "Just leave us alone."

I watched them move slowly toward the bench. I was shaken, but I waited until they were seated before I left. I wasn't sure why Samuel had made his confession, but I guessed that he believed two erroneous facts. One, that because I had stopped by their house last night, I had singled him out as a prime suspect. And two, that I had the ability and resources to dig up a manslaughter conviction in another state that was more than fifty years old. So he had decided to preempt me, to show that he had nothing to be afraid of, because he had *not* murdered Win.

I didn't know Samuel Booth very well. Fern was the outspoken spouse in the Booth household, and I was sorry I knew *her* as well as I did. But now I was pretty sure Samuel had spent most of his life steeped in regret for a death he may or may not have been able to prevent. Then, as if that hadn't been enough of a burden, the one outsider he had trusted with the truth had betrayed him. I felt a surge of sympathy. Samuel had made two bad decisions in his life, and both would haunt him until he died.

I just hoped he hadn't made a third right before Easter and deprived the world of the man who had blackmailed him into silence.

I had lost my appetite for dessert; instead I went to see if Ed was ready to go. Hildy found me before I could find my husband. She gave a nearly full plate of food to one of the servers before she caught my arm.

"Geoff is looking for you. He's going to see if he has copies of any of Win's sermons."

If anything, she looked more wan than she had earlier. I had really expected to see people surging around her, offering comfort, but they all seemed busy elsewhere, and Hildy was alone. I didn't want to leave her standing here by myself. Not today.

"Why don't you come with us?" I suggested. "If he has more than one, you can go through them and pick the one you think Win would have wanted to go into the history."

She nodded. It seemed to take extra effort. "His office is in the back. I'll show you."

We intercepted Geoff on the way to a building about thirty yards behind the house. The construction looked newer, but the same dark siding set off dark green shutters, and the office favored the house in its casual, sprawling style. It was exactly the kind of office I would like myself, if I had a job and a reason. Oh, and the money for a lakeside estate.

Geoff chatted as we closed the distance to the door, and once we were there he patted his pants pockets and grimaced. He leaned down and felt between two decorative boulders on the right, produced a key, and held it out sheepishly. "I keep a lot of personal and business records out here, so I compromise between laziness and common sense. I lock the door, then I hide the extra key in the first place any enterprising thief would look for it."

I smiled to show I was in on the joke. "That would be the second place. The first would be under the mat."

"Crime's not much of an issue out here. If I worried, I'd worry about my boats, not my computer files, but the cops do a good job of keeping trouble at bay. They even have a lake patrol."

We followed him inside. The casual ambience of the house hadn't made its way here.

This was all business. Wall-to-wall file cabinets on one wall, another wall with shelves of supplies, and a comfortable seating area. In the middle a desk as large as my mother's quilt frame, and the Death Star of computers, a black monstrosity that probably blew up friendly planets whenever Geoff left the room.

"It's really more or less records storage," he said. "Most of these are old documents and files. Our real office is in town above the store."

I noted the Emerald Eagle logo on the wall above a leather sofa. The design is a series of green lines, four of them, shaped to look like an eagle soaring. Both simple and clever, kind of like Geoff.

"Win told me you were the best treasurer he ever had," Hildy said. "He wished he could take you along to every church."

"I'm glad I had time to serve when I wasn't as busy with the business. Otherwise he wouldn't have been so impressed." Geoff walked to one of the filing cabinets and selected a drawer. He opened it and began to page through files.

"Can we help?" I asked.

"No, I have miscellaneous records organized by dates. If I have them, they'll be right here."

I spent the next minutes wishing I could say that about everything in my life. Although I'm not a slob, I am far too creative to believe that just one destination per object ought to be the norm.

He finally straightened. "Nothing." He turned up his hands in apology. "I really thought I might have kept at least a couple in with all my records from the years I was on the board. His sermons were so memorable. I'm sorry."

"It's too bad all Win's files are packed away," Hildy said. "But it would be much too difficult for anyone else to go through our boxes at the storage facility. And I'm not supposed to —"

I heard what she didn't say. "Leave town." Hildy was not supposed to leave town because she was the top suspect in her husband's murder. I hurried to fill the space. "I haven't even started asking around. Somebody will have one."

Geoff slid the drawer closed with a bang. "It's too bad Win didn't have the chance to write his —"

Somebody knocked on the door, and before Geoff could finish what might have been an interesting sentence, Ed nudged it open. "I was told you kidnapped my wife."

After a moment of polite chat, Ed asked if

I was ready to go. We had almost an hour's drive, and he wanted to make sure we were home in time to greet Teddy.

"Thanks for looking," I told Geoff. We invited Hildy to ride back with us, but she said she felt she ought to stay and go home with Esther and Dolly, who had brought her. Ed shook hands with Geoff, kissed Hildy's cheek, and we left.

"What did you say to Samuel Booth?" Ed asked, when we were just a few yards from the office door.

I was sorry he'd learned about the altercation so quickly. "What do you mean?"

"They left, but on the way out, Fern told me you nearly gave him a heart attack."

And here I'd just been worried about a stroke. I considered what to say in response. This was my husband, and I trusted him completely. Still, Samuel's words were echoing through my head. Samuel Booth had trusted two people other than his wife with the truth about his past. One of them had betrayed him. The other was me. Did I have the right to tell Ed what I'd learned? I had to think about that.

"He feels strongly about Win's ministry here," I said, which was certainly true. "He got pretty worked up. This murder's hit a lot of the congregation hard."

213

"That's it?"

"Pretty much."

"They can make a lot of trouble for us, but I trust you. I know you didn't set out to antagonize them."

The vote of confidence felt good, but nothing felt as good as leaving the lake behind us, and at least for the moment, Hildy's problems, too.

11

Deena is one of a group of girls who call themselves the Green Meanies. I've watched them intently since their informal friendship hardened into something approaching a middle school sorority. They're all good kids, some better than others. Some of them worry more about being popular than about grades. Some are brainiacs, and, at least on the surface, still more or less oblivious to the male of their species. They all have other friends and interests. There are no clubhouses, rules, and procedures — at least that I know about — or initiation rites. But a week rarely goes by that they don't get together at somebody's house. The Meanie Moms haven't made any real attempts to discourage this, although we meet occasionally to make sure we're on the same page, so that none of the girls can legitimately claim somebody else's mother is cooler than her own.

On the day after the reception, I opened my door with Moonpie in my arms to prevent escape, and found Grace Forester, Shannon Forester's mother, standing on my porch. I assumed she had come to enlighten me about some Meanie madness I wasn't yet privy to. Grace, with her Alice in Wonderland hairstyle and pale green eyes, looks demure, even shy. She appears to be that accommodating somebody you want behind the counter at a hotel or shop making certain you get everything you'd ever wished for. In truth Grace is a pit bull, the Meanie Mom most likely to scent problems in the making and snarl, snap, and lunge until they're fixed. She's as subtle as a pit bull, too.

"My whole world will come crashing to a halt if you don't do something, Aggie!"

I was only on my second cup of coffee, not quite up to saving the world. I motioned her inside, and after I freed the cat, Grace followed me to the kitchen where she flopped down at the table that dominates the room and thankfully covers much of our sad old floor.

I poured her a cup of coffee without asking and freshened my own. Then I plopped down in a chair across from her. I was dressed in sweats, but my feet were covered in fuzzy bunny slippers, a Christmas gift from Teddy. I wiggled my toes to make sure I was really awake.

"This is about Shannon or Deena? Is Shannon on the debate team?"

Grace frowned. She tasted the coffee before she spoke. "I'll give you the name of a good place to order beans. You ever grind your own?"

"Maxwell House is a family friend."

"You have better taste than this. Did you ever try cold brew? Even grocery store coffee is good if you cold brew."

"My oldest sister's the gourmet. She roasts and grinds her own beans, and her coffee is fabulous. She has no children or husband."

"Make Deena do the work. None of those girls work hard enough. Slackers, all of them."

I was used to Grace's rants. "Is that why you're here? Cracking the whip before breakfast?"

She drank half of her mug of substandard coffee, which tasted like life-giving nectar to me.

"I'm going to be ruined," she said at last. "If you don't figure out who murdered Win Dorchester, I'm finished. You know this economy. Who's going to use a caterer who poisoned a guest?"

This was a surprise and news to me, big news. "You? *You* catered the party at the Dorchesters' the night Win died?"

"Emerald Excellence. You didn't know?"

I wasn't sure how I'd missed this bit of gossip. "How long have you been catering?"

"Three months. I bought the business from the former owner. She threw up her hands and said good riddance, and I got it for a song, pots, pans, recipes — not that most of them were any good — the whole works. That's why Hildy Dorchester called me. The name was familiar. And we did such a good job. The food was fabulous, only some bozo poisoned the shrimp dip. And I told Win Dorchester to throw the stuff out because it had been sitting on the table all evening. If he'd listened to me, he wouldn't be dead right now!"

I figured that would teach poor stubborn Win, although unfortunately, he was no longer all that teachable.

"Haven't the police given you a pass already?" I asked. "They don't seem interested in pursuing anybody but Hildy as the murderer."

"I don't have any connection to the Dorchesters except that they hired Emerald Excellence for their party. Why would I kill the man? He only paid a deposit. He was going to mail the rest. You see if I do that again!"

"So why are you worried?"

She ran her fingers through her light brown hair and looked as if she was trying to calm down. "Because I can't go all over town protesting I had nothing to do with this. That makes me look guilty. But until the police arrest somebody, people will wonder anyway. I had a cancellation the day the news got out that Dorchester died from my shrimp dip. Had another yesterday. It's a slow bleed out. I'm dying here."

"I'm sorry." I like Grace, I really do. A person who says exactly what she thinks is rare. One who says it with gusto is rarer still. Energetic Grace had probably put a lot of herself into revamping Emerald Excellence in the months she'd owned it, and now somebody's vendetta against Win was going to ruin her, if the poor economy didn't get her first.

"I need more than consolation from you, Aggie. You're good at figuring this stuff out. If you spend a little time, you can tell the police who killed him. You're not flipping houses these days are you?"

"Not so anybody would notice."

"Then what are you waiting for?"

"You know any private investigators selling out? I could do what you did and buy a business."

"Aggie!"

I raised my hand, palm out. "I'm already working on it, Grace. I'm trying to help Hildy, because *she* didn't murder him either."

She sat back. "Well, what do you know so far? Give me something to hang on to, okay?"

I got up and made toast while I thought about this, using the orange bread I'd finished late last night when thoughts of Hildy and Win had kept me awake. It was rich with zest and pecans and a family favorite.

I brought it to the table with the last of the jam Teddy and I had made from local strawberries the previous June. Grace slathered a slice with butter and jam.

"Maybe you can help *me*," I said. "I know you had nothing to do with Win's death, but you were right there at the party. Emerald Excellence was on my list to interview. I just didn't know Emerald Excellence was *you*."

"The police asked a bunch of questions. Did you make this bread?"

"Uh-huh. What did they ask?"

She held up her half-eaten slice. "It's really good. You honestly made it?"

"Just because I can't make coffee to your specifications doesn't mean I can't bake bread."

She still looked suspicious. "They wanted to know my life history, that's what. Whether I knew Win when he was here before —"

"Did you?"

"No! I lived in Scranton until I married and moved here. I never met Reverend Dorchester until the night of the party. Mrs. Dorchester made all the plans, and wow, is she picky."

I could relate. "What else did they ask?"

"About my employees."

"What about them?"

"How many were in the house that night, whether they had access to the food. Stuff like that."

"What did you say?"

"It was a small party. I have an assistant who helped me prepare, but she was busy that night, so she wasn't at the party. I only needed one other person to help serve and clean up, so I used Red —"

"Red?"

"A local guy, Red Brown. He lives out in the county somewhere. He serves, tends bar, does preparation, whatever I need. Next to Hannah, my assistant, I use him the most. I hired a couple of other people who serve when they're needed, but Hannah, Red, and I are the core. Nobody's making a fortune at this, I'll tell you, least of all me. Everybody but me works other jobs, too. This is extra for them."

"Hannah helped make the food?"

"But she wasn't there, so how could she have put anything in it later in the evening? That must be what happened, you know. The dip was more than half eaten by evening's end, and nobody else got sick."

"What about Red? Was he alone with the shrimp dip at the end?"

"I didn't keep track every minute, but I was the one who brought the dip into the kitchen. Red left early. And before that, people were milling around the table, so it would have been hard for him to doctor it."

"Did you sample it when it came back to the kitchen?"

"Trust me, after you've cooked and cooked and served, eating the leftovers is the last thing you think about. Besides, I was too busy."

I was glad she'd been too busy. "Red left early?"

"He didn't ask to leave. I told him to, because we'd cleaned up as the evening went along, and there wasn't enough left to do for two of us. I paid him and sent him home. I promised we'd split the tip, if there was any. He's moody, and that wasn't one of his better nights. I was glad to get rid of him."

"Was he giving you trouble?"

"Nothing like that. Just sullen. Annoyed at little things. He probably had a bad day. He drives a wrecker for a BP station, and he doesn't like that job. He acted tired."

"Can you give me his phone number? I'd like to talk to him."

"He's hard to reach. He doesn't have a phone, so he calls in every couple of days from a pay phone to see if we have something coming up. If he doesn't call, I have to leave messages at the gas station, but they're not all that cooperative. The next time I hear from him, I'll give him your number."

I just bet old Red never got around to calling me. He sounded like a loner who was happier without human contact. If I was right, I'd have to find a better way to talk to him, like haunting the BP station.

I moved on. "Anybody else come to mind when you think about that night? Anybody who hovered around the table? Or came into the kitchen when they really didn't belong there? Or had anything to do with the food?"

"I've been thinking about this a lot. There was one guy, kind of overweight. His wife is something else. One of those women whose face would crack if she smiled more than once a night. He hung around the shrimp dip, like he was leashed to that corner of the table. He seemed to like it as much as Mr. Dorchester did. One or the other of them was over there a lot. I made a ton of it. Mrs. Dorchester told me to. But between those two guys, I'm surprised anything was left to poison."

The Booths. The description was unmistakable. I made a mental note that Samuel had been near the dip most of the evening. Maybe he hadn't been as fond of it as he'd seemed. Maybe he'd just been waiting for a chance to load it with digoxin. Maybe Samuel had his own supply. He could well be on the drug himself, or at least be savvy about the results if he "borrowed" some of Win's for the dip.

"There was a woman there," I said. "Pretty, dark-haired, designer clothing. Looks rich, *is* rich. Does that ring a bell?"

"There was a woman like that, yes."

"Anything odd there? Out of the ordinary?"

"If it's the same woman, she didn't eat a thing. I noticed that, all right. Frosted me, too, like the food wasn't good enough for her. Drank a lot, though. Even Red remarked on it. He said we might need to cut her off, but I told him that wasn't our business. Of course we were watching, to be sure she didn't try to drive home. But she didn't. She left on foot."

"She left before you did?" If Marie Grandower was the woman Grace remembered, then the timing was off. I'd been under the impression Marie was there after the catering staff departed, because that's when Hildy reported seeing her in the yard with Win.

"Yes. She was wearing a sweater trimmed in silver fox. The coat closet's right beside the kitchen, and I got it for her when I saw her fumbling with the closet door. She took off without a word of thanks, like that was my job, too."

Marie must have waited out front until everyone else was gone, then slipped back into the side yard to talk to Win. Either that or she came back later.

"How much of the time were you in the kitchen?" I asked.

"A lot, unfortunately. I was waiting for things to warm, setting up trays. You know.

I came and went, but Red was out in the room with the guests more than I was."

I determined to talk to him.

"The murderer must have been somebody who was there," Grace said. "Don't you know most of those people, Aggie? Aren't they all members of your church?"

Unfortunately, as far I knew, they were. I wondered if Ed's ministry could survive if I found another murderer right in our midst. How far would parish goodwill stretch if I kept putting our members in jail?

"You've got to do something," Grace said, getting to her feet. "You just have to."

I knew it, too, but I was afraid that the something I had to do might well land my husband among the unemployed.

I walked her out, and as we were saying good-bye I realized Grace might be just the person to ask about Stephen Collins. Grace was always on the lookout for trouble. She was convinced all teenagers were on the road to perdition and had to be corralled and detoured. Had anyone ever said a bad word to her about Mr. Collins, she would have it filed away.

I edged into the subject, asking about Shannon's extracurricular activities for the spring. Then I told her Deena had quit the debate team, and I asked what she knew about Mr. Collins.

"Just wondering if he was giving Deena a hard time," I said.

For once Grace's store of gossip failed me. "Shannon's not exactly debate material. And nobody else has mentioned anything about the guy to me."

I knew I was in good hands here, but I was sorry.

"Of course you need to check Right in the Middle," Grace added. "That's the place to get all the dirt."

"What's Right in the Middle?"

She looked as if she was questioning my right to have children. "How can you not know about that?"

"Can't answer that until I know what it is."

"It's a *blog.* Nobody knows who's doing it, but it's a big deal at the school. You didn't know?"

Me? I barely know what a blog is. I have a sinking feeling it involves turning on a computer, which is why Deena probably hadn't bothered to tell me. I confessed my ignorance, and Grace shook her head.

"I shouldn't like it," Grace said, "but it's hard not to. It's insightful and funny. Whoever puts it together is analyzing every-thing that's going on at the school. It's kind of like a newspaper gone ballistic. All the kids are reading it, and they're hanging on every word."

"How did you find out about it?"

"I track everything Shannon does online. You don't do that with Deena?"

"Not exactly." Not at all, as a matter of fact. I wouldn't have the slightest idea how, or the conviction it was a good idea, either.

"You can't trust her, Aggie! There's a whole world out there you don't know anything about. Where have you been?"

"Not online, that's for sure."

"I'll send you the link. You can check it out. What's your e-mail address?"

I have one. I know I do. My sister set up an account for me somewhere. But the last time I looked at it, I found fifty notices that the IRS was auditing me, with special links so I could see what they'd discovered. It was about that time that the old peasant woman began to haunt our computer, and now I wonder if she was an IRS spy. I still look out the window before I go outdoors, just to be sure no one's waiting with hand-cuffs.

"That's okay," I said. "Just tell me the name again."

"Right in the Middle." She looked at her watch. "You're going to figure out who killed Win Dorchester, aren't you?"

I certainly hoped so, but I made no promises.

I had set aside late morning to wash and wax the kitchen floor. I love getting up close and personal with archenemies. The old floor isn't good for much, but it does provide me with an outlet for hostilities. Being down on my knees also gives me time to think — something religious folks discovered a long time ago. Call the floor my version of a police evidence board, but I'd planned to use my time going over and over what I knew about Win's murder, to see if new connections appeared.

I was just stripping off the old wax when the doorbell rang. I considered ignoring it, but of course, this would be the one time I shouldn't. Besides, instead of thinking about Win's murder, I would spend the rest of my morning wondering who I'd missed.

I was still wiping my hands on a rag when I opened the door to find Hildy. She looked slightly better than she had yesterday, and I hoped she was eating. I'd had a little luck scaring up casseroles for her, but after delivery, nobody stayed around to be sure she actually warmed them and brought them to her mouth.

"Ah, I remember that smell," she said. "You're stripping the kitchen floor. You are taking such good care of the church's property."

I'm never happy at reminders this house isn't mine. We are, in effect, renters here, and subject to the whims of our multiple landlords. But I smiled anyway and motioned her inside. Hildy is Hildy, and unlikely to change.

"I won't keep you from your duties," she said, "but I've taken over the reception after the Sunday service, and I'm not sure if the church has a punch bowl or where it's kept. I was just there, and Norma isn't in this morning."

Ed could have told her, of course, but Hildy would never disturb the "minister" with questions like this. This was strictly minister's wife stuff. Who would know more about the punch bowl?

As a matter of fact, this time Hildy's assumption was true. And most of what I know isn't pretty. The punch bowl and I go way back. Hildy would not believe the stories.

Instead, I just answered the question and ignored the juicy details. "It's locked up in the closet under the parish hall stairs. January will have the key, and he'll be in this afternoon."

"A big one? A good one?"

Big yes, good? Evil exists in many guises, including punch bowls.

"A lovely cut-glass bowl," I said, since every other description makes me sound like a candidate for the loony bin.

"Good. I'll make the punch myself."

I had to question the wisdom of this. Not using the punch bowl, although that was always dangerous, but Hildy doing the reception.

"I'm ready for a break," I lied. "Would you like some tea?"

"I'm fine, but I'll sit with you a moment."

I washed my hands, then I flopped down on the sofa, and she joined me. "Who put you in charge of the reception?" I asked.

"When Sally brought me a casserole, she mentioned that the woman in charge had to fly to Minnesota on a family emergency. She was looking for a volunteer, so I told her I would do it."

I wish Hildy had consulted me, but, of course, that was ridiculous. Hildy doesn't consult anybody. "You just buried Win yesterday," I pointed out, as I put my hand on her arm. "Are you sure you want to plunge right in?"

"Somebody needed to do it."

We have many somebodies in our congregation, and General Sally would have found a willing volunteer, if Hildy hadn't jumped on it. I wondered how this was going to look to outsiders. Hildy should be playing the grieving widow. Instead she was back to business as usual.

Hildy is not a mind reader, but she answered the question I didn't ask. "It will give me something to do. I don't want to just sit around and think about how terrible things are."

I knew there was more to it, too. Hildy already missed her role as minister's wife. This was a way to stay connected to the church, a way to remain in charge.

"I have big plans," she went on. "John Hammond is a lovely man. He and his wife were friends of ours. Of course, she's gone now, poor thing, but John deserves the best."

John, the minister right before Ed, was going to be preaching on Sunday as part of our 150th anniversary celebration. He was due in town today, and would be staying with a church family not far away. I wasn't surprised Hildy knew him. Hildy knew almost everybody in the denomination.

"John will understand if you keep it simple." I flashed my warmest smile. "Really, Hildy, you don't want to overdo."

"I thought tea sandwiches, of course, and vegetables and dip, cut fruit, some really fine cheeses with crackers." She continued, and by the time she had finished describing a meal that made tea at the Ritz sound like soup kitchen fare, my mouth was hanging open.

"We usually just do cookies and punch," I said. "Maybe some pound cake, like we did for Win's Sunday. I think that's what was planned."

"Yes, but this is the church anniversary. More should be expected. We need to prepare for the next 150 years, don't you think?"

Don't you think? It was a figure of speech, and I knew it. What I thought, what anybody thought, wasn't going to matter. This was a freight train picking up speed. I hoped it wasn't also a train wreck about to happen.

"Who's going to make all the food?" I asked, afraid I knew the answer.

"I have lists. I'll be sure everyone does their part, and if they don't, I can make up the difference myself."

I was trying to figure out how to gently remind her that people had lives and couldn't actually drop everything to make bite-size crabmeat quiches, when the door-bell rang again. I jumped up to answer it, hoping it might be somebody who could help me nudge some sense into Hildy.

A moment passed before I recognized the man standing on the doorstep.

"John?" I smiled and motioned him in. "We were just talking about you."

John Hammond stepped inside, and leaned over to kiss my cheek. He's probably in his early seventies, with sparse white hair in something that approximates a halo around his head, and the kindest blue eyes I've ever seen. John is not a fiery preacher, or a Napoleonic administrator. He's a sage, and well respected in the denomination for it. He's the kind of man you'd like to sit with in a quiet room just to soak up the goodwill.

"I stopped by the church. I wanted to say hello, and Ed told me that Hildy was visiting you." John was already looking across the room, and his smile deepened.

"Hildy?"

Hildy was coming toward us, and John opened his arms to enfold her.

"I'm so sorry," he said. "I wrote you. Did you get my note?"

She stepped away. "I did. I just haven't had time to reply to any of them."

"Take care of yourself first."

I decided this would be the perfect moment to check my floor and let the two old friends discuss Win.

My floor was still there, more's the pity. I counted tiles for a minute before I returned. "Have you had lunch?" John was asking Hildy. He looked up at me. "And you, Aggie?"

"I'm in the middle of scrubbing a floor. But please take Hildy out and make her eat something, okay?"

"May I?" he asked her.

She looked unsure. "I'm not fit company."

"That I can decide on my own."

They said good-bye and I watched them leave together. Hildy needed old friends. I just hoped that after Sunday's reception, the ones she had left in Emerald Springs were still speaking to her.

12

I never would have checked out Right in the Middle, but I realized Stephen Collins might be mentioned, and this was a chance to discover something important. If the blog really was an uncensored look at middle school life, maybe there were warnings about teachers.

When Ed came home for lunch, I asked him to find the site and leave it on screen for me. He looked skeptical and asked if I remembered how to use the mouse, but he found it easily. I was pleased to see there were no longer odd intrusions of Polish folk songs and said so.

"We had a virus," Ed said. "One of the girls probably clicked a link she shouldn't have in a bogus e-mail. We finally got rid of it."

"I'm sure you explained the dangers of clicking links," I said, my gaze sweeping the room for a new place to land.

"*You* know better, don't you?"

I had been just the tiniest bit suspicious. After all, the IRS should be able to match verbs with nouns and spell more or less correctly, but Ed's a busy man and doesn't have time for small talk. I kept details to myself.

I saved wrestling with Right in the Middle for the lull between stripping and rewaxing. While the floor dried, I scanned the site.

Forty minutes later I was impressed. The student or students who'd put the blog together were clever and resourceful. The content was much more extensive than random editorials. Right in the Middle had surveys, lists of favorite teachers, photographs, places for students to comment, critiques of school policy, and yes, complaints about classes and teachers.

I'd expected rants and lots of complaining. There was certainly some of that, but somebody was struggling to keep the tone even and fair. It was definitely more honest and therefore more controversial than the official school newspaper, which reported on school activities and tried to mention as many students as possible. Some teachers were singled out for unfair grading practices, or an excessive number of detentions. One I'd never heard of was said to be looking for a new job because she didn't like middle schoolers, a sentiment she'd apparently shared out loud in class.

The only mention of Stephen Collins was as a favorite teacher, and there were lots of comments. From what I could tell, a number of students, mostly girls, thought the man walked on water.

Disappointed I'd learned so little, I exited, but left the computer on, happy to bask in my success without ruining the glow.

By the time the girls got home, the floor was dry. Deena grabbed an apple and told me she was checking e-mail. Teddy and a friend went up to her room to work on a homework assignment about global warming.

Since I'd found fresh tomatillos at the grocery store on Monday, I was making salsa to top black bean enchiladas for the night's dinner when Deena came into the kitchen and poured a glass of milk.

"Who was looking at Right in the Middle?" she asked.

"How could you tell somebody was?"

"If I showed you, you might screw up something."

It's hard to fault a child for being honest. "Shannon's mom stopped by —"

Deena rummaged for a cookie to go with

238

the milk. "How come?"

"Did you know she's a caterer now?"

"Is this a contest to see who can ask the most questions without answering any?"

I smiled. "I don't know, is it?"

"Why did Mrs. Forester come here?"

I sacrificed my chance at first prize. "She catered the party at the Dorchesters' house the night Reverend Dorchester died."

"Yeah, Shannon said something about that. Her mom's like, you know, all whacked out."

That was another accurate statement. "It wasn't good for her business, so she came over to see what I knew. And while she was here, she told me about Right in the Middle."

"How come?"

I certainly wasn't going to admit I'd been checking up on Stephen Collins. "We were just talking about school. She mentioned the blog. She said it's a great way to keep an eye on you and make sure you're doing your homework, brushing your teeth, and dotting your *i*'s."

Deena looked disgusted. "You're hilarious."

I smiled modestly. "You've read it, I trust?"

"Duh . . ." Deena finished cookie number

239

one and rummaged for a mate. "Everybody reads it. Nobody knows who's doing it. It just showed up one day."

"Whoever's doing it is keeping the tone on the up-and-up."

"When you say that, it's time for a change."

"I'm kind of surprised nobody at the school's trying to shut it down."

"How can they if they don't know who's behind it?"

"I can't believe the school can't find out. Whoever's doing it has to get their information somewhere. People would know who was asking questions, right?"

"There's an e-mail address, and the bloggers ask for comments when they're putting together a story. Nobody knows who the address belongs to."

I wondered. I thought somebody could probably trace the address, if they really needed to. As long as the blog remained relatively rant-free, maybe the school thought it was a harmless way to blow off steam. And, of course, there was that pesky First Amendment, too.

"You really don't know?" I asked.

"Some kids think it's this group of three guys in Computer Club. Only, I think if it was really them, they'd have a lot more techie stuff. You know, they'd be showing off."

Ed came home for the afternoon; Deena left for the afternoon; Teddy and her friend transformed Teddy's room into a South American jungle complete with endangered species, corporate kidnappers bent on destruction, and crusaders trying to save the rain forest while establishing a pedestrian mall.

Ed promised to listen for ransom demands from Teddy's room and bargain for her release with cookies, and I took a shopping list to the grocery store.

I hadn't intended to stop by Emerald Eagle, but when I saw Geoff Adler outside examining the sign, I remembered how badly we needed dental floss. After all, we might go through the six packages I had in reserve, then where would we be? I pictured huge dental bills as I braked hard.

Down on my hands and knees doing floor duty, I'd thought about the minutes in Geoff's home office yesterday. He'd started to say something just as Ed walked in, something about Win not having enough time to write something or other. I had no idea what Win hadn't had time to do, probably a lot, although sadly it seemed he'd done more than his share of some things during his years on earth. But just in case Geoff's musings were relevant, I decided to probe a little further.

Inside the store I found the dental floss before I went to look for Geoff. I didn't want the guy to think I was stalking him. Holding the floss up like a badge, I wandered the store until I saw him behind the pharmacy counter, then I wandered that way.

He saw my approach and came around the far end to greet me.

"I didn't expect to find you here," I said, although that had only been true *before* the moment when I'd spotted him outside.

"I drop by all our stores frequently. It keeps staff on their toes, and I can help if the pharmacist on duty gets backed up."

"How many stores do you have now?"

"Four. We're hoping to open another next summer. Depends on the economy."

Geoff had his back to the shelves just below the counter, and I had my back to the aisles behind me. He didn't appear to feel cornered. My luck was good, since he seemed to be in a chatty mood, and we were far enough off the beaten path that we weren't in anybody's way.

"It was really nice of you to host yesterday." I went on to tell him how much I'd liked his house, etc. I was careful not to lay this on too thick, since these days when I'm too nice, people are generally wary I might be swinging into interrogation mode.

"How's Hildy doing today?" he asked.

I told him about John Hammond, and he looked pleased. "Old friends will help. Win's death will leave a large hole in her life."

That was a great lead-in to my next question. "You knew Win better than most people. And you were at the party the night he died. Can you remember anything that happened that might be suspicious?"

"You mean like somebody pulling out a bottle of pills and dropping them in the shrimp dip?"

"That would be helpful."

"Except for the unpleasantness between Hildy and Marie? Nothing, and I only heard about that later. I was already gone."

"I've been told Marie had a lot to drink."

"She *was* drinking a lot, but at the time, I had no idea why. I've been thinking about our conversation, and I guess I'd better set the record straight. I told you Win was like a father to me? Well, that's not exactly true. He was more like an uncle, you know, the family rascal who's the favorite of all the nieces and nephews? Win was like that, quite a storyteller. We used to go out for a

243

drink sometimes after board meetings, and after a couple of drinks, he'd let loose with stories that would curl your hair. He made it clear he liked women. A lot. And that he more or less collected them."

"Collected?"

"Had affairs. I was left to fill in the details."

I must have shown my distaste, because he backpedaled. "At the time I wasn't sure whether it was just talk. I'm still not. But who knows? Maybe that came back to haunt him?"

I wondered about this new, disturbing revelation. Because if it was true, it certainly opened new possibilities. Had another of Win's old flames been at the party? Somebody Hildy didn't know about? Somebody with passion burning so brightly in her aging breast that it finally erupted in murder?

Maybe Geoff read my mind, because he shook his head. "You know, Aggie, if word of multiple affairs got out, that would be even more reason to suspect Hildy. That much more motive."

It was time to change the subject. I didn't want Geoff dwelling on this and reluctantly taking this new development to the police. "Yesterday you started to say something about Win not having time to do something.

244

Something about writing?"

He searched his memory banks. "Oh, right," he said, when he got to the relevant one. "His memoirs."

"Memoirs?" This was new to me.

"I'm not sure what he meant exactly. But he announced it at the party, although some people seemed to know already. He said he'd had a long, eventful career with lots of wonderful stories, and he was thinking about writing his memoirs. It's too bad he waited so long, isn't it? If he had written them, you'd have a lot more to go on."

"Do you think he was serious?"

"I got the feeling he thought it might be a good way to spend his retirement. He still had an awful lot to say."

I wondered exactly what Win would have kept to himself. Samuel Booth's stint in jail? Or would he have created a Hollywood style tell-all? With everybody's secrets, including his own, laid out for the world to enjoy.

Geoff raised a hand in greeting to somebody behind me, and of course, out of curiosity, I turned. Curiosity really should be one of the seven deadly sins.

Fern Booth stood behind us, and until that moment, I'd always thought "smoldering gazes" was a ridiculous description. But the look in Fern's eyes could have set a rain forest on fire.

Geoff said hello, then he glanced at his watch. "I've got to be somewhere in a little while. Nice talking to you, Aggie." He nodded to Fern and moved around us and back behind the counter. In a moment he'd disappeared.

"I want to talk to you," she said. It was not a request.

"We can talk —"

"Outside," she demanded. "Now."

I held up my pathetic package of dental floss. "I still have to check out."

"I will meet you in the parking lot." She took off, head held high. I wondered if there was a rear exit and gauged how long it might take me to skulk home through back alleys. Ed could always come back for the van. Of course even if he came at midnight, Fern would probably still be waiting beside it.

I sighed, paid for the floss at the pharmacy counter, then took my tiny bag and my misgivings outside. Just as I'd expected, Fern was standing beside my van.

Fern wastes no time on pleasantries. "Samuel told me he confessed his past mistake to you."

Now me? I tend to think killing another human being, no matter what the circumstances, deserves a stronger word than *mistake.* But this was not the time to quibble.

"He did," I said, and waited.

"You just wouldn't leave Win Dorchester's death alone!"

"That's right, too," I said, standing a little taller.

"So, now you know. Of course you would have discovered Samuel's mistake eventually. You can't stand to just let the police do their jobs. You have to tamper with everything. And you're not quiet about it. Oh, no, you can't stay quiet about anything."

"Fern, I —"

"I don't trust you. I don't trust you not to just tell anybody who might be interested in my poor Samuel's past. You'll blab it all over."

She was working herself into a frenzy. I tried to interrupt again, but with no success.

"Well, here's what I've got to say about that," Fern said. "If you so much as mention one word of what Samuel told you to anybody at all, I'll make sure your husband loses his job. Is that what you want? To be ridden out of town on a rail?"

Emerald Springs hasn't had a train come through in years, but I got the picture.

"I really, really hate threats," I said, lowering my voice as she raised hers, something I'd learned from Junie and more recently, Hildy. "I don't respond well to them, in fact I don't respond at all. They're a last resort, and you're a long way from needing to make one."

"What exactly does that mean?"

"It means that unless I have some other, better reason to think Samuel" — I hesitated, but I decided to be honest — "or *you* murdered Win, I have no intention of repeating what your husband told me."

"I'm sure you've already told that husband of yours."

"I haven't." And it was true. Ed's job demands that he not reveal "confessions" unless someone is at risk or a crime's been committed. I have no job. Instead I have principles. Mine told me that for now, this was something Ed didn't need to know. Samuel would never allow Ed to comfort or counsel him, so I believed that the less my husband knew, the more likely Samuel was to stay in the church.

Although that, of course, was a mixed blessing.

Fern was sizing me up. "Why not?" she asked at last.

I'd expected her to call me a liar, so this was a step up. "There's no reason for him to know," I said. "Samuel should be the one to talk about his past, not me."

"Samuel should never have told you."

"Samuel told me because he thinks I have better detective skills than I actually do. After all these years, it would be very difficult for somebody like me to find out about his conviction. I'm not a police officer. I don't have access to files and computers" — which was a good thing for the world in general — "and I don't have friends who do. But Fern, I think maybe Samuel just needed to tell somebody what his own minister did to him. He's suffered a lot over this."

She looked surprised, even, for a moment, vulnerable. Then she snapped back. "Well, I don't know why he told you! He didn't even tell me about what that rotten Win Dorchester did to him until the day of the burial."

Now I'm sure I looked surprised. "*You* didn't know?"

"No!" She puffed out a long breath. "I knew about the manslaughter conviction, of course. He told me before we were married. But I didn't know about the blackmail, or whatever you want to call it."

"I call it shameful," I said quietly. "And I'm really sorry."

"All those years I thought he was the finest minister our church could ever hope to have. And I was so glad when I heard Win and Hildy might retire here. I couldn't understand why Samuel had so little enthusiasm."

"I can't imagine facing Win was much of a pleasure."

"Maybe not, but my husband did not kill him." She stared at me. "Not even if Win *did* announce that night that he might write his memoirs."

That, of course, was the elephant in the middle of the Emerald Eagle parking lot. What would Win have said? Whose life would he have ruined? Would he have told Samuel's story? Even if he'd used an alias for Samuel, people in town would most likely have figured it out. Unfortunately, Samuel Booth had a powerful motive for murder. And if Fern was lying and had known about Win's subtle extortion on the night of the party, so would she.

"Samuel didn't kill Win," Fern repeated with conviction, "memoirs or not. But maybe somebody else who was there that night had something to hide. Maybe somebody else shut him up. Maybe somebody else had everything to lose."

As little as I like the Booths, I really couldn't see either of them as murderers.

And Samuel's revelations made it even less likely. Had he really been worried about my digging too deeply, he could have killed me, too, which was more likely to shut me up than an emotional confession.

But I've learned from experience that people do the darndest things when they're under pressure. I still couldn't discount them as suspects. Fern said she hadn't known about Win's blackmail, but how did I know that was true? And, of course, Samuel himself might have told me about his background just to make me less willing to go after him.

"We're finished here," Fern said. "I just hope you learn your lesson someday and stay out of these things."

I watched her stomp away, and I wished I *could* just walk away from Win's death and let the police handle it. But that was like wishing I'd been born blonde and willowy. No, it was worse. I could bleach my hair and lose fifteen pounds, even visit a plastic surgeon. But I don't know any way to take the *busy* out of *busybody.* If I did, that just left a *body,* and unfortunately that's how my snooping came into being in the first place.

13

Russell House had a cheerful lobby crowded with artificial ficus and banana trees that screened seating areas, so families could have more or less private conversations with loved ones. The furniture was rattan with tropical print slipcovers and pillows, and a cage of screeching parakeets adorned a corner. I thought the lobby might be a consolation prize for elderly patients who hadn't been able to afford retirement in Florida. Maybe retirement homes in Naples and Boca Raton are decorated in Ohio Amish chic.

It was mid-morning on the day after my confrontation with Fern, and half an hour ago, I had called Flo at home to see if she had time to talk. Her husband told me she was filling in at work until someone showed up to relieve her. I'd decided to approach her in person rather than make another phone call. Just to get a feel for the place.

Win had spent a lot of time here, and although I didn't expect to find his spirit lingering in the hallways, seeing Russell House up close seemed like a good idea.

Last night after Geoff's revelations, I'd gone home to tell Ed that Win might have had multiple affairs. I know how busy a minister's schedule can be. When had the guy found time?

Ed hadn't disputed the possibility, although when it comes to a nose for clerical gossip, his nasal passages are permanently clogged. He told me that Win's short church tenures might be something of a clue. When the going got risky, maybe Win got going. I asked him to check with some of his older colleagues to see if they knew anything, but he looked at me as if I'd asked him to raid their pension plans.

"Just ask Hildy," he'd said. "She knew about Marie. From that moment on you can bet she was on the lookout. She needs to be straight with you if you're going to help her."

I planned to do that. But right now I was more interested in whether Win had engaged in an affair with either Ellen Hardiger or Zoey — or, heaven help us, both. With this newest bit of gossip, it seemed more likely, and I'd gotten up this morning with the goal of finding out. If he *had* indulged, this was worth taking to Roussos, a strong connection between Win's death and Ellen's.

Zoey was supposed to come to town to make arrangements to transport her mother's body or ashes. I hoped Flo might be able to put me in touch with her. I wasn't sure how I would bring up such a delicate subject, but I was determined to try.

On the far side of the lobby, I found a woman in a lavender flowered lab coat with a chart under her arm and asked where I might find Flo. The woman was in her forties, graying curls and a snub nose. I liked the laugh lines around her eyes and figured she must be a favorite with patients. She checked her watch.

"She's probably on rounds with a doctor. May I help you?"

I debated. "I'm trying to find out if Ellen Hardiger's daughter is in town," I said. "Ellen used to be —"

"Oh, yes, I know who she was. All our residents loved Ellen." She examined me more carefully. "Why do you want to know?"

I figured Zoey's story must be well known here. No one was going to give out her whereabouts, unless they were sure her ex-husband wasn't in the picture.

"It's a long story." When she didn't say

anything, I went on. "I already talked to Flo. My husband's the minister of the Consolidated Community Church —"

"Your husband?" She sounded shocked. "The man who died?"

"No, no, my husband's the present minister. Win Dorchester, the man who died, was a former one."

"Oh." She placed a hand on her chest in relief. "Well, you're certainly too young for him, of course, but you never know, do you?"

I almost went right past that. Then I backtracked. "Um, how do you know how old Win was?"

"Well, I don't know exactly. Except that when he was here the week before he was, you know . . ."

I knew. "Murdered," I supplied. "He was *here*?"

"Yes, apparently he had a nice chat with one of our staff, Cinda."

This was getting interesting. I introduced myself, and we shook. "Look, I'll just come right out with this. I'm looking into Win's murder. His wife asked me to help. I, um, have a little experience. Could you possibly tell me what he was doing here? It might help."

"He wasn't a patient, so it's not confidential, but I'm afraid I really don't know. Cinda never said, and she's away on spring vacation."

That was too bad. I wondered if Win had been checking to see if Ellen still worked here. Maybe he'd wanted to see how Zoey was doing. Or maybe he'd wanted to pick up on yet another old affair.

"She'll be back in a couple of weeks," she added. "Cinda's got family in Jamaica. I wish I had family in Jamaica."

"Wouldn't that be cool?"

"Flo should be done in a few minutes. Why don't you make yourself comfortable and I'll send her out."

I had hoped to see more of the facility, but there was no good reason to ask for a tour. I thanked her and took a seat.

I was engaged in a killer game of War with an ancient woman in a powder blue housecoat and curlers when Flo entered the lobby. I apologized for leaving, and the woman pointed out that I'd been losing anyway. I vowed a rematch.

Flo and I walked outside. She looked tired, but she told me someone was coming to relieve her soon. We stood together on the porch taking gulps of fresh spring air to replace the antiseptic tang of the home.

I explained why I had come. "But I found

out something interesting while I was waiting," I told her. "Did you know Win Dorchester was here right before he died?"

She looked surprised. "I had no idea."

Again I wished Jamaican Cinda was returning sooner. "Any suspicions why he might have come?"

"I can't imagine, unless he was hoping to find some of the people he used to visit. But he must have known they'd be gone by now."

I didn't want to ask Flo about a possibly more intimate relationship between Win and Ellen or Ellen's daughter. I was afraid if I did, she would shut down and stop being helpful. I just repeated that I hoped to ask Zoey a few questions when she got to town.

"You're in luck. She's already here," Flo said. "She's not staying with me. That seemed too obvious, in case Craig shows up looking for her. Ellen's death *was* in the papers, and they did interview me."

I hoped she was about to tell me where Zoey was, instead.

"She's staying with a friend of mine, but she did say she'd be at the funeral home this morning making final arrangements. You can probably find her there." She lowered her voice. "Ask for Zoey Salvo. I'll give her a call when I get home and tell her you want to talk to her. If you don't find her first, I'm sure she'll call you back."

I appreciated Flo's concern for Zoey's safety and told her so.

"I doubt all the cloak-and-dagger stuff is necessary, but you can never be too careful," Flo said. "I couldn't live with myself if that animal found her because of something I said."

The Weiss-Bitman Funeral Home isn't far from the parsonage, on a quiet street in the most historic section of Emerald Springs. The house was built in the mid-nineteenth century and said to have housed a steady stream of sadly childless couples, until Mr. Weiss or Mr. Bitman discovered its true calling. I'd been here before, and as funeral homes go, it offers less service and more arm-twisting. Ed and most of his colleagues try to steer grieving families to another funeral home on the edge of town.

Inside, canned organ music was coming from a room at the end of the hall. Mourners were signing a guestbook in that doorway, and a funeral home employee was lethargically directing traffic. I waited until he'd herded the group in front of me in the right direction before I asked him where I might find Zoey Salvo. He pointed to the staircase up to the second floor.

Upstairs a woman about my own age was just coming out of a door marked Business Office. She was tall and thin, with short blonde hair and a sad expression. I made my best guess.

"Excuse me, are you Zoey Salvo?"

She looked beyond me before she answered, as if she wanted to be sure no one was with me. She gave a short nod.

I explained who I was and why I was there, and made sure to explain how I was connected to Win Dorchester. "Flo told me I might find you here," I finished. "Do you have time to talk, or could we make time later?" She had, after all, just made arrangements to send her mother's body to Florida for burial.

"I don't know what I can tell you."

I suspected sitting in a downtown coffee shop was out. Most likely Zoey didn't want to exhibit herself in public places. "We can sit in my car," I said. "There's a little park at the end of the street."

"If it won't take too long. It's been a hard morning."

I asked her about the arrangements for her mother, and she told me that Ellen had wanted to be buried in Ocala, where she

259

had retired. Zoey planned to honor her wishes.

Zoey checked the street before she stepped off the porch. I was parked right in front and got her into my van without fuss.

"I'm driving Flo's friend's car. I parked a few streets over," she said. "Then I called the home on my cell phone to be sure no man had been there asking about me and nobody was lurking."

I couldn't imagine how tough returning here must have been for her and told her so. Not only had she lost her mother, now she had to worry about her stalker ex.

"My husband wanted to come," she said, "but his father's been ill, and he took a turn for the worse yesterday. Frank needs to stay close by, just in case. I don't have any reason to think Craig's still hanging around Emerald Springs. About ten years ago I heard he turned over a new leaf, went into counseling, and left town to start over. But I'm not willing to assume the best, not after what he put me through."

The lead-in was perfect, and I told her so. "I met your mother at Win Dorchester's memorial service. She told me then that Win had helped you."

"He saved my life. Craig had convinced me I couldn't live without him, and he was always so sorry, you know. He would promise not to ever touch me in anger again, and like a fool, I'd believe him. Reverend Dorchester helped me see it was all a lie, that Craig didn't want to change and didn't know how. Craig insisted he didn't need help, and in the end that no longer mattered to me. Because I did, and I got it."

Zoey had an expressive face. She wasn't really pretty, but her big brown eyes made up for a wide mouth and jutting chin. It was easy to tell what she was feeling, and I saw she was proud of herself for changing.

"Did Flo tell you I'm trying to see if there's a connection between your mother's death and his?" I asked. "Maybe it's a huge stretch, but it seems worth exploring."

"She mentioned it. I can't imagine how they're connected, not unless Craig's involved. But why now? If he wanted them dead, he had plenty of time to make it happen."

"Who knows how a man like that thinks?"

She nodded, and I could almost read her thoughts. She had lived with him, and not only had he lied to her repeatedly, she had believed him.

"So I have to ask you a question you don't want to hear," I continued. "Please understand I'm not trying to pry. But I need to know if either you or your mother had anything more than a counseling relationship with Win. Did it ever get more intimate? Because if it did, that could explain a lot."

"Intimate?" She turned to look me fully in the face. "Like an affair?"

I didn't want to tell her about Marie Grandower, or about Geoff's suspicion there had been more women. She had enough sadness to deal with. I didn't want to knock Win off the pedestal she'd placed him on.

"I know it's a rotten question," I said instead. "But if there's any chance his death and your mother's are related, we need to know."

"He never in any way stepped over the line with me," she said emphatically. "And I'm sure there was nothing happening with Mom, either. I would have known. She thought the world of him, but he was always Reverend Dorchester to her, the man who helped me get away from Craig. She was a very strict Catholic. She never even divorced my father, even though he deserted us."

I believed her, and I was glad. It's easy to see shadows everywhere after the first one's been spotted.

"Thank you," I said. "I hated to ask."

"Well, I hated to hear it."

"Can you think of any other way your mother and Win might have been connected?"

Zoey was silent a moment. "Reverend Dorchester visited patients at Russell House, and he counseled me. That's it. Mom thought highly enough of him to come back to hear him speak at your church. She e-mailed to say that she'd chatted with him for a few minutes during the reception."

"Do you know about what?"

"She told him I was doing well, and he told her to tell me how happy he was that I'd finally gotten the life I deserved."

"I'm glad. Was there anything else?"

"Not that she mentioned."

"Do you have any additional information about your ex that the police could follow up on?"

"Other than that rumor from ten years ago that he'd finally gotten his act together, I haven't heard a thing. I don't even want to think about Craig. Never again."

I knew we'd reached the end. There was nothing else to ask about. I offered to drive her to her friend's car, and she let me. Once there we parked and waited a few minutes to be sure no one was about. Then Zoey said good-bye and took off for a small Chevrolet, beeping it open, so all she had to do was throw the door back and jump in.

Watching her, I was more grateful than usual that I had met and married the right guy the first time.

I own a cell phone. It's the most basic model, and even I can open it to listen to a phone call and close it when the call has ended. The biggest problem is that I never remember to bring it with me.

So it was no surprise when I arrived home from my conversation with Zoey to find Ed in the doorway holding it up, like an award he was about to bestow.

"This is your cell phone. It's supposed to go places with you."

This was not the first time I've been chastised, although it never seems to help. The real surprise? The unmistakable sounds of workmen in our house, which matched the beat-up white van with two ladders on the roof that was parked in our driveway.

"Hot water heater? A sudden roof leak?" I looked up to the skies to see if it had been raining, and I hadn't noticed.

"You're finally getting your new kitchen floor."

"Are you kidding me?" For a moment I was thrilled. I had given up hope the church

264

board would ever find the money to put in a new floor. Every time the subject came up — and I made sure it came up frequently — a new problem came with it.

"What about the asbestos?" That had been the most recent reason to stall.

"No asbestos after all."

I envisioned all the books I could read in the time I'd spent scrubbing and waxing. I envisioned knees without calluses.

The thrill lasted only moments. Then I sobered. "Why didn't somebody alert us?"

"It's a surprise."

I'll say it was a surprise. Not only hadn't I been alerted, now that I thought about it, I hadn't even been *consulted.*

"Do they have samples with them? Doesn't it usually take time to order the materials?"

"That's all been taken care of."

I didn't like the sound of that. "Without us?"

"Apparently Hildy claimed there was no need to bother us. She said you liked the old floor so well, you'd love to have another one just like it. Only a new one you don't have to spend so much time taking care of. So they're putting in black and white squares again."

"Hildy?"

"There's a lot that can be said about Hildy, including the fact that she gets things done. She called every member of the board and told them they owed us this."

I was stunned. I could only imagine how much the board had wanted to hear that. What I couldn't imagine? Living with that dreadful new floor when I could have had one I loved for the same price.

One that I picked out. Me, the *present* resident of the parsonage.

"Where is she?" I demanded.

"She left for home once she was sure the crew was doing their job according to her specifications."

"Tell them not to put down a single piece of flooring."

"Don't worry about that. They'll be tearing out the present floor for the rest of the weekend. We won't be able to use our kitchen without cleaning every single thing in it."

"I'll be back eventually."

Ed didn't ask where I was going. He rested a hand on my arm. "She just lost her husband. She's under suspicion of murder."

"I may be, too. If I'm not home by six, call Jack and withdraw our life savings. You'll need to bail me out of jail."

■ ■ ■ ■

Hildy answered the door so fast I thought she'd probably been waiting for me to appear.

"You don't have to thank me," she said, putting her arms around me and pulling me close. "You're trying so hard to help me, I wanted to return the favor."

"Hildy, I —"

"Come in! I'm baking treats for tomorrow's reception." She had a real smile on her face, a pre-shrimp-dip smile, and for just a moment, I considered forgetting the whole thing. Then a vision of the new floor danced in my head, a floor I didn't want and hadn't chosen. A floor that Hildy had chosen out of nostalgia, and a sad desire to still have her say about what happened in our parsonage.

I followed her inside, but not all the way into the house. Just far enough that the neighbors wouldn't hear me.

"I'm really upset," I said, once we were both in the foyer. "Really, really, really upset, Hildy. I know you're going through an awful time right now, and I've tried to cut you some slack. I really have. But what were you thinking badgering the board that way, then choosing a floor for *us?* Ed and I live in the parsonage now. And we deserve to have a say in what happens inside it!"

She stared at me. It was clear my words were not computing. "You're unhappy?" she asked at last.

"You don't live there anymore, Hildy. It's not your house. It's mine. You have a different life now. It can be a great one if you let it. But this life is mine and I want it back. I don't want you choosing my floors. I don't want you telling me how to be a good minister's wife. I don't want you cutting the crusts off my bread! My bread is wonderful. People love my bread, crusts and all. And nobody but you cares what I pay for my living room furniture or what that says about Ed's paycheck."

Okay, I was getting out of line, I was getting weird. I could hear it. I could feel it all the way to my toes, but my tongue was tap-dancing to its own rhythm.

"I like you," said my tongue. "I like your energy and your genuine kindness and your desire to do the right thing. But you need another project. You need a new life, Hildy. Because the one when you were the wife of the Tri-C minister is over, and you can't get it back by taking charge of mine."

I was finished. I knew it, and so did my

tongue, which seemed to wilt in my mouth. I just threw up my hands as a final statement.

"Aggie!"

I didn't want to argue, and I didn't want to stay and listen to her side. Even now I could feel guilt beginning to spread its shaky tendrils. I so rarely lose my temper I was already unsure I'd had a right to confront her, or if I should have swallowed my anger, stayed home, and served lemonade to the workers tearing out my floor.

My floor.

I stiffened my backbone.

"I'll talk to you tomorrow," I said. "When and if I'm calmer."

I turned and left before I could say one more thing. This time she didn't try to stop me.

All the way home I replayed our scene. And every time I told myself I shouldn't have confronted her, I envisioned our brand-new floor, a shinier, unscarred version of the same darn floor Hildy had walked on and waxed and loved in her years in our house. Hildy's reminder that the parsonage still belonged to her.

I told myself I'd better get used to that vision. Unless the board was willing to pay the fees for returning Hildy's floor and purchasing mine, I might be seeing black and white for all the years we spent in the parsonage, too.

14

Here's the problem with anger. It's easy to feel righteous when you're venting. After all, I did have cause to be unhappy with Hildy. She'd been trying to "improve" me since the moment she came back to Emerald Springs. And choosing a new floor for a house she no longer lived in? *My* house? She'd been wrong. No sweat.

But so had I. By the time our takeout pizza was eaten in our relatively dust-free living room, and everyone in the house but me had gone elsewhere — Ed to Columbus for a colleague's retirement party, the girls to sleepovers — I was feeling hugely guilty. Wasn't Hildy going through enough? I'd promised to stick by her, and didn't that mean more than finding her husband's murderer? Didn't it mean understanding who she was and accepting her? I didn't have to tolerate her choice of floor, but there had been many nicer ways to tell her so.

And bread crusts? Who cared about bread crusts?

I wasn't sure how I was going to get myself out of this one. Ed had already called the board president and explained that as nice as it was for the board to put in a new floor, we had hoped to choose the pattern and color ourselves. Our prez promised to get us the floor we wanted. Call me skeptical, but I'll be poring over Ed's paycheck for the next six months to see if the shipping costs are deducted.

So my torn-up kitchen would be an inconvenience for at least ten more days while a new floor was ordered, but the problem wasn't permanent. Dust could be wiped away. We could walk on the uneven, sticky subfloor. But my relationship with Hildy wouldn't be so easy to fix. I was afraid maybe I had damaged it beyond repair.

With hours alone stretching in front of me, I didn't want to go over and over the scene in Hildy's foyer. I needed to make amends, but I didn't know exactly how. I wished my mother was in town. Junie would listen carefully, then put her finger right on the best way to fix this. Others might think she's flighty and, well, odd — okay, she *is* flighty and odd — but she has a deep understanding of human nature that transcends both.

I decided to spend my evening working on the church history. I wanted to see exactly what I had and what I needed. And one thing I needed for certain was more information about Win's ministry. Without a sermon, I had very little to put in his chapter, but I did have board reports.

I'll confess I had another reason for reading through board reports, too. I'd met Win, smiled and laughed at his jokes, and stood beside his wife when he was buried. But I really only knew him through the things others had said about him. I hoped that by reading more about his ministry, I'd learn more about the man himself. I wasn't expecting anything major, no "If I die, it will be at the hands of John Smith" revelation deep in the middle of a report on the annual church canvas, but maybe something would trigger a new direction to investigate. More than ever I wanted to catch Win's killer. Frankly I couldn't imagine any better way to make up to Hildy for my outburst.

I threw on a sweatshirt, grabbed Ed's church keys, and locked our door behind me. The sky hadn't deepened into night, although it was well on its way. A few stars were twinkling, next to a silver sliver of moon, and the air smelled like unfurling leaves, fresh and new. There were lights in the parish house, most likely some meeting or other, possibly even Hildy and crew setting up for tomorrow's reception. I would be friendly, but I wouldn't apologize tonight. I needed quiet for that, and somewhere the two of us could have a heart-to-heart.

There were three groups meeting at the church, but Hildy and whatever helpers she had commandeered weren't among them. An AA chapter was in the social hall, our hunger task force was in the kitchen making sandwiches to take to the homeless shelter, and the flower committee was decorating the church for tomorrow's service. My potted hydrangeas were now gracing a flowerbed at the side of the church, and it was time for tulips and pussy willows.

I said brief hellos to people I knew and started up the stairs. By the time I got to the third floor, I was panting. The last flight is narrow and steep, and I was looking forward to having the archives one flight down in a room where they would have more protection. There was nothing between the present storage area and the roof except a shallow attic with wiring that had seen better days. An overhaul was in the budget, and I just hoped my new kitchen floor wouldn't delay that repair yet again.

I unlocked and went inside to search for the file. Despite the substandard conditions, the room's in much better shape than it was when I first took over. In addition to our new dehumidifier, last year we installed an attic fan, so the heat's not so fierce in the summer. I spotted the cardboard file box right where it was supposed to be. Even if none of our past historians were much for organization, they did save every little thing, and there were boxes and boxes of material going back into the 1800s. The older the material, the more carefully I'd tried to organize and preserve it, although by now, some of the papers were nothing more than fragments.

I lifted the top and pawed through the box, searching for the correct years. I was on my way back to the door with everything under one arm when I stopped. Something was wrong. I could sense it, something out of the ordinary, something different. I did a 360-degree turn, looking carefully around me, but nothing looked out of place. I hadn't heard noises, nothing except the possible featherlight scurrying of tiny feet in the space above. Squirrels aren't unheard of in the attic, nor are mice. I would have to tell January, since mice in particular are fond of dining on wiring, a problem we don't need. January has a shelf filled with live traps and removes his prey to abandoned buildings far, far away, making country mice out of city mice because he has such a kind heart.

I listened harder, wondering if I'd heard something else, something more suspicious, but just off my radar. But the storage room was quiet now. No creepy footsteps on the stairs. No creaking of floorboards.

The air felt the way it always does in spring. Cool, almost cold. Not as damp as it had been before the dehumidifier. Nothing there.

I sniffed, since I seemed to be going through a list of my five senses and there was nothing to taste. At first I only noticed the sweet decay of old paper, and the stale air of a confined space. These scents were so familiar I knew they wouldn't bring me up short. I was about to admit I'd imagined the whole thing, when I realized there was more. I took a deeper breath and identified that hidden extra, which was no longer quite so hidden.

Smoke.

I froze. I'm not sure how the species has survived this long, since freezing right before panic sets in gives wild animals time

to leap, storm surges time to sweep everything away, and fire time to take hold and
spread. I was frozen only moments, but they
were terrifying enough to seem like hours.

The second I recovered I ran to the door
and down the first flight of steps screaming
"fire!" By the time I got to the first flight,
people were gathering at the foot of the
stairs to see who was making such a ruckus.

"Fire! In the attic! Call the fire department."

Two men I didn't recognize stared at me
a moment, then one took off for the telephone, unfrozen and helpful. The other
thawed, as well, grabbed a fire extinguisher
from the case just across the hallway,
wrestled it off the wall, and started up the
steps.

I didn't think a fire extinguisher was going
to be much help. My best guess was that
this was an electrical fire in the space above
the storage room, old wiring that planned
to go out in a blaze of glory. But I ran back
up in hopes I was wrong.

"I . . . think it's in here," I said, puffing
from having taken the steps so fast both up
and down. I threw open the door and saw
there was no question I was right. The storage room was filling with smoke.

One thing about living in a "city" as small

as Emerald Springs? Fire, police, ambulance? They're only minutes away. I thought I heard sirens in the distance.

"What's *in* here?" the guy shouted.

I'd been so worried about the church, I hadn't thought to worry about my precious records. Now, horrified, I realized that if the room caught fire, they would all be ashes. And once the fire department arrived, whatever was left would be washed away.

"Records!" I screamed. "Our church archives."

I have the good sense not to run into a burning building. At least I think I do. Unless, of course, someone had to be saved — pretty much anybody, if it comes right down to it. But this was just paper. No one cared all that much about our church history except me, and I wasn't sure why I did. As a child I wasn't baptized, christened, dunked, confirmed, or even assigned my own mantra. Not until I met Ed did formalized religion have much of a draw. So this wasn't my heritage going up in smoke. But Tri-C and all the people to whom it had been so important through the century and a half since the doors were flung open?

They mattered.

I ran inside the room. No flames were visible. Had there been, I'd have said a sad farewell to all those good people and shed a tear or two. Instead I began to grab boxes and haul them out the door. I literally threw them outside to the top of the steps, and my unknown cohort grabbed them and heaved them to the landing below.

The smoke was thickening, but I kept going back. Back and back and back again. I heard heavy footsteps on the stairs, but I kept going. I ignored everything else in the room, costumes from plays our religious education department had staged years ago, Christmas decorations for the sanctuary, and kept heaving boxes.

"You've got to get out, ma'am," a man in a firefighter's uniform said. I hadn't even heard him enter the room.

I had two small files and three more boxes. I told him so.

"Out!" he said.

"Help me with these, then!"

I'm sure he was violating all kinds of firefighter edicts, but he'd probably dealt with intractable women before. He grabbed one of the files and sent it out into the hallway, where my knight in shining armor grabbed it and sent it tumbling down the steps. In a moment the other had followed its path and I emerged with the last box. More firefighters were running up the steps, cursing the roadblock of boxes and files. I got to the landing and found a bucket brigade of committee members, handing boxes and the scattered contents down the steps.

By the time I got to the bottom with the last rescued box, most of what we'd removed was piled high in the downstairs hallway. Two men were bringing the small file boxes, and once I'd really caught my breath, I saw that the stairs were emptying of everyone but firefighters who were shouting at us to get out of the building. Everything that had been removed from the storage room was at my feet.

Unless the parish house burned to the ground because I had caused a delay, the archives were safe.

I started the process of moving all the boxes and files into my husband's study once the all clear was sounded. It was only when I was carefully setting loose papers on a bookshelf to be settled in their proper home when I had the time to reorganize, that I realized the file in my hand entitled Christmas Readings held more than a collection of poetry and scripture. In the middle of the file was a neatly bound packet of sermons, and the top one was titled "On the Night before Christmas," by Reverend Godwin Dorchester.

■ ■ ■ ■

I stayed around long enough to oversee moving all the boxes and files into Ed's office. With John Hammond in our pulpit tomorrow, Ed might be home from Columbus late. I tried to call his cell phone but got voice mail, so I left a message telling him what had happened and not to worry. One of the firefighters had told me that by the time they pulled down the ceiling, the fire had only just ignited and was quickly contained. As I had suspected, it looked as if old wiring was the culprit, although it was hard to tell much, since the wiring had shriveled and melted.

He'd also said that if I hadn't been there and discovered it, the entire parish house would have been at risk. He said it must have been my lucky night.

I didn't add that to my message.

I shuddered to think of the mess we would have to clean up this week, not to mention all the filing and reorganization that would be left to me. Also at issue was how we would cope without lights and power in some of the building tomorrow, but I shuddered more when I considered what might have been.

Back home, after a shower I made cocoa as a treat and a sedative. Every joint and muscle ached, and it was still too early for bed and my hot date with Win's sermons, which had been misfiled for more than a decade. I wandered into Ed's study and noticed the computer was still on. I made myself comfortable and typed in the address for Right in the Middle, to see if anything new had been added about Stephen Collins. Here I was, spending my evening with men I had serious questions about. I wished Ed was home instead.

The computer did not explode. No strange messages flashed across the screen. The website came up without fuss. This really *was* my lucky night.

I was surprised at how much had been added since I'd looked at the site yesterday. There seemed to be dozens more comments about teachers, and Stephen Collins had garnered a couple new raves. There was an updated blog entry, too, about summer jobs. Deena would be looking for one this summer. With a few state regulations in mind, she and her classmates were old enough, and I knew she was looking forward to earning money we had nothing to do with.

I almost skipped over it, but the first few

sentences snagged me and I finished the post.

"Wow." I read it again. According to the students who were publishing this blog, there were only a few good places for middle school graduates to work this summer. A couple of fast-food chains on the outskirts of town, a landscaper who hired kids to mow lawns and paid them fairly, and about half a dozen other possibilities, including one of the chain drugstores, where kids were treated well, but paid a bare minimum.

The list of places *not* to look for a job was lengthier, and uncomfortably familiar. A dry cleaner where I usually took our winter coats. A pet-sitting service that had cared for Moonpie when we were off on vacation. Our most upscale retirement home, where dishwashers and busboys were treated like slaves and many of our older church members resided.

"Ouch."

Of course, the information was based on the experiences of last year's crop of eighth graders, but a lot of thought and research had gone into it. The lists were presented in a factual, unemotional manner. Each example was followed by quotes, although sources weren't named. Whoever had written the blog had been careful to point out the lists were based on opinion, and that, of course, opinions can be exaggerated and situations can change over time. But still, I figured there were going to be some unhappy business owners in Emerald Springs when this blog entry made the rounds.

Maybe even some unhappy enough to change their ways.

I just hoped this new post didn't vault the authorities at the middle school into containment mode.

I exited, and feeling courageous and competent, I turned off the computer. When nothing frightening happened, I considered dressing to hit the grocery store for a lottery ticket. Instead I went upstairs and got into bed with Win Dorchester.

First I zipped through the board minutes I had brought home. Nothing astonishing there. The same names kept appearing, many of them names of people who had been at Win's final hurrah. Geoff Adler had been our treasurer. Samuel Booth our president. Nothing new there. I saw that Yvonne had been in charge of flowers, and I wondered why she never did them now. Esther, our organist, had actually chaired the religious education committee. I even spotted reclusive Marie Grandower in two positions, our endowment committee — possibly the most boring committee in the church — and building and grounds. I could just imagine Marie down on her hands and knees weeding flowerbeds. What had all that dirt done to her manicure?

There were no death threats mentioned against anybody, more's the pity. I set the minutes aside as useless.

I moved on to the sermons. An hour later Ed wasn't yet home and Win, at least the Win who had populated our pulpit, and I were old friends. Only I had discovered a sad truth. Win Dorchester was a man I would probably never have been friends with. He'd been something of an egotist, with a habit of playing down his accomplishments in such a way that they stood out even more clearly. He never confessed doubts about anything. He seemed certain he had the answers to all life's questions, the absence of which is something our denomination is famous for. We embrace many possibilities, and although Win gave lip service to that ideal, I read a certainty, perhaps even a perceived superiority, into much of what he said.

Of course, I had been primed not to like him. I did realize that. This was the man who'd had at least one affair and possibly many, while his wife struggled to serve his congregation in her own way. And if Samuel Booth was telling the truth, this was the man who had used a confession to blackmail his board president.

I reminded myself that Win had been a faithful visitor at Russell House, he had helped Zoey Salvo to a new life, and there had probably been many lives he had changed for the better. Win Dorchester was a human being, both obtuse and insightful, cowardly and courageous. A man, not a god.

I didn't want to read more. Instead I picked one at random, set it beside the bed, and put the others back in the box to return to the church once we had a new home for our records. I had a sermon. I had a new understanding of Win Dorchester.

What I didn't have? A murder suspect.

I fell into a restless sleep and dreamed an angel was speaking to me. Unfortunately, I sat at her feet with my hands clapped firmly over my ears.

15

Ed came home about midnight, and I woke up just long enough to fill him in. Before I opened my eyes on Sunday morning, he was gone again. I knew he was at church making sure everything was set for John Hammond's morning in our pulpit, or figuring out what to do about religious education classrooms with no electricity. Exhausted by last night's events, I seriously considered staying home, but if I was going to repair my relationship with Hildy, I couldn't skip the service and reception. I needed to be there, saying wonderful things about the work she had done, even if I felt the extravagance was unwise and unnecessary.

I dragged myself into the shower, then I looked for something to wear, settling on a lavender cotton sweater Junie had crocheted for me. By the time I was ready, I had only minutes to get to church. I found a seat in the back and listened as our board president reported details of last night's near catastrophe. I was thoroughly embarrassed when he acknowledged my role in saving the archives and most likely, the entire building. Then he made me stand.

At least I was happy I hadn't slept in, since everybody would have known I wasn't there.

John Hammond turned out to be a terrific speaker, genuinely humble and thoughtful, with insights I would be mulling over for the rest of the week. For the second time, I was glad I had come.

I was less glad when the service ended, and it was time to go to the parish house and face Hildy. I hadn't seen her in church, which was no surprise, since preparation for the reception had probably started at dawn. A couple of people had mentioned they were making food at home and bringing it in, but I hadn't heard anyone say they were actually coming this morning to set up. Now I was sorry I hadn't volunteered. That, too, might have earned points to get back into Hildy's good graces, even if it would also have shored up her belief that the minister's partner should have her hands in every single thing.

Right now I was willing to take a hit on that one, just to see her smile again.

By the time I exited, people were grouped

outside, on the lawn, on the sidewalk, on the steps up to the parish house. I saw John surrounded by people, most likely thanking him for his sermon, but also keeping him from moving inside. This was unusual. Most of the time people are in a hurry to have their next cup of coffee. When food is served, as well, there's usually a stampede.

Today nobody seemed in a hurry. In fact, they seemed oddly reluctant. I was sure everyone knew what was waiting inside. The reception had been announced in the service, and Hildy had been lauded for all her hard work.

As I passed I greeted people, and squirmed while more than a few congratulated me on my heroism. Little did they know that the same firefighter who had grudgingly congratulated me on spotting the smoke had also warned if I ever again failed to take orders, he would personally haul me off to jail. I'd had to bite my tongue not to tell him he should compare stories with a certain Detective Sergeant Roussos.

By the time I got into the social hall, there were, at most, a dozen members milling about. I hadn't yet seen Ed and suspected he might be talking with visitors in his office. I glimpsed Hildy across the room looking flustered. She was behind the demon punch bowl, dressed in a sunny yellow skirt and blouse, and entirely alone at that table. As I wished Hildy had raided her closet for cocoa brown or even shipyard gray, signs she might still be mourning Win just a little, Yvonne McAllister came out from the kitchen carrying a plate of tea sandwiches, and several people headed in her direction.

"Don't these look good," one person said loudly enough for me to hear. "Did *you* make these, Yvonne?"

She nodded and suddenly a flock of inner vultures was released. In moments the sandwiches disappeared. Yvonne didn't even get the plate to the table.

"Goodness, what a hungry bunch," I said to a man whose name I couldn't recall.

"For some things."

He wandered off as I tried to figure out what he'd meant. Were people turned off by the sheer amount of food Hildy had prepared? Had there been a pancake breakfast at the local American Legion post before the service, and the whole congregation had stopped there first?

Hildy was looking straight at me, and there was nobody to duck behind. I strolled to the table, which she had beautifully draped with a pale green cloth in the center covered by a soft drift of lace and crowned by the punch bowl. The punch was a soft grapefruit pink, and the ice ring had clusters of pansies and violets frozen inside it. White and pink roses and sprays of baby's breath flanked the bowl, and silver trays of sandwiches and assorted goodies anchored each end.

"Everything looks scrumptious," I told her. "You did a beautiful job."

Her eyes were sad. "I worked all day yesterday, and I've been here since six."

I was so relieved she was speaking to me that I didn't know what to say. I pulled myself together. "I would love some of that punch."

"You'll be the first." She looked even sadder.

"I'm sure you'll be swamped in a moment. People just don't seem to be in a hurry to come inside."

"None of the children are coming at all."

I had to admit it seemed strange no children were here. I'd noticed it myself and wondered. "Maybe classes are taking longer than usual."

"One of the teachers told Yvonne they would be serving the children outdoors today. A special treat, she said."

"Oh, maybe they want this to be an adults-only event."

She shook her head. "You're certain you want *my* punch?"

"Of course I do. Who else's would I want?"

"Anyone's, it seems." She picked up a cup.

I felt chastised, and for good reason. I started to apologize, then and there, but Hildy was looking into the distance.

"Anyone who isn't accused of poisoning her husband," she continued. "Anyone whose punch is safe to drink."

I stared at her. "No . . ." I shook my head incredulously. "I'm sure that has nothing to do with it," although even as I said it, I wondered. Could all these people possibly be staying away because they thought that they, like Win, might be poisoned by something Hildy had prepared with her own hands?

"Yes, it does," Hildy said. "I heard a couple talking. People are afraid I might be planning to take out the whole congregation, like that crazy Jim Jones in Guyana with his poison Kool-Aid."

"That's ridiculous."

She lifted her chin. "I know what I heard."

"Not you, Hildy, *you're* not ridiculous. The sentiment. And I bet whoever said it was exaggerating." Of course if this was true, it would explain why the sandwiches Yvonne had prepared had been eaten before landing on the table.

She poured punch in the glass and held it against her chest. "They said I had prepared the punch myself, and that nobody should assume it was safe. And here it is, looking so delicious in this beautiful punch bowl, and no one will even have a taste."

I couldn't help myself. My gaze drifted down to the bowl. Bathed in light from the nearest window, it seemed to wink malevolently at me, as if to take credit for scaring everyone away.

"Make mine a full cup," I said. "And I believe I'll stand right here and have several. All that smoke last night made me thirsty."

"You don't have to do this."

"Of course I don't. I'm being entirely selfish. I need punch, and lots of it."

Hildy sighed and handed me the cup. I smiled at her, then I turned with my back to the table and made a point of drinking it, smacking my lips, as if I was actually living in a country where an audible concert of enjoyment was considered the height of good manners.

"Hildy," I practically shouted, "this is the best punch I've ever had. I have got to have this recipe. What did you put in it?"

"Arsenic. Strychnine. Lye."

She'd spoken low enough no one could

have heard her words but me. I turned and glared. "Don't you do this. There are always a couple of doubting Thomases. Don't play to them."

"My life has been a terrible failure."

"I need more of this," I said loudly, for everyone else's ears. "I could drink the whole punch bowl dry."

"You'll have ample opportunity," she said.

"Yvonne!" I waved with the resolve of a navy signal man. Yvonne, who was delivering another plate of sandwiches to the wolves, turned to stare at me. Yvonne was the mother of Hildy's lawyer. She, of all people, would be on Hildy's side.

She started over, then she saw my empty glass. She glanced at Hildy, then back at me, and suddenly I saw recognition dawn in her eyes.

"I am *so* thirsty," she said at top volume while she was more than ten feet away. She began fanning herself. "Will you pour me a cup, too?"

Hildy's eyes misted over, but she did. Yvonne downed it in one gulp. "I think I need some of your wonderful food to go with it," she said. "Aggie, dear, will you make me a plate while I have another cup of Hildy's fabulous punch?"

"I'll make us both one." I went to the end

of the table and started distributing items on two pastel paper plates. Tiny quiches. More sandwiches. A mixture of spiced nuts and dried fruit. Vegetable crudités.

No shrimp dip, thank the good Lord. I'm loyal and faithful, but I'm not stupid.

I brought a plate back to Yvonne, and we stood side by side eating and laughing too loudly. When we had finished, we held out our glasses to Hildy and asked for another round.

Yvonne drank hers in one big swallow, although by now, she was looking both bloated and glassy-eyed. I waved her back to the kitchen, and I asked for yet another.

John Hammond came through the door and straight over to the table. He didn't ask for punch. He circled the table and put his arms around Hildy for a long hug. Then he reached around her, once he'd released her, and poured his own cup. He held it out in toast, then drank it dry.

"I'll have another, too," I said, since more people were coming into the room. "John, will you fill my glass?"

By this time I'd had enough liquid to irrigate a grove of olive trees. I hoped that if and when I was able to turn over the drinking of the poison punch to willing members whose bladders were not yet stretched to capacity, I'd have a clear path to the down-stairs restroom. There was no way I'd make it one step farther.

I saw Ed come into the room, and I beckoned wildly. He frowned, but he made his way in our direction. The room was beginning to fill up now. Some hardy souls were even hovering nearby, but as yet had not dived into the available goodies.

"Ed," I said with unusual volume and exuberance, "you have to try this punch. Hildy made it, and it's delicious."

Ed's no dummy. He understood immedi-ately. He stepped up to the table and took a glass. "Make mine a double," he boomed. "And pour me one for Teddy. She loves punch. I'll take it outside."

I could swear the room went silent for a moment. Nothing is louder than the com-plete absence of speech when a room's been buzzing. I even thought I could hear atoms colliding or splitting, or whatever atoms do when they think nobody's listening.

Then the noise began again, and more people started toward our table.

I recognized a choir member, a woman on the board, a man who trims the shrubs and plants our flowerbeds in spring. They got into line and held out cups for Hildy to fill.

Then, and only then, did I make my

beeline for the door.

And just in the nick of time.

After that I didn't have a chance to talk to
Hildy again, but the reception was enough
of a success that I hoped she felt vindicated
and supported. I doubted it. Unfortunately,
now she knew that some people in the
church suspected her of her husband's
murder, at least enough not to take chances.
I was sure the punch bowl had whispered
doubts loudly enough to be heard, but
punch bowl perfidy is hard to prove. Believe
me, I've tried.

We had what was for our family, an un-
eventful afternoon. I didn't find clues or
question suspects. The board prez didn't arrive to tell Ed that half the congregation
thought his sermons were too intellectual
and the other half thought they weren't
intellectual enough. Deena didn't ask to
have her tongue pierced, and Teddy didn't
tell her father all the answers on the *New
York Times* crossword puzzle before he
opened the paper.

Lucy arrived an hour before dinner with a
panini grill a client had given her as a thank-
you gift for selling his house. Lucy doesn't
cook, so she offered to give it to me if I
would make paninis for dinner and invite

297

her to stay. Since she has a standing invitation to dinner, this was no hardship. We set it up in the dining room and experimented for the next hour with different breads, spreads, and cheese, then when every combination had been consumed, I pulled out my Jane Austen video tapes. Lucy, Deena, and I settled in for the night, and Ed and Teddy went upstairs to disprove Einstein's theory of relativity.

At some point Deena went to bed. At some point I threw Lucy an afghan, because the evenings can still be cold this time of year, and we are too aware of the church finance committee poring over our gas and electric bills to heat the parsonage unless we absolutely have to.

I woke up when the telephone rang. Disoriented, I sat up slowly. On television someone in silly-looking Regency garb was expounding about the latest fashion. This, of course, wasn't much of a clue about which novel we'd graduated to. The phone rang again, as I remembered where it was and how to answer. I saw that Lucy was waking up, too. The clock insisted it was almost midnight. Or possibly noon, although that seemed unlikely.

I caught the phone right after the fourth ring, and to my credit, I remembered what

I was supposed to say, although it came out as a croak.

"H'lo." I cleared my throat.

"Aggie? Mrs. Wilcox?"

I am actually Aggie Sloan-Wilcox, but it was too late at night to explain the importance of not getting absorbed into the identity of one's spouse. "That's right." I cleared my throat a second time.

"This is Florence Everett. From Russell House? Ellen Hardiger's friend?"

"Of course, Flo." I was beginning to sound less like a beached whale and more like a sentient human being. Flo just sounded worried. "What's up?"

"I hate to trouble you, but I just got a frantic call from Zoey. She was planning to leave tomorrow evening, on the same plane from Columbus as her mother's body, you know, but she thinks maybe she saw Craig outside my friend's house."

I tried to piece this together. "Her ex?"

"Yes."

I remembered that Zoey was staying with a friend of Flo's, to thwart her maniac ex, in case he learned she had come back to Emerald Springs.

"How would he trace her there?" I asked.

"Who knows? He might have seen her at the funeral home or elsewhere, and followed her back. Or maybe somebody else did. He had friends, macho guys just like him. One of them might have spotted her and told him."

"But it's been years since she lived here."

"Anyone who knew her well would probably recognize her."

"Did she call the police?"

"They drove around the neighborhood. They didn't see anyone or anything. They said they'll come back in a couple of hours, just to make sure. But Zoey's really spooked."

"I can understand that." And I could. After what she'd been through, this must feel like dropping back into a nightmare.

"I hate to ask, but Zoey wants to go to Columbus tonight and wait for her flight at a hotel there. My husband and I can't drive her, because that's too obvious. Someone might be watching us. My friend, same thing. But she liked you. She said you really were trying to find out what had happened to her mother. If you could do it . . ."

How could I say no? Zoey had been through enough, and I wasn't about to hang back while her ex moved in for the kill. "How can we get her out of the house without being seen?"

"If you park on the street behind the

house, Zoey thinks she can sneak out the back way next time the police drive by. We'll tell them what we're doing, and ask them to stop at the house. That should scare away anybody who's watching. Then Zoey can just cut through the yard and the neighbor's behind it, and you can whisk her away. I think you'll be safe. I wouldn't ask if I thought different. I have a neighbor who would do it, only he has problems with his night vision and can't drive after dark anymore."

I needed someone with good night vision to help keep watch while Zoey sprinted to my car. I wondered if I should wake my husband and ask him to come along. But Ed was exhausted, and he'd made that drive to and from Columbus on Saturday. Lucy was frowning in my direction. I covered the receiver.

"Want to help me whisk a woman out of town under the nose of her abusive ex?"

Lucy's eyes lit up. She can always be counted on if adrenaline's involved. I uncovered the receiver. "When should we come and where?" I jotted details on the pad beside the phone, then I scrawled a note to Ed, who might wake up and wonder where I'd gone.

I hung up, and filled Lucy in.

301

Lucy is happiest if she's able to dress for a part. In this case that meant ninja costumes, maybe, or Army Rangers. Just to please her I found a dark shirt of Ed's to put over her much too sparkly tunic, and I fished a black T-shirt out of the clean laundry I hadn't yet taken upstairs. The shirt reads "Two-for-one burgers on Wednesday," which is an odd thing for a vegetarian to wear, but it was free, and I'm neither proud nor fanatical.

We were ready when the phone rang again. Zoey had called the police station, and they'd agreed to send an officer by the house as cover while she stole out the back. Afterwards, the officer would meet us on the street behind Zoey's and escort us out of town. I figured that the local cops had wanted to escort me out of town any number of times, and this was no hardship. I told Flo what we would be driving — Lucy's red Concorde — and hung up. I put Ed's note on the banister, and off we went.

The night was perfect for covert operations. What moon was left was shadowed by clouds, and all the galaxy's stars must have been beaming down on somebody else's planet. Of course the night was also perfect for an ex-husband stalker to exact his revenge on the woman who'd left him. Craig would be invisible if he simply crouched behind a tree. I had the presence of mind to go back inside once I realized the situation and grab our heaviest flashlight out of the basement. Now it resided like a police baton at my feet on the passenger side of Lucy's Concorde.

Lucy knows every house in Emerald Springs. When I told her where Zoey was staying, she gave me a rundown on the woman who now owned the house and when she'd bought it. She also knew which agent had listed it for sale and who had represented the buyers.

"You could call Roussos and let him know what we're doing," I said, like the good conversationalist I am. "Just in case he wonders where you are."

"You're not going to leave that alone, are you?"

"Of course not."

"Even if I was ready to tell you anything, I probably wouldn't. I hate interfering with your vivid imagination."

"I could spend all my free time imagining world peace and an end to hunger. Think of the beneficial effects."

"Should I cut the headlights? We're just about a block away."

"I think if you do, you'll probably drive into a ditch."

As a compromise she switched to her parking lights. We stopped on the side of the road right between two yards. I peered between them, but the houses behind were dark, at least from the rear. The better, of course, for Zoey's escape.

"Should be any time now," Lucy said.

"It's nice of you to do this with me. You didn't have better prospects this evening?"

"Fishing, fishing, always fishing." She glanced at me. "Let's just say I had a lovely morning."

"This is *so* unfair."

"My lovely morning? Or needing to know everything about everybody?"

"I don't need to know everything. Just major details."

"About everybody."

"Not everybody." I struggled. "For instance, I don't need to know about the boy who bags my groceries at Kroger." Although, come to think of it, I have noticed that sometimes he favors his right hand and sometimes his left, so I do wonder if a set of nearly identical twins is taking turns at the store.

But I don't *really* need to know.

Lucy greeted my example with surprising enthusiasm. "The kid with the braces and the black crew cut? Have you ever noticed sometimes he wears his school ring on his left hand and sometimes his right?"

"You're kidding!" We compared notes and theories, until I thought I saw something moving just beyond us.

"Get ready for liftoff," I said. "I think she's here."

A woman materialized out of the darkness just in front of the first of the two houses. She wore jeans, and a dark hoodie drawn up to cover her hair. In the glow of a street-light half a block away I could just make out that in one hand she carried a small overnight case, and on her back, a pack the size of the one Deena carries to school. Clearly we had the right fugitive in our sights.

I jumped out and threw open the rear door. I'd had the good sense to bring sofa pillows and one of Junie's lap quilts to make Zoey comfortable on the trip to Columbus. After her harrowing evening, she deserved nothing less.

She'd paused a moment when the door opened, but now she waved and started forward.

She was nearly to the car when another figure materialized from the shadows of the second house and streaked across the yard, directly into her path.

"Zoey! Wait! Zoey! Stop!"

I didn't need fingerprints or a driver's license to identify the man standing between Zoey and freedom. He was close to six foot, broad-shouldered and even in near darkness, looked to have a full head of hair, maybe several shades redder than Lucy's. He wore a sweatshirt, sweatpants, and running shoes, and filled them out the way a weight lifter might. I hoped that was an illusion, that he was just fat or bloated, and that if I was forced to conk those red curls with the flashlight I was scooping off the floor of the car, he would go down like a tree struck by lightning.

Zoey froze, then she did something I would never have expected. She didn't cower, and she didn't scream. She slapped her hands on her hips and faced her tormentor.

"You skulking, cowardly creep! Who do you think you are, stalking me?" She started by shouting and only got louder. "What gives you the right to even come within a block of me, Craig Brown? I despise you. I wouldn't have you if you were the last man on earth! You can beat me into a bloody pulp, and I still won't have you. You can kill me, but don't imagine we'll be reunited in heaven, because I'll be there all by myself.

So clear out. Get a life. Get an ego. Get help!"

I'm not a counselor, but I honestly don't think this is the correct behavior for dealing with stalkers. It didn't matter. Zoey was beyond caring what was correct or what might enrage him further. She had lived in fear of this man for her entire adult life, and now she seemed to realize she'd moved through fear and beyond it forever. When she said he could beat her or even kill her, those were the words of a woman who realized that standing up to her ex was worth any risk. She would not live in the shadows, and she would not tolerate his control over her life ever again.

"I don't want to beat you." His voice was one half step from a whine. "I just want you back."

"You are sick and you need help."

"I got help! I'd never hurt you now. No chance. We could try again. We could —"

"We could nothing! You're wasting a perfectly good life trying to get something you'll never have. Never. Never. Never!"

When I'd opened the door of the car, the inside light had come on. Now that bulb shed just enough glow on the scene for me to see Craig reaching into a pocket. I envisioned a gun. I envisioned the death of an innocent woman before the police escort arrived. Lucy was out of the car now, too, and standing behind it. When I lunged at Craig with the flashlight over my shoulder, ready to bring it down on the back of his head, she jumped forward, too.

He twisted just in time to avoid my swing, but that left him off balance, and in a moment he hit the ground hard. Lightweight Lucy had tackled him.

Lights flashed and I heard one blast of a siren. Then I heard a door slamming and feet slapping rapidly over the sidewalk. I turned to see the double barrel of a shotgun.

"Hands over your head. Get up nice and slow," a man shouted.

Lucy had already managed to extricate herself, and she backed away. I'd never been prouder of her.

"I didn't do anything!" Craig shouted.

"He was reaching in his right pocket," I told the cop, a young man with glasses.

"Those hands get anywhere near that pocket again, you'll be sorry," the cop told Craig.

"It's just a ring. A ring! I was going to give her back her wedding ring. That's all!"

"You really are nuts," Zoey said contemptuously. "Taking off that ring was the best thing I ever did."

I'd expected a lot of things from Craig, the abuser. More violence. Vicious words. Even an attempt to drag Zoey away. I hadn't expected tears. But tears we got. He began to cry. Loud, choking sobs that would have touched almost anyone. Only it didn't touch any of the women standing together in the darkness as the policeman cuffed Craig, or as another officer arrived to assist and helped the first one put Craig in the cruiser.

Charity and forgiveness are worthy goals. Neither Lucy, Zoey, nor I came close to embracing them that night. Not then, and not on the way to Columbus, where we delivered Zoey safely to her hotel and out of the clutches of her obsessed ex-husband, hopefully forever.

Zoey's ex-husband, Craig Brown, who was — not surprisingly — known to some of his friends as Red. The same Craig Brown who, according to Zoey, had always worked in food service and according to me, was now working for Grace Forester and Emerald Excellence.

16

Roussos had a new jacket, and I was sure a woman had picked it out, since the charcoal color looked great with his black hair, and the cut was perfect, casual with flair. I suspected Lucy's hand in this, yet another sign that Roussos was the man of the hour.

"Great jacket," I said. "New?"

He looked suspicious. "Why, are you cold again?"

"I'm wearing wool." I held out the hem of another of Junie's sweaters, this one a raspberry knit, as proof. "Not cold, just observant."

"I'm going home for Easter, and they'll make me go to church. I figured I'd better be dressed for it."

"You're late. Easter's over."

"Not for us."

"Gotcha. Home's in Athens, maybe? Santorini?"

"Try Tarpon Springs. Florida."

This was more than he'd ever told me. Greek Orthodox. Florida boy. Autocratic family. I almost had enough to write the man's biography.

Roussos wrote "the end" to the story of his life and turned back to the reason my seat was firmly planted in the extra chair in the cubbyhole that passed for his office. "Brown claims he was with friends the morning Ellen Hardiger was run down. He says he was up in Michigan on a fishing trip."

"Do you believe him?"

"I don't form opinions."

"If he was with friends, then they can vouch for him, right?"

"Could if they were around. Brown says they took off somewhere or other and probably won't be back for a couple of weeks. We'll make some calls and see if we can track them down."

I already knew the cops hadn't charged Craig Brown, although they had held him for the night. There was no restraining order in effect, so even though he'd gotten up close and personal with Zoey, no crime had actually been committed. He had never threatened her; he hadn't even touched her. He had only begged her to return. The cops had questioned him, but this morning, they'd had to let him go with a warning not to leave town.

As for the murders? Roussos had listened carefully as I told him about the link between Win, Ellen, and Zoey's ex, and he hadn't even told me to find a new hobby.

"I'll interview Grace Forester again," Roussos said, "just to see if she thinks there was enough time during the party for Brown to find Dorchester's meds, figure out an overdose would kill him, and add them to the shrimp dip. But it sounds like a long shot to me. You said yourself that *she* carried the dip into the kitchen after he left."

"He could have poisoned it before he ditched."

"Nobody else at the party got sick."

"Maybe that was just luck. Maybe nobody else had any after he poisoned it. It was the end of the evening."

He didn't look convinced, and I didn't feel convinced. But my scenario was possible.

"We're going to keep an eye on the guy," Roussos said. "I've already advised the sheriff's department, since he lives in the county."

I got to my feet. Slowly. I'd gotten a total of four hours sleep after dropping Zoey off in Columbus, driving home with Lucy, and falling into bed in my clothes. This morning Ed got the girls off to school, then headed to the church to wait for the electrician who was supposed to repair the attic wiring, but once sunlight was beaming full strength through our curtains, I'd driven here to tell Roussos my pet theory and relay the events of last night from my perspective.

"You know the big problem with everything you told me?" Roussos said, standing to see me out, like the proper gentleman he is.

"His motive?"

"Yeah, why he'd wait so long to kill either of them, much less both so close together. You have any thoughts about that?"

It almost sounded like Roussos was asking me for help, which just goes to show you the tricks ears can play. "Not yet," I said. "Unless having both Win and Ellen here at the same time just set him off. Maybe he's been simmering all this time, but he was too disorganized to find and kill them."

"Weak. Very weak."

"Yeah, I know. I'm working on it."

"Don't bet the farm. Sometimes you connect dots, and there's nothing to show for all that effort except a lot of straight lines leading nowhere."

We had been heading back toward the

reception area. Roussos opened the door, but I didn't move.

"Hildy Dorchester's innocent," I said. "I'm going to connect dots until I can prove it to you."

He opened the door wider and gestured. "You start seeing some shapes, you come back and tell me. Just don't try to figure out what they are all by yourself."

A sensible person would have gone home for a nap. No one accuses me of being sensible. Yesterday morning I'd chalked up a few pluses with Hildy when I'd imbibed untold quarts of suspect punch. I figured that gave us a place to start again after my unfortunate temper tantrum, but I had to take advantage of her goodwill right away.

I also needed to tell Hildy about this new development, not to raise false hopes, but to let her know I was still working hard to find her husband's murderer. And truthfully, I had another reason, too. A couple of questions had occurred to me, and if I could find a way to ask them, I needed to. If I was going to find a new and better suspect than Craig Brown, I needed, at the very least, more information. More likely I was going to need a whole new theory, and questioning Hildy was a place to start.

I filled the gas tank of my van at the cheapest station in the county, and when I went inside to pay, I fortified myself with a cup of coffee brewed — at the latest — on St. Patrick's Day. I drank it anyway, checking out the magazines so I could delay getting back into the van. Who knew there were so many ways to skin a deer or drain a radiator? By the time I'd jacked up my courage to go see Hildy, I'd picked out three likely tattoos and several great topics to discuss with my father next time I visited his compound in Indiana. Did he know, for instance, that a simple fruitcake wrapped in cheesecloth, soaked in brandy and buried in powdered sugar, could save his life and sustain him practically forever once the world falls into chaos? Did I want to tell him and risk a fifty-pound package on my front porch on Christmas Eve?

The drive to Hildy's took fifteen minutes, but only because I took back streets and braked for winged insects. I parked in front of the house and tried to tell myself I was investigating. Of course nothing much had changed. The trees, and what looked like a snowball bush, were a little closer to leafing out. A newspaper adorned the driveway. Ace detective that I am, I knew this meant either Hildy just hadn't bothered to pick it up this morning, or she had gone away. Knowing Hildy, I discarded the latter possibility. She would cancel the paper rather than waste her carrier's time. Besides, she wasn't supposed to leave town.

Not picking up the paper? Either she'd slept late because she had finally come to the sad conclusion that nobody in town was ever again going to request her help early in the morning, or she had simply lost all interest in the world around her.

I felt worse than ever.

I finally ambled up the sidewalk. I told myself I was still investigating. For instance, I'd never noticed that the lots on this side of the street were somewhat unusual. The front yards are surprisingly deep, giving welcome privacy from the street, as well as long, lush stretches of lawn. To compensate most side yards are narrow, and the houses set close together, almost as close as town houses. Hildy's yard is a good example. There's almost no lawn to Hildy's right, and on her left, the driveway extends beyond the house and up to her backyard, bordered along its outer edge by the neighbor's identical drive.

The front windows of Hildy's house are deep and wide, and the shrubs beneath them are trimmed low. Again, the airy effect

316

offsets the close proximity to neighbors, but I wondered if Hildy ever opened curtains on the right side of her house.

On a whim I strolled across the yard — still wasting time — and peered into the side yard. The architect of Hildy's house was no dope. He'd solved the problem of peeping Toms. I could only see one window on this side of the house, in a peculiar-looking extension that jutted out nearly to the property line. The window faced front, and a picket fence stretched from the extension to the front of the house, creating a narrow garden with a flagstone path and no gate leading into it. Perhaps originally this had been a clever secret garden, but now, without a gate, it was simply one of those quirky features that make old houses interesting.

I reminded myself that due to the lousy real estate market, I was no longer flipping houses, and Hildy's windows or lack of them were no longer of professional interest. I had delayed the inevitable too long. I took a deep breath and walked back to the front and up to the porch. After I rang the doorbell the fourth time, Hildy finally answered. She was as neatly dressed as ever, her hair pinned into a tidy knot on her head and face scrubbed and shiny. But she looked tired, as if sleep was no longer her friend.

I should have prepared a speech. Instead I just turned up my hands. "I'm sorry. Can you forgive me?"

She shook her head. "For what? Telling the truth?"

"How about for exploding when I could have told the truth with the respect and consideration you deserve?"

Tears filled her eyes. She held out her arms, and I stepped into them. We hugged hard.

"I always say it's best to just come clean," Hildy said. "But you already learned that from somebody else."

I laughed, and okay, I wiped my eyes, too. "That darned floor's just been such a sore point. I guess it's my Achilles' heel."

"And I have a terrible habit of taking over. I knew it, and now I know it even better."

"I just had the worst cup of coffee in the entire world. Any chance you have something to chase it while I tell you some news?"

I followed her into the kitchen, and she made a pot of coffee while I told her about the events of the previous night and the links to Win and Ellen Hardiger.

"So they're looking at Craig Brown as a possible suspect," I said, ending with the good news.

"Goodness, you do get yourself into tense situations, don't you?"

After all we'd been through, how could I fault her for stating the obvious? And, besides, wasn't that just the nicest way of summing up my life?

"Putting my life in jeopardy seems to be my way of establishing a separate identity," I told her. "I guess it's about as far from what's expected of a minister's wife as I can get."

Hildy took down two mugs from the cabinet beside the sink. "In the long run, you'll be the best kind of role model, won't you? A good marriage and happy family. Your own place in the community, and well loved in the church anyway. All because you made yourself happy doing what you're good at."

I waited until she served the coffee, with a pitcher of cream, cloth napkins, and sugar cubes, to boot.

"You were happy doing what you're good at, weren't you?" I asked when she'd seated herself across from me at the kitchen table.

"I really wanted to be a doctor." She took a sip, then she smiled. "I should have, was going to, then I met Win. I loved him enough to put that behind me, only, once I made that choice, I knew I had to be the best minister's wife out there, just to prove to myself I'd done the right thing. Maybe we'd all have been better off if I'd just gone ahead with my plans, and Win had been forced to make some adjustments for *me*. Maybe if I hadn't put him at the center of the universe, he wouldn't have settled there so comfortably."

I was surprised how clearly she saw her life. I wondered how many people were able to look back at decisions they had made and see them for what they really were.

"But I helped a lot of people, a lot of churches," she said, after a pause. "I did a lot of good. I just never learned when to pull back. I guess I'll learn that now."

"I'm so very sorry you're having to learn anything from this situation, Hildy. I promise, I'm still looking for Win's murderer."

"Do you think it really was Craig Brown?" She gave a visible shudder. "To think he was here in my kitchen doing who knows what?"

I told her the questions Roussos had raised about Zoey's ex, questions I'd already considered. She sighed.

"There is something else, another avenue to explore," I said. "But it's not pleasant, Hildy. I don't want to make you unhappier than I have already."

"Why don't you let me decide where to go with whatever it is?"

I debated. But if we were really going to find out who killed Win, I had to know more.

I decided to edge into it. "Win's memoirs. How serious was he about writing them?"

"I don't know. I really don't. He was having as much trouble letting go of his ministry as I was. I suppose that would have been one way to relive it. But he also talked about publishing his sermons, maybe in some sort of self-help, popular theology format. I think that was more likely. He was a practical man. His sermons might have found a home with a publisher. But memoirs? Who would have been interested in his life as a minister, except the people who'd known him as one?"

"Then you're doubtful he would have written them?"

"Why is this coming up now?"

I thought about Samuel Booth. "Maybe somebody was afraid he might."

"Somebody with something to hide? There was no reason to be afraid. Win would never expose a parishioner's secret."

I hoped she was right, and Win's threat to Samuel had either been unintended or just a bluff. "Maybe whoever this was didn't believe that."

"What kind of secret?"

When I didn't answer, she set down her cup. "Let's have it, Aggie. If you and I are going to be honest with each other in a good way, this is the place to start."

"Somebody told me Win may have had more than one affair, and you probably know."

She looked stunned. Then she shook her head so hard wisps of hair escaped their carefully pinned home. "No. I know no such thing, and furthermore, I don't believe it."

She was telling the truth. I had no doubt of that, but was she just closing her eyes to an unpleasant possibility?

"Here's why I'm sure," she said, correctly reading my expression. "Because after Marie? I never trusted him again. Not fully, anyway. Once trust is breached, nothing's ever the same. I tried to have faith in him, but I finally realized I never would. Not completely, and not unless I had proof. So I watched him. Checked up on things he told me. Kept an eye on our finances, on his trips out of town." She lifted her shoulders. "You're not the only minister's wife with detective skills."

"Wow."

"Do you think I would have come back to Emerald Springs if I thought Win was still involved with Marie? Or if he had given me more cause to suspect him of infidelity? Win was a great storyteller, and he liked to shock people, just to see their reaction. He liked to throw them off balance. He was far from perfect, still an adolescent in some ways, right up until the moment he died. But with Win, it was mostly talk. I'm almost certain Marie was his only affair, and no matter what she says, I don't think it continued after we left. In fact I'm almost sure he was glad to say good-bye to her. She was a complication, and he didn't need or want emotional complications. That's why he loved me. I made everything run smoothly, so he could just go on being Win."

"You changed churches so often. I thought maybe . . ."

She shook her head again. "No, he wasn't in trouble. Win just loved whipping churches into shape and moving on. Everybody knew he was good at taking troubled congregations, setting them on their feet, and looking for a new challenge when he'd finished. It was a rare talent, and I liked moving to new places and fixing things, too. That was something we shared."

"What about the night of the party? Marie was a pretty big complication."

"When I confronted him in the kitchen after my scene with Marie, he told me she had drunk too much, so he went outside to talk her into leaving. He was afraid she would upset me. He said he offered to drive her home, but she refused."

"That's when you saw them together?"

"So he said. He claimed he told her as nicely as he could that he didn't want to pick up where they left off, and she needed to move on."

I was trying to imagine this. "Where were they exactly?"

"On the side of the house."

"In the driveway?"

"No, the other side."

I was glad I'd wasted time by examining the house more carefully. "I only noticed one window over there, Hildy. Is that little extension part of your bedroom?"

"No, our — my bedroom's upstairs. Win's study was down here, in the back of the house with windows looking over the backyard. Then there's a guest room in the front, and a little hall between them, ending in an alcove with the only side window, and it faces front. I was standing in the alcove when I spotted them."

I was trying to imagine this. Hildy could

tell, and she got to her feet. "Come, I'll show you."

I put down my coffee and followed her on what turned out to be a fast trip. Through the kitchen into the living room, then into a short hallway that ended in the extension I'd noted. A tall secretary rested at the end beside the window I had seen looking over the narrow side yard.

"What were you doing here?" I asked. "When you saw them?"

She bit her lip, then she pointed to the phone sitting on top of the secretary, a note-pad beside it, a calendar on the wall behind it. "I think the phone rang. I'm almost sure it did."

"It's kind of a strange place for a phone, isn't it?"

"I think this little nook was used as a study of sorts by the owners, to pay bills and such. The phone jack was here, so we put the secretary here and hooked up a phone when we moved in."

"Why did you take the call here instead of the kitchen?"

"I was in the living room turning off lights and straightening up. The caterer was gone by then, and I was waiting for Win to help me put away the leftovers, since he had insisted on keeping them. I thought he'd gone outside to walk the last guests to their car. This was the closest telephone."

"Who called, do you remember?"

She frowned. "Why?"

"Trying to get a picture, that's all."

She bit her lip again, and I worried about blood loss. "I can't remember. I just remember seeing Win and Marie and losing my temper."

"If that was the end of the party, it must have been pretty late. Do your daughters call at that hour because they're on the West Coast?"

"Not usually . . ." She was still nibbling, then she nodded. "Nobody."

"Nobody called you?"

"No, nobody was on the line. I answered the phone, and there was some kind of background noise, then the line went dead. By then I'd seen Win and Marie through the window, and I wasn't paying attention to the call anymore. For all I know, I even left the receiver lying on the desk."

"What happened next? Can you tell me?"

"I stepped back here" — she moved against the wall beyond the window to demonstrate — "so I wouldn't be seen. And I watched them for maybe a minute. No, probably even longer. I was frozen in place. They were standing close together, and I could hear their voices, but not their words. Finally Win hugged her, then he set her away." Hildy put her hands up in the air and pushed, as if she was pushing on somebody's shoulders. "He moved past her and around the house, but he didn't come in the front door. When I realized he wasn't going to, I used it myself, went outside and confronted her."

"You didn't see him?"

"No."

"Where do you think he went?"

"I don't know. Maybe he went around the house and in through the kitchen. I didn't see him again until I went into the kitchen myself. By the time I did, he was cleaning up. He'd put some of the food into containers by then, thrown some away. I was furious . . ." She swallowed. "I told you the rest."

"Right." I stepped toward the window and peered out. "If the phone hadn't rung, you never would have seen them together."

"Not likely, no."

"How long were you out of the kitchen altogether, would you say?"

"Counting the time I was straightening things and turning out the lights? Maybe five minutes. Why?"

"Five minutes until you went out the front

door and confronted Marie?"

"About. Maybe more."

"You weren't in the kitchen, and Win wasn't there, and the caterer was already gone. The last of the guests were gone, too. The kitchen was empty, you were across the house in the alcove, and you were unlikely to return immediately, since you were busy watching your husband with another woman."

"That's all true. Are you saying . . . ?"

"That somebody may have taken advantage of your absence and used it to poison the shrimp dip? I think I am. I may even be saying that whoever made that telephone call, did it to get you to the one place in this house where you could see Win talking to Marie. And Hildy, that could be the person who murdered your husband."

17

Deena and Ed would have been proud of me. I let my fingers do the walking, and while I was still sitting in front of Hildy's house, I made two calls on my nearly virgin cell phone. The first was the easiest. I called Roussos, who, to his credit, didn't point out that I just left his office. I asked him if he would find out who had made the call to Hildy on the night Win died, and explained why. He told me I was reaching, but he didn't refuse. I was satisfied he would get around to it, but would he tell me what he discovered? Unlikely.

The second call was less pleasant. I considered going to Marie Grandower's house to talk in person, but in the end I decided she would be easier to tolerate on the telephone so I looked her up in the church directory under my seat.

Marie was not happy to hear from me and told me so immediately. I followed up that excellent start with a question — as if she hadn't just called me a meddler and a pain in a place from which her surgeon husband had probably removed a lifetime of hemorrhoids to keep her in diamonds.

"Marie, can you tell me why you and Win were in the side yard talking on the night of the party? Why there?"

"What's this? You're trying to implicate me in his murder?"

"Absolutely not. In fact, if I'm right, your answer will make it clear it couldn't have been you." Which was more or less true. If I was right and the murderer had guided Hildy to that spot with a phone call in order to have the kitchen empty to do the deed, the murderer couldn't have been Marie, who was busy talking to Win and not making prank calls.

"Why don't you get a real job? Who do you think you are?"

"The person who's trying to make sure nobody suspects you of killing Win Dorchester."

Okay, I confused myself with all the double talk, but luckily it seemed to be having the same effect on her. She actually answered. "Well, Win wanted to meet me there, that's who. It was *his* idea. I just did what he asked."

I thought that was too bad, since I was pretty sure Win didn't kill himself. Suicide by shrimp dip is always suspicious.

"You're sure?" I asked.

She hung up, which probably meant she was.

For the moment I gave up and went to my favorite little Italian grocery, DiBenedetto's, where the produce is always fresh and the hunky son of the proprietor spends some unknown amount of time in Manhattan visiting my older sister. I say unknown, because even though Vel admits that she and Marco DiBenedetto see each other now and then, she refuses to tell me how distant now is from then. Days, weeks, months? I am surrounded by secretive women.

Among other goodies, I bought glistening asparagus, aged Swiss, and farm fresh eggs to make a quiche for dinner, since our stove was still hooked up, even if it had been pulled into the middle of the kitchen by the floor guys. Marco himself walked me through the checkout line and asked about our family as I tried not to swoon. In turn I asked about his two young sons, who, in my opinion, desperately need a mother with Junie's extraordinary parenting genes. Vel, of course, fits that description, since we have the same mother, if not the same father. To

331

my credit, I didn't add that suggestion to the conversation. My busybody reputation is undeserved.

The radio was on when I returned home, and it wasn't a station Ed would willingly choose. I opened the door to a song that was some combination of R&B, salsa, and punk. I might have suspected burglars, but I'm pretty sure they have better taste in music.

"Deena?" I called. "What are you doing home?"

Deena poked her head through the kitchen doorway, pale apricot hair swinging around her face. "Getting something to eat. It's almost lunchtime."

I joined her in the demolition site formerly known as a kitchen, a grocery bag in each arm. "You know that's not what I mean. Why are you home when you're supposed to be in school?"

"Half day today, remember? Teacher training."

Now I *did* remember, although it seemed like years since I'd seen the notice in the school newsletter. I supposed forgetting was a sign that Win's murder was taking over my life and shoving my family on their own resources.

Too bad.

"How long have you been home?" I asked, as I set bags on the counter.

"I don't know. Fifteen minutes." She peeked into the first bag. "How come you never buy potato chips?"

"Loaded with fat, salt, and preservatives."

"I just go to other people's houses and eat them."

"I'll see if our health insurance covers that."

We made sandwiches with tofu turkey and fresh tomatoes. I haven't always been a vegetarian, and I still remember what real turkey tastes like. I'm still hoping someday the tofu turkey folks will remember, too. But how can they compare if they're vegetarians and don't eat meat? How will they ever know?

We took our lunch into the living room, where our shoes didn't stick to the floor, and we didn't have to view the mess.

"When's the new floor coming?" Deena asked.

"I have to go back to the dealer this afternoon and pick out something else. Turns out the one I like was discontinued."

"Great. We're never going to have a working kitchen, are we?"

"Never is a stretch. Just probably not in your lifetime."

333

"So, have you been reading Right In the Middle lately?"

I studied the question silently, wishing I could throw my sandwich into the air and run for the computer.

"Something on there you'd like to tell me about?" I asked, as nonchalantly as I could.

"Not really."

"Why'd you bring it up?"

"Just making conversation."

Girls Deena's age do not make conversation with their parents. In fact avoiding conversation is on the first page of the "You're a Teenager Now" handbook.

"Okay," I said, topping my last try at nonchalance.

"What do you think of it?"

I'd already told her, so this was yet another clue. But I played along. "It's well done. Clever. Not mean, which it could be. Why?"

"You ask that a lot."

"It's rooted in my DNA."

She chewed a moment, and I stayed silent. I've known her since birth, nine months before, in fact, and I had a pretty good idea something was about to gush forth. I swallowed to prepare, so I wouldn't choke.

"It's just that Mr. Collins . . ."

I stayed perfectly still, and did not compress my sandwich into a sphere the size of a Ping-Pong ball. When she didn't continue, I ventured a guess.

"Somebody's reported him for something? Another student?"

She frowned. "No. What do you mean?"

I backtracked. "I was trying to finish your sentence. You kind of left it hanging."

"Mr. Collins said I should talk to you."

That was completely unexpected. I had swallowed for nothing. "Did he?"

"I just said so, right? I mean, I heard myself say it."

Patient Aggie disappeared. "Deena, what's this about?"

She wrinkled her nose. I've been careful not to tell her how cute nose wrinkling is, just in case she tries it on some pimply adolescent of the opposite sex.

"Mr. Collins knows . . ."

"What does he know?" I demanded. This time I didn't finish her thought and prayed she'd get around to it eventually.

"Well, he knows Tara and Maddie and I are the ones behind Right In the Middle. It's our blog." She narrowed her eyes. "And don't go all ballistic, okay?"

"Yours?"

She nodded.

"But I asked you all about it. I asked you who was doing it!"

"And I told you who everybody *thought* was doing it, and why they probably weren't right. I never really lied to you. I just said nobody knows who's doing it, and that's true, well, except Tara, Maddie, and me. And Mr. Collins."

"Why does *he* know?"

"You aren't going to get this part."

I leaned forward and gave her my best Mom look. "Better try me."

"Well, I told him about Right In the Middle when I went to talk to him about quitting the debate team. See, I hate debating, only I didn't want to tell anybody, because Daddy loves it so much. I wanted Daddy to be proud of me. And you don't have to tell me he's proud of me anyway, like I don't know that. But it was something we could share. Teddy's not the only one in this family with a brain."

"Whoever in your short life said she was?"

"It's just that the two of them like all the same stuff. They have everything in common. Church stuff. Finding out about everything, even stupid stuff. And Teddy loves being in front of people the way Daddy does."

"You don't." It was not a question.

She nodded. "I hated being up there. I liked writing and researching, you know, and putting ideas on paper. I just hate being up there presenting it. I can't think. I feel like I'm talking underwater."

"But you didn't want to tell your father? You thought he wouldn't understand?"

"He won't, not exactly, because we don't really think alike, him and me. I'm more like you, and you always think way outside the box and drive him crazy. I guess I will, too."

"Wow," I said. What else could I say? It was more or less true.

"So I kept going to the debate meetings and hating them more. I tried the school newspaper a couple of times, thinking maybe I could switch without anybody getting upset, but the meetings were so stupid, all about staying positive. Then one day Tara said we ought to start our own blog with real news about school. We messed around with it and I realized how much I liked doing it. It was so different. Plenty of time to get everything right and think it through, and nobody's watching me. That's when I knew I had to quit the team and do what I wanted instead."

"So you went to Mr. Collins?"

She nodded.

I was ashamed of myself, but I couldn't quite let go of the idea that Stephen Collins had somehow acted inappropriately with Deena. The possibility had haunted me too long. "I bet he was sorry to lose you," I said.

"Not very. He already figured out I wasn't all that into it and needed something else to do. He's a good teacher. He always says every student has talents and just needs to try different things to find them. That's why we all like him so much. He doesn't push, and he doesn't make us feel bad. But when he saw me this morning in the hall, he took me aside and told me I needed to tell you the truth, because it wasn't fair to worry you. I guess he was right about that, too."

I finally let go of what had been a huge, nearly catastrophic, misjudgment. Stephen Collins had obviously never by word or deed hurt or upset my daughter. He had, in fact, just encouraged her to do what her father and I had always told her to do. Follow her heart. This had never been about sexual misconduct. Deena had simply worried she might disappoint her father.

As if.

"I wish you'd told me sooner," I said. "I could have told you Dad doesn't care one bit whether you debate or write or join the pep squad. He's always proud of you."

She cocked her head and stared at me as if my brain had shrunk to walnut size.

I retrenched. "Okay, he might not be all that understanding about the pep squad. He's a guy. But Deena, he's nuts about you, and that means the real you."

"He and Teddy are always doing stuff together."

"Because you have your own life now, and not as much time for us. Teddy still likes hanging around with us. When you were eight, we did a lot of things together, too. That's how it works."

When she didn't look convinced, I reached over and patted her knee. "I'll tell you what. I won't say a word to him. You talk to your father tonight and tell him yourself. Watch his face. He'll be completely blown away, I promise. You never had to keep it a secret."

Deena finished her sandwich and went into Ed's study to turn on the computer, most likely to report our conversation anonymously on the blog under "Dumb Things Parents Say." I tried to deal with all her revelations.

The big revelation and relief, of course, was that Stephen Collins was an innocent man and a good teacher. I had incorrectly assumed the poor guy had made advances. Deena's secrecy, her obvious reluctance to tell us why she really ditched the debate team, and his refusal to discuss the situation had led me to one conclusion. Sex.

But wasn't sex in some form or the other, often a culprit? What kind of mother would I be if I refused to consider this possibility and check it out? Still, how often do we jump to that conclusion, when something else is in play?

That sounded familiar.

I stopped and tried to figure out why. When recently had I assumed that something had to do with sex, without really looking at the other possibilities? The answer wasn't hard to find.

Win's murder.

Fifteen years ago Win Dorchester engaged in an affair with Marie Grandower. From that indisputable fact I had widened the net, looking for all kinds of sexual indiscretions in the man's past. Yet nothing I'd found so far had led to any. Zoey had insisted Win was nothing but helpful, and that neither she nor her mother had ever had anything more than a counseling relationship with him.

Then I had immediately jumped on Geoff Adler's suggestion that Win may have had other affairs. Hildy had set me straight on that this morning. She staunchly believed, and now I supposed I did, too, that Win had made one mistake, not many.

340

So twice in the past weeks I had been led astray. I had gone right for the sensational, when the answer had had nothing to do with sex. At least not when it came to Deena and her debate coach. Now it was also time to remove sex as a factor in Win's death and see what was left.

If Win had *not* died because of an ongoing or previous affair, then why had he? And what was the connection between Win and Ellen Hardiger? Helping Zoey leave town, of course, and perhaps the answer was that simple. Maybe Craig "Red" Brown really had murdered them both, because of his sick obsession with his ex-wife. But Roussos didn't think so, and more and more, neither did I.

We had missed something important. I could feel it deep in my bones. If the two deaths were linked — and I refused to believe they were not — then there must be another way in which Ellen and Win were connected.

I got a pencil and started scribbling in the margin of the *Flow*.

Ellen worked at the nursing home.

Win visited patients at the nursing home.

Ellen thought so highly of Win that she asked him to counsel her daughter, in hopes Zoey would leave her abusive husband.

Win counseled Zoey. Zoey left town.

Both Win and Ellen were murdered within days of each other here in Emerald Springs, after long absences.

Zoey's ex-husband was living in town and was present at the party where Win died.

What else had Ellen said about Win? I tried hard to remember our brief conversation at the memorial service reception. She had told me how she knew Win, that he had visited patients at Russell House, and not just ones who were connected to the church.

Hadn't she said something about the way he listened so carefully, and compared Win to her priest, who'd charged in only at the end, most likely because he had a much larger congregation and more duties?

That felt right, although obviously the priest was not a suspect. And what else? I remembered feeling annoyed, that her praise was another manifestation of St. Godwin, who I hadn't really liked all that much.

What else?

I remembered that Ellen had talked about how much her patients loved Win. This caring, patient man was a side of Win I hadn't seen, and I'd been reluctantly impressed. How had she put it? She'd said they were so grateful. Hadn't she said that some of them even made him little gifts in their craft classes? I remembered, because I had envisioned Popsicle-stick birdhouses and crocheted coasters.

I'd been tired and frustrated that day. Charity had been at a premium.

There was nothing helpful here. I closed my eyes and tried to envision Ellen, with her pale eyes, her papery white skin.

"Some of them even wanted to leave your church money in their wills," Ellen said in my imagination.

I opened my eyes. Had Ellen *really* said that? I'd been surrounded by noise and confusion, plus I'd been on my way to put out fires and explain why the burial had been postponed. I'd explained that to Ellen, too, and she'd said she was going to stay in town long enough to see Win buried properly.

A decision that cost her her life.

"Money in their wills." That still sounded right to me, as if Ellen had actually verbalized this, although of course, it was all too hazy for me to be sure. But what if somebody *had* left the church money on Win's watch? I couldn't imagine what that might have to do with his murder, unless an angry relative had killed him for derailing an inheritance, but at least this was a detail I could follow up on. And this was a connection between Ellen and Win of sorts. After all, Win had been at the nursing home before he died asking Jamaican Cinda questions.

I knew this was a long shot and a weak premise, but it should be possible to find out if anybody from Russell House had actually left the church a bequest. Church records were still jumbled in boxes, waiting to be returned to the third floor after the wiring was repaired, but I wondered if Ed had separate records in his office. Financial reports, maybe, or budgets presented at our annual business meeting?

I tried his cell phone, since this was Monday and the office was closed. I knew after he let the electrician in, he'd planned to attend a ministerial luncheon, then stop back by the church to check progress before he came home for the day. I hoped I could catch him before he did.

He answered on the second ring. I wallowed in his rich baritone before I told him why I was calling. I expected a delay in getting my answer, even a pile of files by our bed for me to go through on my own, but he told me to hang on a moment, and he would see.

He came back on the line well before his battery could go dead. "We have a legacy list," he said. "Kind of an honor roll of people who left money to the church or the endowment. It's been in force for a couple of decades. We publish it in the newsletter every year during the pledge campaign to show how many people have left money in their wills."

"I don't remember seeing it," I said.

"You don't read the newsletter, Aggie, don't deny it. But we have a committee designing a plaque with all the names to hang in the back of the sanctuary next fall."

I imagined the plaque was one part to honor past generosity and one part to encourage more.

"Are the names arranged by dates?" I asked.

"Right."

"Can you isolate the years of Win's ministry?"

"Easily." He paused. "There *were* a couple of bequests back then, but I recognize the names. Members of long standing. People still talk about them."

"How about after he left?"

Ed was silent a moment. "Somebody donated a large sum to our endowment about ten years ago, but again, I recognize the name. Her husband's still alive, and she would have been somewhere more upscale than Russell House. Everything since then looks familiar, too."

I thanked him and told him to expect a quiche in his future. He said he'd be home as soon as he spoke to the electrician, and we planned a quick bike ride once Teddy got back from school, because he was going to be at a board dinner all evening.

No records of any unusual bequests during Win's ministry and none right after. My theory was a long shot, and I knew it. I nearly discarded the whole line of thinking, but a new thought nagged at me.

Was it possible Win had embezzled a bequest, before the church received it? He was a hands-on administrator, so it seemed possible. He could have made sure the information and the check made it into his own pocket. In the guise of kindness and pastoral care, had he convinced some poor old person to leave money to the church, just so he could steal it?

I hated to think this way, since Win's kindness at Russell House was an image I wanted to preserve. But still, whether I liked the idea or not, I needed to follow up on all connections to Ellen and the retirement home. Wasn't it possible that somebody had discovered Win's deceit and murdered him for it?

But why murder Ellen, too? Had she known, and because of her gratitude, failed to report it?

Ellen's compliance just seemed so unlikely. So did Win's stealing money from the church. But stranger things have happened in ministries. Every denomination has its stories.

Stories. Win had been a great storyteller. I'd bored myself silly reading sermons filled with them. And I'd only read a fraction. The rest were still waiting for me.

Whether Win had inspired a bequest or even embezzled a bequest, a clue to what he'd done might be in a sermon I'd never got around to. And if not, maybe I'd find something else, some hint that led me to his murderer.

I was afraid that after the girls went to bed, I had another long night ahead of me. I just hoped that this time, I found something of lasting value in Godwin Dorchester's words.

18

An octogenarian named Daisy Dreyfus owned a lot of real estate in Reverend Godwin Dorchester's sermons. On Monday night after Greek salads with my daughters, I plunked myself in the middle of our bed and began to sort them. Not by date or subject, but by whether Russell House was mentioned. After an hour of scanning pages and making piles, I found ten sermons that qualified. Of those nine, Daisy was mentioned by name in seven.

By the time Ed came in and was ready to go to sleep, I cleared the bed and took the sermons down to the living room. I didn't really intend to read and take notes on all of them that night, but that's what I did. Call me committed or call me obsessed, I wanted to be sure I kept all the facts in my head without sleep erasing them. It was two AM before I made my final notes. Daisy Dreyfus dominated them.

Through dogged pursuit, I had pieced together her story. Her childhood had been tough. Alcoholic parents, frequent upheavals, an uneven education, because even as a young teen, she'd had to help support her family. When she left home at last, she fell in love with a man she couldn't have, and after that disappointment, she never found another she wanted. She lived frugally, cleaned houses and waited tables, and once she had saved enough to buy a little house in Weezeltown, a rundown section of Emerald Springs, she took in foster children.

That decision marked the moment when Daisy's life changed for the better, and she found her true calling. By the time she entered Russell House, Daisy had raised eighteen children and set them on the road to adulthood. Some were marvelous successes, some not so much, but according to Win, all were better off for having had her love and support. The "kids" visited Daisy frequently at Russell House, and she continued to dispense love and stern advice, as if she wasn't sitting in a wheelchair and far too fragile to make sure any of them followed through.

Win was at his best when he talked about Daisy, and what he had learned from observing her. Respect shone through every word, and by two AM, I liked the man better. Of course now that I'd absolved him of a slew of extramarital affairs, it was easier.

Wills and bequests were not a part of these sermons, at least not until the next to the last one that mentioned Daisy. Then I sat riveted in my chair and read and reread his words.

"Daisy Dreyfus will leave a lasting legacy. Not in the funds she claims she will leave Russell House because of their kindness to residents, and not in the funds she threatens to donate to our church because I visit the home each week. Not even in the small bequests she will leave each of her foster children, small enough, she insists, to make sure they will keep working hard and never look to others for rescue. No, Daisy's legacy is even more lasting. It comes from a life well lived, in spite of a difficult start, a life dedicated to service and love. A conversation with Daisy is a lasting legacy for anyone lucky enough to have engaged in one. I count myself among the privileged."

I stared at the words written more than fifteen years ago. I was sorry I had never met Daisy Dreyfus, who must surely have died by now. I was more sorry that I hadn't read all of Win's sermons on Saturday. Two days had passed when I could have looked at his life with clearer vision, and when I might have checked out this possible new link between Win and Ellen. I still had no idea what any of it meant, if Daisy had actually had money to leave our church, and if so, why someone would kill Win and Ellen because of it. By this time it was nothing more than a cloud in my head, made wispier by the late hour. I turned off the lights and went to bed. There was nothing I could do at two in the morning except get some sleep.

The girls were gone by the time we sat down to muesli and strawberries I'd bought at DiBenedetto's. Ed and I caught up a little. He told me that the electrician thought mice or squirrels must have stripped the wiring directly above the storage room archives. The rest of the wiring needed to be updated, but nothing looked imminently dangerous. In return I told Ed what I'd learned from the sermons.

"Russell House caters to people with few resources," he pointed out after I finished. "It's unlikely Daisy Dreyfus had anything to leave anybody. Look at what you know. Waiting tables, raising foster children. Nothing very lucrative there."

"True, but we don't know all there is to know about her."

"Are you planning to check it out?"

I was, and by the time he left, I had showered and dressed for the trip across town. The best place to find out about a resident of Russell House was at the home itself. A call to Flo's turned up the fact that she was now permanently working mornings, so if nothing else, I could talk to her.

The parakeets were screeching at full volume when I walked into the lobby. My War opponent was just going out with a young woman and small child, and all of them were smiling. I wasn't sure if they were just glad to be together, or if they were breaking out my card-playing buddy for good.

Today a woman in a blue lab coat sat at an unobtrusive reception desk by the door, and when I asked for Flo, she lumbered off to find her.

I didn't have to wait long. Flo arrived before the other woman returned and greeted me with a smile. My stock had risen since removing Zoey from Craig's clutches. Even if I never solved Ellen's murder, at least I'd done that.

Flo looked better this morning, more rested. She had taken time for a new haircut and some reddish highlights, both of which suited her.

She invited me on a tour, and we walked

through the first floor looking at the communal living area with a big-screen television and tables for games. A group was gathered around an upright piano singing Beatles songs, and in another room without carpeting, about two dozen residents were doing a complicated line dance to a country tune. The smells from the dining room were a forecast of things to come. Spaghetti, I thought. Or maybe lasagna.

"The new wings contain apartments with microwaves and refrigerators," Flo said. "Not large, but large enough for residents to keep some of their own furniture when they move in. The two floors above us are for people who need a more structured environment and skilled nursing care, and the addition at the back is our Alzheimer's unit."

How many people can tour a facility like this one and not wonder if a similar ending is waiting in their own future? I appreciated the cleanliness, the number of staff, the recreational opportunities in a facility run on a shoestring, but I was glad at the end of the visit that I could turn around and head back to the parsonage.

"I went through a lot of Reverend Dorchester's sermons last night," I told her, when we were sitting in the staff lounge drinking coffee. "He really liked coming here and talking to the residents. He mentioned one in particular. A woman named Daisy Dreyfus. I assume she's no longer alive?"

"No, bless her. Daisy passed on a long time ago, about two months after I arrived. She was memorable, though. No one here will ever forget her."

"Why not?"

"Every comfortable little touch you see? The cheerful decor in the lobby, the piano, that fabulous television? And a lot of things you won't see, like our recreational therapist, and the beautician who cuts and styles hair three afternoons a week? Courtesy of Daisy."

I felt a tiny electric charge. So somehow, Daisy had managed to accumulate enough money to leave some to Russell House when she died. Quite a bit, if my calculations were on the right track.

"She left that much money?"

"It was quite a surprise. Most of the staff knew Daisy paid her own way, not, I hope, that it made any difference in the way she was treated. Most of our residents get Medicaid assistance, but Daisy didn't need it. Of course, most people able to afford their own care choose another sort of facility, one with more to offer. Daisy was just different. She had friends from her neighborhood living here, so this is where she wanted to finish her life."

"Reverend Dorchester painted the picture of a woman who had a difficult road to follow and very little money," I said, as tactfully as I could. "I'm just trying to figure out how that translated into large bequests in her will."

Flo smiled. "You won't believe it. Her father hardly worked a day in his life, not a regular job anyway. I gather the family was practically homeless a time or two, but apparently when he was sober, he was brilliant. He invented some kind of special valve for heavy machinery. He died before he reaped any reward, but the idea was picked up by some manufacturer, and Daisy was his only heir. She took a lump sum as payment and invested wisely, so she could put her foster kids through college or vocational school. She kept quiet about the money — she didn't want to change the way she lived. But she still had quite a nest egg when she came here."

"What a story."

"You're no more surprised than we were. All of us. We had no idea there was a real bequest. She used to talk about leaving us money, but we all thought it was just talk, or maybe just enough for a new Ping-Pong table. Daisy loved her Ping-Pong."

"What did Ellen say about this?"

"Daisy died about six months after Ellen left town. I wrote her, and she was as surprised as everyone else."

Surprised and not on site to get details. Details like whether Daisy had also left money to our church, as she'd intended.

But maybe once Win left town, too, Daisy had lost interest in us. Maybe we had been in her will, then she removed us when her contact with the congregation ceased, or at the very least decreased.

And maybe not . . .

I didn't voice my suspicions. "Any news on when Cinda will return? I'd love to find out what she and Reverend Dorchester talked about."

"You could ask the administrative assistant. She's covering social services while Cinda's away."

"Social services?"

"Cinda's our social worker."

Which meant Cinda would probably be the person most likely to have information about Daisy's final plans, including her will.

I stood. "I'll see if I can get her contact

information in Jamaica. You've been a big help."

"This can't possibly have anything to do with Ellen's death, can it?" Flo asked.

I couldn't imagine how myself, but at the rate I was uncovering new information, anything seemed possible.

Our county courthouse is plain and functional, not exactly the finest moment in local architecture. After asking a few questions of bored clerical staff, I ended up in the applications department, at a counter tended by a bald man wearing wire-rimmed glasses. He stared at me as I explained that I wanted to see Daisy's will, and for a moment, I was sure he was going to deny me a look on general principles. But after a not-so-discreet sigh, he looked up Daisy's name on his computer, jotted down the case number, and came back after a few minutes with a reel of microfilm.

"Reader's over there." He motioned with a jerk of his head.

"I'm technically challenged," I said. "You don't want me threading microfilm through a reader by myself."

"You're kidding."

"I'm not." I dimpled appropriately. "Graduate school was a nightmare."

He softened at the dimples, only he tried not to show it. "I'll set it up for you. Do you need somebody to read it to you, too?" He smiled a little to offset the sarcasm.

"I can do that part."

In a few minutes I was staring at a copy of Daisy Dreyfus's will. Wills are so much legal gobbledygook, and I scanned until I got to the good stuff. I'd been prepared, so I wasn't surprised at the amount Daisy had left Russell House, although I gave a low whistle. This was an honest-to-goodness lasting legacy, and I was just sorry I'd never met her. There are so many people like Daisy we never hear about, people who make huge contributions to the welfare of others and are never recognized for them.

As Flo had said, there were many smaller bequests, and I guessed these names were the foster children she had raised. The amounts were not tiny, nor were they large enough for a fabulous week in Las Vegas with the high rollers. I hoped her kids were using the money wisely.

The only other bequest was several thousand dollars to the SPCA, in the name of three dogs Daisy had likely owned and cherished.

The church was not mentioned at all.

So dead-end number . . . I had lost count.

I'd known all along that this avenue of investigation was a long shot, but at least I'd only wasted a morning.

I got up and stretched. My stomach was rumbling, and I realized it was lunchtime. My bald buddy came over to check on me. He had warmed up nicely.

"Find what you needed?"

"I guess, but not what I wanted."

"You know, you're not the first person to check that particular will lately. A guy was in a couple weeks ago looking for it. I had to help him, too, that's why I remember. That and the name. Daisy Dreyfus. Nobody's named Daisy these days."

What were the chances someone else had just happened to come in to check Daisy's will? I forgot my craving for a panini with my best seven-grain bread, our Swiss cheese, a slice of fresh tomato.

Well, I almost forgot.

"Do you remember who it was?" I asked, hoping this kind of information wasn't confidential.

"Did I ask *you* for a name?"

He hadn't. I guess anybody off the street can come in and play with the microfilm.

"Can you describe him?" I countered.

"It's been a couple of weeks or more."

I dimpled and cocked my head. Nose

wrinkling next, if I needed it. Like I haven't told my daughter, it's a powerful weapon.

He relented. "Tall guy. Older, in his late sixties maybe? Could have been older. A little frail I think, like maybe he'd been sick and was recovering. Oh, yeah, he had this booming voice. I remember, because he sure didn't sound sick."

Win. Reverend Godwin Dorchester. Right here in this room. Looking at Daisy's will.

"You wouldn't have that exact date, would you?"

He shook his head. "But it was a week, no, more like two weeks before Easter, because I went away on vacation right after he came in. I just got back."

Win had died about ten days before the holiday. The timing was right.

"Do you remember if he said anything, asked anything?"

"Uh-huh. There haven't been a lot of people asking me questions 'cause I've been away. In fact it's pretty quiet in here all the time. He asked about life insurance."

"What about it?"

"Why it wasn't in the will."

I hadn't thought about life insurance. After all, Daisy had been well off, with enough to leave her foster children without keeping an insurance payoff.

"I just guessed if it wasn't there, she didn't have any," I said. "She had lots of assets. No need."

"You'd be guessing wrong. A lot of old people bought whole life policies when they were young. You know, the kind you start paying a little on every month? Unless the estate itself is the beneficiary, the insurance goes directly to the person named in the policy. Say she leaves it to her Aunt Matilda. The company sends it to Matilda directly. It doesn't show up in the will at all."

"So Daisy could have had a policy, and we'd never know?"

"Right, but you can find out. You know the name of the company, it's pretty easy. Or you can ask the state to search for a lost policy, if you don't. There's a form you can fill out. It takes a while, but it's usually fruitful. The company will contact you if they have information, as long as you have some good reason to be asking. That's what I told him. The other guy."

I thanked him for all his help, then I left him to wrestle with the microfilm, which was mysteriously tangled, even though I had cranked it with extreme care, just the way he had showed me.

My brain was overflowing. Even with the lure of my new panini grill, I didn't want to go home, where I would find a million distractions to keep me from piecing together what I had learned. I knew I was going to have to glue this together with a lot of "what ifs." I left my van in the parking lot and crossed the street on foot to the worst coffee shop in town, where I ordered egg salad on toast and hot tea. Not surprisingly, I had the place to myself.

While I waited for the owner to burn the bread and mysteriously transform the eggs into rubber, I sipped my lukewarm tea and scribbled notes.

By the time I had managed to consume half my sandwich without gagging, I had a scenario.

It went like this.

Win preaches his anniversary-year sermon. Ellen hears about it in advance, and because she's been planning to visit Emerald Springs anyway, she schedules her visit to coincide. She attends the service, and afterwards, she speaks to Win at the reception.

Had Ellen actually told me they had talked? I couldn't remember, but Zoey had mentioned it. I remembered that much and believed it, too. After all, Ellen had come up to me for a chat after Win's memorial service, and I was a stranger.

Okay, they had almost certainly talked. And here's how it went, at least according to my inner detective.

First Win: "How's Zoey doing, yada, yada, yada." Then Ellen: "I'm sure you heard Daisy Dreyfus left Russell House quite a large sum in her will. Remember all the times she said that's what she planned?"

Win, shocked: "I hadn't heard. A lot?"

"Yes, an amazing amount, really. Did she leave the church anything? She always said she was going to."

Win, recovering: "If she did, I never heard about it."

Ellen: "Didn't she say she was making the church the beneficiary for her life insurance?"

Okay, that last sentence? Pure imagination, and my inner detective was shaking her finger in my face. But, darn, it could have happened.

And what proof did I have that this conversation was rooted in anything except my fertile imagination? Well, several bits. One, I knew Win *had* been at Russell House asking questions after that service, and he'd talked to Jamaican Cinda, who was the most likely person on staff to have known the secrets of Daisy's will.

So after his conversation with Ellen and

chat with Cinda, Win trots over to the courthouse to see if he can look at a copy of said will. Microfilm challenged, he, too, needs help and establishes a relationship with my bald friend, who tells him life insurance payments are not usually included in wills. But if he really needed to find out about one, there are forms to fill out.

These, too, were facts.

From there? No facts, and right now, no theory.

I wished Cinda would call me. After explaining the urgency of reaching her in Jamaica, the administrative assistant had reluctantly given me Cinda's cell phone number. I had called from the parking lot and left a message, but so far, there'd been no return call. Cinda was in paradise. Why would she be checking her phone?

One thing was now completely clear to me without anybody's help. Win Dorchester was not a serial adulterer nor a thief. Daisy had died *after* his ministry ended here, and Win would not have had access to any bequest. No, I was almost certain Win had gone on a mission to find out if Daisy had left the church money, money that hadn't showed up in our budget. He had been suspicious, but of whom and for what reason?

And how would he have known Daisy's bequest had never ended up in the budget after all?

I didn't have to ponder that for long. The answer came easily. Because Win would have asked his valued former treasurer, the best treasurer he had ever had in his long ministry, the man who stayed in that position for several years after Win's departure.

Geoff Adler.

Had Win questioned Geoff? Geoff had never said anything about that to me, but that particular subject had never been raised, either. So it was possible that conversation was simply a blip on Geoff's horizon, one he hadn't remembered? I was reaching for my cell phone to call Emerald Eagle and ask, when my hand stopped midair.

Who better to have embezzled Daisy's money than Geoff himself?

Church finances are notoriously loose affairs. Audits? They cost money. In a church the size of ours, if audits are conducted, they're conducted by church members, usually anyone willing to spend countless evenings going over dull figures. Needless to say, they don't happen often.

No, churches rely on goodwill. We preach honesty and brotherly/sisterly love, and we hope our members and everyone who has business with us will abide by the rules. Money arrives and goes into the treasurer's files to be logged and deposited. Sure, most outgoing checks usually need two signatures, but nobody's standing nearby making certain that two different people are really signing. I'm as honest as they come, and in a pinch, I can forge Ed's name or my mother's if I need to deposit checks for them. Banks rarely look twice, and I do good imitations. But I put money into accounts, not take it out without Ed or Junie knowing.

Geoff had been our treasurer, an official representative with all kinds of power to deposit and remove money from our accounts.

Win departed Emerald Springs in a hurry after Hildy gave him an ultimatum. I wondered if there had been time for the church to get an interim minister as his replacement. Or had they muddled through a year without one. Without a minister. Without supervision. With no one looking over our treasurer's shoulder.

Without oversight, the very year that Daisy died and left her insurance money to us.

I got to my feet. "Yikes!"

"What's wrong, you don't like the sandwich?" My waiter looked surprised, as if nothing like this had ever occurred at the coffee shop.

"No, I don't like what I just figured out," I told him.

"Can't help you there," he said, clearing away my plate.

This I knew, but I had a pretty good idea who might be able to. I left money on the table and headed out the door.

I had been looking for connections between Ellen and Win, and I might well have struck the mother lode. It seemed more and more possible that Win had suspected or even discovered that Daisy Dreyfus left Tri-C money that never made it into our coffers. And who had aroused his suspicions? Ellen Hardiger. Where had it happened? At our church, during his anniversary reception, in earshot of anybody lingering nearby.

It was possible someone — the murderer or someone who reported it to the murderer — had overheard Ellen telling Win about Daisy's bequest, or asking if the church had gotten one, too. Such things do happen. But it was also possible that Win had just been caught snooping and killed for it. Maybe he had asked questions of the wrong person. Maybe Ellen had asked a few, as well. Or maybe her name had been mentioned by Win in conversation with his murderer, the person who later staged a hit-and-run, because Ellen might grow suspicious and mention Daisy and her bequests once again.

I tried to remember what I knew about Geoff Adler. I ignored the basics. What else did I know? That he had single-handedly pulled Emerald Eagle out of the hole and was now creating a chain. When? Close enough to his stint as our church treasurer to give me pause. Where had he gotten the funds for that miracle? Savings and good business sense? Or something more sinister?

What else did I know? That Geoff and Marie Grandower were close friends, often appearing together when she was in town to shoo off potential matchmakers. But what had Geoff told me? That despite this long-term friendship, he'd had no idea that Marie and Win had ever had an affair.

At the time I'd thought this odd. Now I thought it was probably bogus. They were members of the same church, ran in the same social circles, and close friends, to boot. And Geoff had never suspected? Even strait-laced Samuel Booth had seen Win coming out of Marie's house and figured it out. How could Geoff not have known?

And if he knew, why did he bring Marie

to Win and Hildy's welcome home party? Unless . . . unless . . .

Unless he wanted to create a diversion.

This time I didn't bother with my cell phone. I drove directly to Marie Grandower's house in overblown Emerald Estates and parked in the middle of her driveway — just in case she decided to make an exit. Normally I'm a fan of houses and pay close attention. But today was not a normal day. The house was a large, formal Colonial with a small yard, a large garage, and a Realtor's sign. I disliked it on sight.

I got out and charged up the walk. Marie answered after I finally leaned on her doorbell.

"What are you doing here?" she demanded. "I thought I made it clear I don't want to answer any more of your questions."

"Me or the police," I said. "Take your pick."

She narrowed her eyes. "This does it. I'm going to resign from the church."

To my credit I didn't mention how little she would be missed. "Did Geoff know you were meeting Win in the yard? Did you tell him?"

"Why?"

"You know, if you're not guilty of anything, you're sure making a big deal out of refusing to answer questions. I'm going to have to pass on that insight to Detective Sergeant Roussos. He's asked me to tell him anything I find out."

Her eyes were now slits. "I still have a number of friends in city hall, Aggie. I sincerely doubt your detective will be calling."

Confusing her had worked before. I gambled. "In other words, Geoff didn't know, and so he can't back up your story. Too bad."

She looked surprised. I nodded, as if victorious. "Right. I thought so."

"What are you saying?"

"It's simple. If you told Geoff, then you have a witness."

"Witness to what?"

I looked at my watch. "Darn, Roussos is going to call any minute. I was certain you had coverage on this."

"What are you talking about?"

I cocked my head, as if she'd just proved my point. "So nobody knew where you were meeting Win. It's just your word?"

"Oh for God's sake. Geoff told me where to meet Win and when! All right? You can ask him yourself. He's the one who told me Win wanted to meet me in the side yard."

My stomach used my toes as a trampoline.

For a moment I felt disoriented.

I recovered quickly. What choice did I have? "Okay, Geoff told you to meet Win in the yard. So he can corroborate if he has to. But did he say why? Because I'm sure he didn't know you and Win ever had an affair."

"Are you a complete fool? Of course he knew! Geoff and I are close friends. He knows everything about my life. Do you think I could keep something like that from him? He's known right from the beginning. Geoff was my rock."

"Wow, my mistake."

"Leave me out of this and leave Geoff out, too. I don't know what you're trying to do, but the two of us have more friends in this town than you'll have in a lifetime. Don't mess with us, Aggie."

I whined just a little. "Like I said, I was just trying to help. I guess I won't mention this to him if you don't. I don't want to embarrass you. I just had to be sure."

"Of course I'm not going to tell him! He has many more important things to worry about than your twisted fantasies. You really are pathetic." She closed the door in my face.

Ah yes, pathetic I was. Pathetically glad that I was finally on my way to something that could finally be an answer. And if I was right, Hildy Dorchester was well on her way to regaining the respect and trust in our little burg that she so richly deserved.

19

Hildy was home, but where else would she be, except in jail awaiting a hearing? She no longer felt welcome here. She still had friends, but nobody was beating down her door to take her shopping or out on excursions. Emerald Springs was in wait-and-see mode with poor Hildy. Worst of all, she knew it.

I didn't have to lean on her doorbell. After one jab I heard footsteps, and in a moment she opened the door.

"Coffee today?" she asked.

"No, but a sandwich would be nice. I just ate the worst egg salad of my life."

"Why do you fill your stomach with bad things? Come in and we'll eat together."

I had hoped so. Not only did I need an internal fencing match with the egg salad, Hildy needed to eat. Taking care of me was the best way to make sure she did.

In the kitchen she took out bread, lettuce

and tomato, sliced cheese, and lunch meat. I stopped her before the ham ended up on my sandwich, and she shook her head. "I worry about you getting enough protein."

I was glad she still had the energy to meddle.

The sandwich was fine, but better yet, she ate, too.

"I'm not here just to raid the kitchen," I said when half her sandwich was eaten. "I wonder if you've found the time to start going through your mail."

"All those cards and letters. I've made a start. But Win was part of so many lives, and everyone wants to tell me how sorry they are."

"No one expects you to jump right on every piece of mail." I paused. "But I was thinking more about something besides a sympathy note. Letters addressed to Win?"

"You have something in mind?"

"I'm wondering if anything came from the state of Ohio. Maybe from the Insurance Division, or something similar?"

"I don't know. I've made stacks. That's as far as I've gotten since . . . since I found out everybody thinks I murdered my husband."

"Not everybody. Would you mind very

much if I sorted through the non-sympathy stack?"

"Of course not, but why?"

I debated what to tell her. I decided some of the truth wouldn't hurt, because it was possible Win had spoken to her about his suspicions. "Win might have been looking into insurance fraud involving the church."

She looked surprised. "Fraud?"

"Did he ever mention anything like that? Any suggestion a bequest to the church never made it into our budget?"

"Somebody stole money from the church?"

I could see this was a total surprise, which was a shame. "I don't know yet."

"We were both so busy. I was planning the party and getting the house in order. Win spent time with some of our old friends, lunch or a drink, you know. He was having tests, too, so our doctor could get his medication adjusted. He was at the hospital hooked up to a heart monitor or giving blood the week before he died."

"So he never mentioned this to you."

"He wasn't secretive exactly, but when Win had something on his mind, he kept quiet. He usually waited until he had answers before he discussed anything. He wasn't one to let other people make suggestions. Too sure he was right, I guess."

I was sorry to hear that, but I hoped the mail would turn up something. I told her as much, and she left the kitchen, returning with a tall stack of envelopes. I thought I'd better winnow out the bills while I was at it. At the very least she needed to deal with those.

I began to sort. Bills in one pile, obvious junk mail in another, anything else that looked vaguely official in a third.

"I know I should take care of the bills," Hildy said.

"I can help if you want."

"No, you stack them, and I'll pay after you leave. I do it on the computer. It only takes a few minutes."

I, of course, do it the old-fashioned way, with stamps and a pen. I am almost sure if I set up bill paying on the Internet, my kerchiefed friend will be singing Polish songs of thanksgiving.

I was nearly at the bottom of the stack, when I found what I was looking for. "Bingo!" I looked up. "May I open this?"

"Be my guest."

Inside the envelope from the Ohio Department of Insurance was a brief note. Unless Win had proof he was an executor, a legal representative, or a member of the immediate family of the deceased, the information he had asked for was not easily available to him. A phone number and name were included, in case he wanted to discuss the circumstances of his query.

Of course I was disappointed, although I had assumed it was too early to get confirmation that the payoff from a policy in Daisy's name had been made to the Consolidated Community Church of Emerald Springs. But I had hoped a search was in the works. On the other hand, this was all the proof I needed that Win had indeed been suspicious.

Now I had a phone number. I could call and talk to the man who had signed this letter, explain my situation, and ask what to do next. If he was sympathetic and not hidebound, maybe he would do the search after all. And if he turned up a payment to the church that never made it into our bank account, then I had something concrete that Roussos could follow up on. For once I would not have to put my body on the line. I could stand back and watch the fun from a safe distance.

Well, not fun exactly. Because this really wasn't one bit fun. Two people had died, and I was about to make sure yet another member of the church went to jail.

"What does it say?" Hildy asked.

I held it out to her. "Win asked them to do a search to see if an insurance policy for a woman named Daisy Dreyfus turned up. I think Win believed it should have been paid to the church after Daisy died."

"Oh, Daisy. Of course. She was a wonderful woman. I used to visit her, too. The stories she could tell."

Duh. Of course Hildy had known Daisy. If somebody in town needed visiting, had Hildy been far behind?

"Did she ever mention a bequest to the church in your presence?" I asked.

"She was a dear old thing, and yes, I think she did. But I'm sure she didn't have money."

I filled her in on the invention and its aftermath. Hildy's eyes widened.

"I'm surprised Win didn't tell you this," I said.

"That would be like him, of course. He'd want *all* the facts so he could make a huge splash when the time came. No doling it out in little pieces."

"It's possible she did leave her insurance to the church. It would have been a simple way to leave money. Clean, no fuss, not even mentioned in the will."

"And it's not in the records?"

I debated, but Hildy needed cheering, and she was, after all, used to keeping secrets. It comes with the "job."

"Not in the records," I said. "And if this is true, I think I know who might be to blame."

"Who?"

"Tell me everything you know about Geoff Adler."

Her jaw dropped a full inch. "Geoff? No!"

Again, I filled her in. On the way over I had done some thinking on how this might have been accomplished. Now I explained how easy it would have been for Geoff to take the insurance check, put it into church accounts for a few days until it cleared, take it out again with an explanation to anyone at the bank, if needed, that the money was going into a brokerage account, then conveniently bury that month's statement. Who would know so much money had come and gone? Who would care? Who would question a sap who plugged on and on as treasurer, a job nobody ever wanted.

"But that's not the only reason I'm suspicious," I finished. "Geoff lied to me about something. He told me he never knew Win and Marie had an affair. Then on the night of your party, he told Marie that Win wanted to meet her in the side yard. That's why she ended up out there."

Hildy's eyes were growing larger. "Geoff did that?"

I nodded.

"Win told me . . ." She licked her lips. "The night of the party, when we fought . . . before he died."

I ached for her, but I nodded again.

"He told me he only met Marie outside because somebody told him she wanted to see him alone. He was told she'd had too much to drink and was going to cause a scene if he didn't talk to her."

"He didn't say who?"

"He was careful not to. I thought he just didn't want to get caught in a lie."

"You never told me that, Hildy."

"I thought he was covering up his real reason for going outside. I didn't believe him, so it didn't seem important. I was sure he'd gone out on his own. After all, I saw them standing just inches apart. I stood there and watched them together."

I just wished that Win had said Geoff's name, but Win probably hadn't wanted to involve Geoff in any way. If I was right, Geoff had informed Marie that Win wanted to meet with her. Then when he was sure she was going to, he had persuaded Win to meet Marie in the side yard. Each one had believed that the other had asked for a meeting. Geoff Adler had made all the arrangements.

Geoff, who may well have murdered Win Dorchester. Geoff, the pharmacist, who knew what an overdose of digoxin could do. Geoff, who wouldn't even have had to steal the digoxin from Win's supply. He could simply have checked Win's record at Emerald Eagle, discovered what medication he was taking . . .

I stopped the wheels from turning. "Did Win get his meds at Emerald Eagle?" I asked.

She was shaking her head, but not in denial. "Yes. I can't believe this."

"Okay, none of this is for sure," I said. "This could all be a construct of my vivid imagination."

"We were so proud, Win and I, so pleased when we heard that Geoff had pulled Emerald Eagle out of near bankruptcy. Win had such faith in his abilities. And all the time, he might have been using money meant for the church to work his magic."

I hardly heard her. I was remembering that Geoff was the one who had misled me about Win's multiple affairs. And his kindness in offering his lake house for the reception? Not kindness, but a calculated effort to be certain he stayed in the loop, as well as a demonstration that his support of Hildy and his love for Win were unchallenged.

"You can't breathe a word of this," I said. "You have to promise me. I'm going to call the Ohio Department of Insurance when I get home and see what they'll do for me. You just have to hang in for a while, Hildy. This may take some time, but we can't let Geoff know we suspect him. The minute I know the church was the beneficiary of Daisy's insurance policy, I'm going to turn this whole new thread over to the police. They can do the rest."

"That could take weeks."

Sadly, she was right. It might. "You'll be fine," I promised. "You can tough this out until we know, right? You're not going to do anything silly like ask Geoff for a confession?"

"A confession?" She huffed. "Of course not. I only believe the best about people until the worst is right in front of me."

"Good." I looked at my watch. "Mind if I take this letter with me? I'll call this man from home, but I promise I'll let you know everything I discover. Just hang tight, okay? Pay bills, answer mail. Before long maybe this will all be over."

Mr. Gleck from our fair state's department of insurance was a lovely man, he just wasn't much for taking chances. I explained who I was and what had happened and told him that the church was concerned that fourteen years ago, someone might have embezzled an insurance payout meant for us. The problem was that we had no record of which insurance company might have made the payment, which is where he came in. Mr. Gleck isn't one to take initiative on his own. He promised he would bring the matter up with a superior and get back to me next week. I pointed out that the publicity would be fabulous for his department if they helped catch the bad guy, but even that wasn't enough of a lure.

Not everybody is as dedicated to fighting crime as those of us in the trenches.

I wasn't sure how much to tell Ed. He has this teensy-weensy problem. Whenever I get close to solving a murder, he worries about me. I knew that even if I assured him I was not going to go near Geoff Adler or do anything to make him suspicious, Ed would still worry. In fact he would worry so much he would begin following me around, calling me to see what I was doing at any given moment, suggest a visit to Indiana where my father's buddies and good old Ray Sloan himself would be sure I stayed safe. I might never be able to leave Indiana again, but at least Ed wouldn't have to worry about my well-being.

I decided not to mention Geoff's name. After all, I had no real proof I was right. Not yet, anyway. Instead, as we cleared off the dining room table after dinner, Moonpie weaving in and out of our feet to make it twice as hard, I explained that I was looking into possible insurance fraud as a motive for Win's murder, but until I got some help from the Department of Insurance in Columbus, I was stuck. By the time we had moved everything into our disheveled kitchen, I had asked him not to mention anything to anybody at this point, until I knew more.

"You don't want anybody on the board thinking the church is about to get some kind of windfall," I said, squirting detergent in the sink, since our dishwasher was still unhooked. "Imagine the trouble that could cause."

He handed me the platter that had held his signature penne primavera. This had been Ed's night to cook, a feat he had accomplished in our church kitchen, where he was less likely to stick to the floor. So what if the food hadn't been hot by the time he transported it home?

"If what you think is true, we'd probably never see a dime," he said. "Fourteen years is a long time, and you can be sure the insurance company will point its finger at the church and our lax accounting standards."

"That would be so unfair to Daisy."

"She'll have to get in line behind Win and Ellen Hardiger."

I winced, because how true was that?

This time he handed me the salad bowl. "So you're done snooping for a while?"

"The minute I know somebody made off with a payout meant for Tri-C, I'll go directly to Roussos. Until then, I've done my bit. We'll let Roussos catch a murderer for a change."

"You mean it?"

I stood on tiptoes and kissed him. "Worry-wart."

"As if I have no reason."

"There's no point in coming up with new lines of investigation. Not when this one's so promising."

"Why do I think there's more you aren't telling me, like who you suspect?"

"Because you're a brilliant man who's been married to me long enough to father a couple of kids and drag me around the country to three different churches."

"You're not going to tell me?"

"I don't want you acting differently if you run into said suspect. And if I'm wrong, I don't want you laughing at me."

"And what if *you* run into said suspect?"

"I plan to stay a million miles away."

I remembered those words when I got Hildy's phone call. It was seven thirty, and nobody was home but me. In keeping with his new resolution to spend more time with Deena — even if she pretended in public that she didn't know him — Ed invited her to a father-daughter softball match at the rec center. Neither of them is that crazy about softball, but they went anyway, and Teddy went with them to cheer them on. Figuring this would not be father-daughter time if I tagged along, I decided to stay home and take a nice hot bath.

Never let those words streak through your head. The nice-hot-bath monsters will make certain it never comes to pass.

I was stripping off my jeans when the doorbell rang. I zipped them up again and ran downstairs to find Lucy. She held out a woven basket wrapped in cellophane. "Cookies, cheese, you name it. I found a renter for one of my clients today."

"What am I, the Island of Misfit Gifts?" I grabbed it, in case she thought I was serious.

"Ha, I can dump anything on you guys. Friends with no scruples are precious."

"We have growing children who need to be fed. And how come we never get good bottles of wine from your grateful clients?"

"It would be inappropriate to bring that much wine to a man of God and his virtuous wife. May I come in?"

I realized we were still standing on my porch. "If you can stand listening to me brag about my investigative abilities."

Of course she did. I was in the middle of explaining all about Geoff Adler and the Great Insurance Swindle, when the telephone rang.

I held up a finger and grabbed the phone.

"I'm just pulling onto Geoff's property," said a soft but familiar voice. "I'm going to prove he stole that money."

"What!" *My* voice was not low or particularly well modulated. "Hildy, are you crazy?"

"Don't worry. He's out of town. I called Emerald Eagle and asked for him. He's at one of his other stores for a couple of days, the one near Wooster. I even called *them,* and they said he was on his way. The man said he'd just talked to him. I know where he keeps his records, Aggie, and where he keeps the key to get in. Remember his office? Behind the house?"

"Turn around and come home. What are you thinking?"

"I'm thinking this needs to end. I want it over. I'm tired of people believing I'm something I'm not. I'm tired of that awful Grandower woman pointing her finger at me. I'm going to go through his business records and see if there was an influx of cash after Daisy's death. I'll make copies if I find anything, and I'll send them to the police anonymously."

"Hildy, finding anything would take the skills of a forensic accountant. You think Geoff made notes in a ledger somewhere explaining that this money came from Daisy's insurance, meant for the church? Once we know there really was a payment, the police can get those records legitimately and an expert can go over them. Or the church will hire somebody if we have to, I don't know. But this is too dangerous, and there's nothing good to be gained from breaking into his office."

"Breaking into his office?" She gave a

humorless laugh. "This is the man who broke my heart."

The line went dead.

"Hildy!"

Of course, no answer.

"She's at Geoff Adler's house?" Lucy's eyes were shining.

"What on earth should I do? I can't call Roussos. He'll have her arrested for breaking and entering."

"If you don't call, Adler might reunite Hildy with her husband, and you'll have to deal with another memorial service."

"She claims he's out of town. She called the store to talk to him on some pretense, and they told her. For a couple of days."

"I've got a full tank of gas, and the night is young."

I really wanted to make an honest woman of myself and stay away from Geoff Adler, his house, and his pharmacy, just as I'd told Ed. I wanted to wait for solid information. I wanted to hand Roussos all the pieces and let him put this jigsaw puzzle together without me. I wanted Roussos to sidle up to an unsuspecting Geoff and handcuff him before Geoff knew he'd been cornered.

"This is such a bad idea." The words sounded like one, long moan.

"You have a better one?"

"Let me grab a jacket and leave Ed a note."

"Dear Ed," she chanted, "Lucy and I have gone for a drive."

"That will worry him enough," I said.

"No flies on that boy."

20

One problem with spring? The sun doesn't set. It leaps into a coffin and pulls down the lid, particularly when rain is forecast. By the time Lake Parsons was supposed to be sparkling in front of us, clouds were gathering overhead, and nothing but darkness greeted us. In another month, summer houses would be opened and aired, and lamps would glow in many of these windows. Now, though, only a fraction of the houses were illuminated, and very few of the drives leading up to them, as if the lights we glimpsed might be there for security only. Summer communities can be victimized by winter burglars, who probably find little to fence besides badminton sets and molding beach towels. Still, since tourism is the mainstay of the local economy, the county police and the lake patrol were well known for routing out jigsaw-puzzle bandits.

I hoped no one in uniform was planning

to drive by Geoff Adler's house tonight.

"Well, one thing," I said as Lucy turned onto the road to Geoff's place. "If somebody has to come out here and rescue Hildy, at least you'll have better luck getting Roussos to listen than I would."

"You're not going to give up digging into my private life, are you?"

"My mother spent time in a sweat lodge while I was in utero. She-Who-Will-Never-Say-Die is my middle name."

"That would explain the damage to your brain."

We were joking because we were nervous, or at least I was. I wasn't certain about my friend in the driver's seat.

"I don't have any clout with Roussos," Lucy said, when I thought we were finished. "Not as much as you do, anyway."

"Why, is he afraid somebody will scream favoritism?"

"Aggie, I don't have *anything* going with Roussos. Never have. You can take that to the bank."

The world as I knew it was coming unglued. "Are you kidding me? You have the man on speed dial."

"Any friend of *yours* has to."

My own cell phone rang at that moment. I fished for it, hoping it was Hildy, and she had regained her common sense. But the voice was a lot deeper and belonged to the man we'd just been discussing.

Roussos never wasted time on preliminaries. "Just wanted you to know that the phone call to the Dorchester house on the night the reverend died? Came from a phone registered to a woman, and not anybody on the guest list. Somebody across town, and from a land line, not a cell phone."

This was not good news. I'd hoped, really hoped, Geoff had made that call. That would have shored up his status as lead suspect and my right to skulk around his house tonight. I wasn't ready to give up. Maybe Geoff had driven to somebody's house and used a phone there. Driven really fast, marched in, and grabbed the phone before the requisite small talk.

How likely was that?

"Do you know why she phoned the house?" I asked, knowing better than to ask the mysterious woman's name.

"We have a call in, but she hasn't returned it."

I thanked him and hung up. I really wasn't sure where to file this disturbing piece of information. I needed to think about it, and think hard. Right now there was no time for that.

I continued my conversation with Lucy where we'd left off. "Then if you and Roussos don't have a thing going on, how did you get word the police suspected Win had been murdered? Before I could even tell you? And who were you with in San Francisco?"

She glanced at me. I could just see her face in the glow from the dashboard. "Grayson Adams."

"The police chief?" I nearly shouted this. I pictured a tall, muscular man who had once wrestled an intruder out of a party I'd attended.

"Do you know another one?" she said.

"I hardly know *that* one. We've spoken once. He pretended to know me."

"He knows all *about* you, that's why."

"Man!"

"We're keeping it quiet, Aggie. Gray's going through a divorce, and not because of me, so don't lecture. I came into the picture well after the lawyers got involved. It's been a long, messy episode in his life. They both want custody, and she wants to take him to the cleaners. We started as friends and now it's more."

"Custody?"

"One boy. Nine and cute as a cocker spaniel. Most likely they'll end up sharing. He'll do all the work, and she'll undermine Gray's authority."

"Oh, Luce."

"Don't be like that. He's a good man, and I think I love him. The kid thing could be tough, but we'll work it out."

Lucy flipped off her lights as Geoff's house came into sight. Of course Lucy had known exactly where he lived and what the house was worth.

"So what's the plan," she asked as she slowed to turtle speed.

"First, you're not going to drive into the lake."

"Agreed. Keep your eyes open. I'm pretty sure we're still on the road."

I had already told Lucy about Geoff's office behind the house, our final destination. "We'll drive up to his office and park. I'll drag Hildy out of there, making sure everything's back in place before I do. Then I'll throw her in the trunk of her own car and drive it back to her place."

"Maybe you really ought to go back with her, just to make sure she doesn't turn around and try this again."

"Agreed. I'll have the whole trip back to

talk some sense into her. You think you love him?"

"He's hard not to love."

Despite a boatload of apprehension, I smiled.

There were no lights in view at Geoff's house. Some might be on in rooms where curtains were drawn, but from here, I couldn't tell. I gave directions to the office, which in daylight was easy to spot. Now the drive that circled the house was almost invisible.

"Do you have a flashlight?" I asked.

"Trunk."

"If you stop, I'll get it and see."

"Or, get this, I could turn on my parking lights and make sure we're on the road the easy way."

"Smart ass."

She did just that. The soft light swept the driveway for just seconds, to prove that Lucy, at least, had the eyesight of an owl. We were exactly where we were supposed to be.

After she crept forward for another excruciating minute, an even larger sign we were on the right track loomed in front of us. We finally glimpsed the office. I could just see the shape of Hildy's car parked under a tree to the side of the driveway. If she thought that would render it invisible, of course she was wrong, but at least it wasn't blocking us from turning around.

"While I'm gone, turn around so you're heading out," I whispered, "in case we need to make a fast exit."

"I'll probably have to put on my lights to do that."

The night seemed to be holding its breath. No sound, no movement we could see, nothing but inky darkness that stretched out to the silent lake.

I grasped the door handle. "Why don't you just wait, then? I'll go take a look around. If it looks safe to turn on your lights, I'll come back and tell you."

"I want to come."

"We might need you behind the wheel in case things don't go well." She might need to drive to the first occupied cottage for help.

"If you're gone too long, I'm calling Gray."

How could I tell her not to? Hildy's future was important, and I wanted to keep her out of jail. But sometimes a good cop comes in handy. Like when a crazy pharmacist realizes he's about to get nailed for murder and embezzlement and probably forgery, to boot. What's another body or three if they guarantee his secrets a little longer?

"What's too long?" I countered.

"Seven and a half minutes."

"How did you come up with that?"

"If I said five, you'd be halfway up that drive, then you'd ask yourself if I said five or ten. You'll remember this. Now get."

I hated that my distractibility had assumed legendary proportions.

I couldn't make out anything on the dial of my watch, so the whole discussion was futile anyway. I opened the door quietly and slipped out, flooding the immediate area with light as I did. I pushed the door closed until the light went off, then started down the driveway.

A click sounded behind me, and I whirled. Lucy had gotten out of the car, too. I heard another click and in a moment she came around, flashlight extended but unlit.

"Forgot this," she whispered.

Sheepishly I took it. I wasn't planning to use it, and unlike the one I'd nearly beaned Zoey's ex with, it was slim and ladylike and not likely to do much damage as a weapon. But in a pinch, at least I would be able to see.

Lucy would get a real head basher next Hanukkah.

I started back down the driveway. My eyes were adjusting, although by the time my pupils strained to maximum width, I still couldn't see beyond my outstretched hand. Despite Lucy's timetable, I had to move slowly enough not to trip, screech, and ruin the surprise of my approach.

I was so relieved when I finally got to the overhang sheltering the office door that I rested a moment. Aware of time, I listened hard for sounds inside, but the night was just as still as before. After I caught my breath, I inched forward and peered through a sidelight. It was shrouded by a thin curtain, but I was almost sure if someone had a light on, it would glow through the fabric.

No glow.

I remembered where Geoff kept the key, and I could make out the shape of the boulders where he'd hidden it. But before I squatted to feel around, I tried the door. No need to worry about spiders or other nocturnal flesh-eating insects on the ground. The door was unlocked.

This was not a situation easily slotted into good vs. bad. Hildy had called to tell me she was nearly here. Hildy's car *was* here, proving she was as good as her word. And now, the door of the office she had planned to search was unlocked, as well. But three strikes or three home runs? I had no clue.

The fact that I couldn't see a light glowing inside worried me. If Hildy was in there searching, she was wearing night-vision goggles.

I really had no choice, and my minutes were ticking down. I opened the door as quietly as I could and stepped inside.

I waited until my eyes adjusted to this deeper darkness. I could make out the desk looming in the middle, the wall of file cabinets, even the seating area on the opposite side. What didn't I see?

Hildy.

Had she arrived here, been scared off, and was now hiding somewhere outside, waiting for the right moment to sprint to her car and make a clean getaway? Did Hildy sprint?

"Hildy?" Not a whisper and not a shout, but if she was here, she would hear me. "Come out right now. You've got to leave. This is a job for the police."

A clock ticked somewhere by the sofa as answer. I noted that there was light after all, a faint red dot at the bottom of the computer monitor. And below the desk, a power strip with a glowing switch that indicated it was on and working. I figured what the heck and switched on my flashlight, training it on the floor as I moved forward.

That was the moment I realized somebody *had* been here, even if they weren't here any longer. All I had needed for the discovery was a thin beam of light. Several file drawers weren't closed all the way, and one stood completely open, files exposed. Under that drawer, several manila folders lay facedown, contents fanning out on the floor. I moved closer and thanks to my light, didn't trip over a straight-back chair lying on its side near the desk.

When I saw the lamp lying across the mouse pad, I knew we were in trouble. I hoped seven and a half minutes had passed, and Lucy had called her police chief amour. We were going to need him.

I was turning back toward the door, when to my absolute horror, I saw it swinging into the room. I switched off my light and scurried toward the wall before the intruder got in. As I did, my mind searched feverishly, hoping I would remember something that could be used as a weapon.

"Aggie!"

My throat was too dry to do anything but croak. "You were supposed to stay with the car!"

Lucy came all the way inside. "I turned around and went back a little way up the drive to prepare, and I saw a light on the water. Moving out into the lake."

For a moment this didn't compute. "Light?"

"It has to be a boat, but I didn't hear a motor."

Geoff's silent boat, his hobby boat, the one he'd built himself.

For just an instant I wondered if Hildy had taken the boat out. But, of course, there would be no point to that. Unfortunately, there *was* a point to having her on board as a passenger. An unwilling passenger for a one-way voyage to the middle of the lake.

"There's been a struggle here," I said. "Somebody caught up with her."

"Do you think . . ."

"Yeah, I do. Let's get down there."

I switched on the flashlight, because I was almost sure our reason for stealth had just left the dock.

We hurried to the door, the thin beam lighting the way. I considered throwing the switch lighting the office and the grounds outside it. Would Geoff see the lights, know we'd caught up with him, and another murder was fruitless? Or would the lights make him hurry even faster? It's not that easy to think like a murderer, and I decided not to take a chance he'd feel compelled to cover his tracks.

"Do you think she's alive?" Lucy asked as we jogged toward her car.

"I don't want to think. You called the chief?"

"Sorry, but yes, I got spooked."

"Good thing. We'll need help." I flung open the passenger door, and Lucy jumped into the driver's seat. In a moment she was barreling down the driveway, lights on. Case closed on whether to let Geoff or whoever was out on the lake know that we were on the way.

Whoever was out on the lake. Something nagged at me.

"Lucy, why would Geoff take Hildy out into the lake and drown her? By now Hildy must have told him I was on to him. Wouldn't he at most tie her up, so he could get a head start out of town?"

"Maybe he's just going to kill her to buy time. More permanent."

"No, that just doesn't work. He has to know they'll drag the lake if she disappears. Besides, Hildy said he was heading to another drugstore, and both this store and that one confirmed it."

"So, he lied."

"No . . . no, he's a very precise, organized businessman. If he changed his mind on the way, he would have called the store to tell them, and they would have told Hildy. No, this feels personal, Luce. He's practical and methodical, and killing Hildy at this point is neither. And that call from Roussos just now? I expected him to tell me that Geoff phoned the Dorchesters' house during the party from his cell phone, so Hildy would go into the hallway just in time to see her husband and Marie together. But he wasn't the one who called the house. Somebody else did, a woman who wasn't even at the party. I thought he was buying himself time to poison the dip while Hildy was spying on Marie and Win, but maybe somebody had already poisoned it. Maybe somebody did it between the time the caterer left and Marie met Win outside."

"You're not making sense. Then who's got Hildy out there?"

I continued to put facts together out loud. "There was no car parked in front of this house when we pulled in, the way there would be if Geoff had changed his mind, headed home, driven up, and realized Hildy was in the office."

"I don't see what you're getting at."

"Let's say Geoff pulls in and either sees Hildy's car or lights in the office. Something to make him suspicious. We know *somebody* was suspicious because Hildy got caught. In that situation Geoff would never open his garage door to park inside before he went to check. That makes noise, and Hildy would have heard him and run. There was a struggle *inside* the office. No, for that to be true, he must have parked in the driveway or on the grass, gone around the office, and caught her red-handed. Only there's no car in the driveway."

"Maybe he reparked afterwards, *after* he grabbed her."

"No time, and why? No, whoever has her must have been on the property already. They were here when Hildy arrived, only Hildy didn't know it. Maybe she didn't see lights, and that person's car was in the garage. She wasn't expecting anyone to be here. She knew Geoff was out of town."

"Who, then?"

Who, then? But the answer was suddenly clear. The woman who had pawed through the coat closet right beside the kitchen door until Grace Forester had been forced to find her sweater. The woman who might even have heard Win, himself, tell Grace to save all the leftovers, particularly the shrimp dip. The woman who had probably gone out the front door, around the side to the kitchen, and waited near the door until she had the room to herself. Doctoring the dip would only have taken moments. And if she'd been caught? She'd needed a glass of water or almost anything else.

"Marie Grandower! Sometimes she house-sits for Geoff when he's out of town. I upset her today. Maybe Geoff told her he was going to be away, and Marie figured she'd get away from what she called my pathetic questions. But I scared her. I must have scared her, and she came out here to avoid me while she figured out what to do."

Lucy gave a low whistle. "Talk about personal."

"She has every reason to want Hildy dead, not just detained while she escapes. She hates Hildy. Hildy was married to the man she loved." A man she had murdered in a rage when he told her what they'd had together had been finished for many years. Or maybe something else entirely. Maybe just a man who had asked one too many questions about an old woman named Daisy Dreyfus.

Lucy was at the dock now. She hit the brakes, and we were both out in a flash. Just as she had reported, I saw a light disappearing farther and farther onto the lake.

"Where are the cops?" I demanded.

"The boat's too far out to swim for it."

For a moment I felt completely helpless.

406

Then in the beam of Lucy's headlights, trained on the water, I saw a possible solution.

"Not too far for a Jet Ski." I started across the dock. Just as I remembered, there were two Jet Skis docked there, on ramps that extended out into the water. I prayed they weren't secured with locks.

"I've never even been on one." Lucy was right behind me. "I could learn."

"Ever driven a motorcycle?"

"How do you know so much?"

"Florida vacation."

I swung my feet over the side of the dock and jumped on the closest ramp. "Single passenger. Stay here, Luce, and don't try to follow. They're tricky, and *somebody* has to tell the cops what's up. If help arrives in time, put somebody on the other one and send him out to help. Call everybody you can."

I didn't stay to see if she listened or agreed, or long enough to talk myself out of this. I slid the Jet Ski back until the rear was in the water and jumped on before it could float away.

I had made myself sound confident, but I was far from it. I'd ridden one of these monstrosities just once, and vowed never to repeat my performance. The whole experience had been too reminiscent of childhood journeys on my father's Harley, only a whole lot wetter. And while I'd felt relatively safe with Ray Sloan's muscular arms around me, by myself on the Jet Ski, I'd felt like diving off and taking my chances with sharks.

No sharks here, of course, but there was one too many murderers on Lake Parsons, which was worse.

I found the kill switch and the spiral loop that fit around my wrist. I was supposed to have a life jacket, but there was no time for that. Hildy certainly didn't have one. If I rescued her and tossed Marie or whoever had Hildy overboard, then I'd don a life jacket from the boat's supply.

I punched the ignition, but nothing happened. I remembered I had to activate the choke and found what I hoped was the right lever near the gas tank. Then holding my breath, I tried again to start the engine. I was glad this model didn't have a key, which would surely not have been waiting in the ignition. The engine caught and I began to move slowly out into the water as I released the choke. So far so good. I turned the throttle and the Jet Ski leapt forward. I eased off immediately.

I was terrified.

The lake was dark; I could easily hit anything floating in my path and launch myself into the water, winter-tinged water that hadn't had time or summer sunshine to warm it to a bearable temperature. I had so little to guide me, the faintest lights from the boat and no moon or stars in a sky filled with clouds. I just had a promise I'd made Hildy, and a simmering fury.

At that thought I increased my speed again. Well away from the dock now, I aimed my water-cycle toward the fading lights and turned the throttle even more.

I felt like I was flying, and not safely. The water was freezing cold and I was saturated almost immediately by spray pelting me. I thought I was eating up the distance between us, slower than I wanted to but steadily. I'd remembered how to board the Jet Ski, and get it moving. Now I was trying to remember what I'd learned about slowing down, crossing wakes, and yes, stopping. This was a craft without brakes. How did I pull up next to a boat without driving straight through it and sending all of us tumbling into the lake?

My bow was rising out of the water as my speed increased. My job was to gauge when to slow and when to stop turning the throttle completely. I remembered vaguely that I wouldn't be able to turn unless I was giving the Jet Ski gas, that if I stopped the gas, it would just move forward. That didn't sound good to me. I had to keep moving when I turned, then stop moving once I was beside the boat so I could jump on board, which meant I had to begin my maneuver just the right distance away.

What were the chances?

I concentrated on my speed, on watching the lights of the boat, on prayer. I was getting closer, but I wanted this over with. I throttled up, and the bow lifted higher. So did my prayers, at least I fervently hoped so.

Finally I was close enough to make out more than lights. I could see the boat now, with a fringed awning stretched on poles above it like a perky pleasure craft off on an afternoon outing. Lights glowed from the deck.

The boat was still putting along, and that was a positive. Marie hadn't weighed anchor and added Hildy to the rope for extra heft. Maybe she'd been too busy trying to get away to worry about getting rid of her.

I was gaining steadily, and as the first waves from my Jet Ski began to pelt the side, the boat slowed considerably. I thought I saw a figure standing at the bow, a small, slender figure, not Geoff Adler, who had temporarily been my candidate for Emerald Springs's serial killer of the month. A woman's figure, and not solid, earthy Hildy's. A woman who dieted and pampered herself and clothed her sleek body in Armani and diamonds. Marie Grandower, who had not taken her husband's job — saving lives — nearly as seriously as Hildy had taken hers.

I let up on the throttle and slowed, hoping I was gauging correctly. I started my turn, but I wasn't turning as fast as I'd expected. Shutting my eyes — my favorite option — wasn't a good one. I turned the handles and leaned farther left. I knew this was the best way to fall off, had done so, in fact, in the warm summer waters off the coast of St. Petersburg. Getting on again had been a production and another reason I'd ruled out more of the same in my future.

I was turning faster now, and as I turned, I throttled down. I nearly swiped the side of the boat, which was rocking wildly, but I stopped just in time.

I cut the engine. "Where's Hildy?"

Marie was facing me, barred from the edge by a cushioned bench that ran along the front and part of the side. I saw she was holding a gun, and now I knew why she'd cut her engine, too.

The better to aim at you, my dear.

Gun. Why hadn't I thought of a gun? Because none had been used in either murder? They were too personal, too immediate. She'd poisoned her ex-lover and hit an old woman with her car, leaving Ellen for dead on the road. But why hadn't I considered how she'd gotten Hildy into the boat?

Because now I could see that Hildy *was* in the boat. Gagged and trussed from the knees up like a suckling pig and lying on the floor, feet flailing.

"You *could* shoot me," I said, guessing Marie wouldn't. "I mean, what are a few extra dead on your hit list, even though shooting people is just so messy? But, so you know, the cops are on their way, and my friend waiting on the dock is good buddies with Grayson Adams. Anything happens to me, he'll take it personally."

"You really do stick your nose everywhere it's not wanted, don't you?" She held the gun out, but I saw how unsteady her hand was. I took heart.

"Here's what's going to happen," I said sounding surprisingly calm. "Unless you toss that gun, I'm going to start my engine, whip around, and ram this boat with all I've

412

got. You can shoot as many times as you like, but it's unlikely you'll hit me."

"You don't think so?" She held out her wavering hand, gun pointed more or less in my direction. "Besides, we'd all go in, and Hildy can't really swim right now, can she?"

"We'll take our chances. Don't forget it would be sink or swim for you, too. Just drop the gun, okay? Everything's over anyway."

"I'll shoot *her!*" She lowered the gun toward the bottom of the boat.

"You do, and you'll blow the boat full of holes and the whole thing will sink."

She swung her arm around and aimed in my direction again. Then she lurched a step toward the stern and Hildy.

I tried to start the engine before my final few words, but what had worked so well wasn't working now. The motor coughed and sputtered. Frantically I tried the throttle again. Marie was closer now, turning, the wavering hand with the gun pointed in my direction. I knew I could try to launch myself at her, although it would be a clumsy attempt, most likely ending with me in the water sandwiched between the boat and the Jet Ski. But I had to do something, and the Jet Ski was no longer cooperating.

"Having prob—" Marie screeched, then

413

she went down on her knees. Just like that. One minute she'd been leaning toward me, and the next she was pitching forward, one arm thrown over the side.

I took advantage of the situation, swung a leg over the Jet Ski, and threw myself toward the boat, aiming for the closest pole. I just managed to grab hold before the Jet Ski flopped away and left me dangling. Geoff's little boat was rocking demonically. I had to get inside, or it would capsize, then Hildy really would go down, Hildy who was now kicking out at Marie again, having already landed at least one blow that had knocked the woman to her knees.

I had a leg over the side and was swinging around to get both feet on board when Marie pushed off the edge and stood. She had dropped the gun when she fell, and no sooner was she on her feet than she was searching for it. Hildy kicked again, and the gun skidded toward the bow. Marie dove for it, but as I swung onto the boat I stuck a leg out just in time to trip her.

She scrambled to her knees, then her feet. She moved forward, as if to push me aside, then her shoulders sagged. I could see she was looking beyond me. I dared one quick glance. A brightly lit boat was speeding in our direction with several figures standing in the bow.

The lake patrol. I'd never been more grateful. I edged backwards toward the gun, just in case Marie was spooked into trying to take everyone with her.

I squatted, gaze still fixed on her face, and felt behind me. My fingers closed on the barrel. I lifted the gun in one swift movement and tossed it over the side.

Then I stood, hands out and arms extended in front of me, just in case, but there was no need. We could hear shouts from the lake patrol, and their directive was clear. Marie slowly raised her hands above her head, and so did I, for good measure.

21

Teddy wasn't the least bit nervous. She had memorized her speech and practiced every inflection. Deena had gotten into the act, giving her some pointers she had picked up from her stint on the debate team. I wondered how much time my oldest would have for tutoring her sister in the coming years. She was now a middle school graduate, and soon enough she would be a working woman. She had snagged a job waiting on customers and making sandwiches at Ahmed's Deli for the summer. I was hoping for a discount on falafel.

Teddy, of course, had no job, but she did have a speaking engagement. She was the token child at a rally on the Oval to promote a pedestrian mall for downtown Emerald Springs. The cause was futile, but the day was lovely and lots of people had turned out. To her credit, Ida Bere had done an admirable job of organizing. Clowns strolled through the audience bestowing balloons with "See Emerald Springs on Foot" printed on them. At booths and tables along the edges local businesses sold their signature wares, and a restaurant grilled hot dogs and popped corn. I'd seen a number of members of our church. Ida was in charge; they were terrified not to show up. Ed was off somewhere chatting and shaking hands. I'd nearly run into Samuel Booth, who hadn't, to his credit, disappeared back into the crowd to avoid me. Maybe he was starting to believe I was not going to share his secret. I hoped so.

My mother had come back from her trip to the West Coast just in time to join us, and now we were standing in the middle of the crowd, waiting for Teddy to speak. My daughter was scheduled after a performance by a local oldies "rock" band that had, so far, performed "These Boots Are Made for Walking," "Walk on By," and "Under the Boardwalk." I thought the last might be a clue that the theme had been milked for all it was worth, and Teddy would be next.

Not so. The band, made up of three men and a woman, all pushing sixty, swung into "Walk a Mile in My Shoes." Teddy didn't seem to mind.

I had been in the middle of telling Junie

some good news, so I finished. "And so, Grace Forester has asked me to bake bread when she needs it for Emerald Excellence. She was so glad I helped catch Win Dorchester's murderer, and so impressed with the loaf I served her, she offered me an exclusive contract. So it looks like I'll be employed again," I finished. "Part-time, though it may be."

"I can't believe all this happened while I was away," Junie said. I had already filled her in on the rescue of Hildy Dorchester and subsequent arrest of Marie Grandower. "At least baking bread won't require any spectacular rescues."

"It *was* quite an event," I said modestly, although I thought that for sheer drama, I would *never* be able to top my Jet Ski rescue of poor, trussed Hildy.

"And Mrs. Dorchester is okay?" Junie's as maternal as she is flighty. Although she'd yet to meet Hildy, Junie already wanted to take her under her wing. That was something I hoped never to witness.

"She's fine," I said. "And relieved, of course, that the real murderer was caught and nobody suspects her anymore."

"But why would this Grandower woman do such a thing? She had so much. Why couldn't she see that?"

Junie's so good at finding the best in people, that someone like Marie Grandower is completely alien to her. She's incapable of imagining that kind of anger or greed.

I tried to explain. "Her husband was wealthy, but unbeknownst to anyone, Marie had a serious gambling problem. When he died unexpectedly — which they're now investigating, by the way — he left her more than comfortable. Unfortunately, after a couple of long vacations in Las Vegas and Atlantic City, she had nothing much left except her house here in town, and their vacation home in Hilton Head."

"That sounds like an awful lot in a world where some people have no roof over their heads."

I nodded for solidarity and went on. "When Daisy Dreyfus died and left her insurance money to the church, Marie was chairing our endowment committee."

Churches remain mysteries to my mother, who can't imagine why anyone feels a need for a building in which to worship. "And these committees do what?" she asked.

"They invest and manage the money that's been given to or left to the church. We have a substantial endowment, because the church has been here so long. Marie got appointed to several committees when Win

Dorchester was the minister, most likely to have more contact with him, although now we have a professional auditing our books to see if she was stealing from the endowment before she stole the insurance money. Things were in disarray after Win left so suddenly, and Geoff Adler, who was still the treasurer, was working furiously to keep Emerald Eagle afloat. Because he was so busy, Marie volunteered to help him. She'd pick up the mail in his folder, for instance. Which is probably how she found out about the insurance. And because of her work on the endowment committee, she was able to forge the papers needed to get the money, then wash the check in and out of our investment accounts without anyone paying attention."

"And you say the total was nearly half a million dollars?"

That part still hurt. Marie had stolen $375,000 from the church, a staggering amount for a budget like ours. The chances we would ever recover it were slim, because Marie's gambling had never ended. Sadly she hadn't put her house in Emerald Estates up for sale because she wanted to live permanently in Hilton Head. Her South Carolina house, too, was on the market. She had debts again, huge ones, and not much else.

"It's all such a shame," Junie said. "But you caught her. You should be proud."

"I'm not all that proud. I nearly blew it. I was sure the murderer was somebody else."

Geoff Adler had been more shocked than anyone to learn that Marie killed Win Dorchester and probably Ellen Hardiger, although Marie had yet to confess to that death. Geoff had also been shocked to learn that he had been my top suspect.

Last week he and I had met at Give Me a Break, our local coffee meet and greet, to hash out the details over lattes.

"A number of things pointed to you," I'd told him after some tense preliminaries. "First, you lied when you said you didn't find out until recently that Marie and Win were lovers."

To his credit, Geoff had blushed. "I shouldn't have lied. If the police had asked, I would have told them the truth. But let's face it, you weren't asking in an official capacity."

I ignored the affront to my dignity. "Why did you lie?"

"I thought I was just acting like a loyal friend. All those years ago Marie asked me not to tell anybody. After Win left she was afraid people would find out about the affair and think she was a tramp. When it came up again, I didn't want anybody to think she'd bragged about it."

"Not just a loyal friend." I looked down at my cup, to eliminate some of the pressure on him. "You were in love with her, weren't you? Maybe you still are?"

He didn't answer. I gave him a few seconds, then I looked up. The truth was in his eyes, as well as embarrassment.

"It clouded your judgment," I said.

"Seriously."

"And the bit about Win having multiple affairs?"

"Protecting her again, I guess. I wanted to blame their affair entirely on him. I guess I even convinced myself what I told you was true, that he'd seduced her and she was just one of many. Win did have an eye for women. He liked to talk about them, man to man. I expanded those conversations in my head, I suppose, to make Marie less responsible. I don't know if he had other affairs or he didn't. I don't want to know."

I didn't either. Furthermore, I believed Geoff, even while I found his loyalty to Marie puzzling. But people in love do the oddest things. Look how many times Zoey told herself her husband would stop beating her,

422

before she finally realized she had to leave him for good.

"Why did you bring her to the party that night?" I asked. "Knowing what you did about their past?"

"Marie heard about the party at church on the Sunday Win spoke, and she told me she wanted to go. She said she wanted to hold her head high and show Win she had moved on without him. I was delighted. I thought if she was finally over him, maybe she was ready for the two of us to be more than friends."

"And you weren't worried about her causing a scene?"

Before he responded I could see him going back over that awful night. "I'm a take-charge guy," he said at last. "I guess I thought I could get her out of there if I needed to. I didn't count on her having so much to drink there was no reasoning with her."

"Except that she probably wasn't even tipsy, Geoff. She was pretending to be, so she could act like she was leaving, then sneak back in through the kitchen door and load the dip with the pills she'd taken off Win's nightstand. Then she went back outside and waited. She'd already told you she was going to demand a chat with Win.

She figured if she lingered in the side yard for a private conversation with him, you would ask him to go out and talk to her. She had already worked out a way to be sure Hildy saw them together, in case later the police suspected murder. She wanted an angry scene with Hildy, so she made sure she got one."

"How could she do that?"

"She made sure the telephone rang at the right moment, so Hildy would most likely answer it in the hallway and glimpse them together. Marie called a friend across town, when she knew Win was probably on his way outside, then she asked the friend to call her back. She pretended she was having problems with her cell phone, so she gave the woman the Dorchesters' phone number. At the same time she warned her the number might not be correct, so if Marie didn't answer herself, the friend should just hang up."

"All because he was so standoffish with her that night?" Geoff asked.

"No. Not at all." That was the part, of course, that all of us had missed. Neither love nor sex had been factors in this murder.

"Marie probably *was* over Win, if she was ever in love with him in the first place," I said. "Frankly, I think he was a distraction.

She liked to gamble. She liked to take chances. She went after him the way she probably went after the jackpot in Atlantic City, and she won, at least until Win woke up and realized he loved his wife and family. Most likely Marie was annoyed, but I'm sure she got over that quickly. No, she killed him because after he talked to Ellen Hardiger at his anniversary sermon and discovered Daisy Dreyfus had left Russell House a boatload of money, Win cornered Marie and asked if Daisy had left anything to *our* endowment. He remembered that Marie had chaired the committee, a three-year commitment, and he assumed she would be the one to know. When she said nobody named Daisy Dreyfus had left the church anything, he must have gotten suspicious. Maybe from the way she answered? Maybe the look on her face? Whatever it was, he started asking questions. Marie knew him well enough to be sure he would ask, and if he asked too many, her theft would be discovered. So she had to take care of him quickly. Ellen was probably an afterthought."

"How do you know all that?"

Because my best friend was in love with the police chief, a man who liked to talk about his work? I couldn't tell Geoff that part.

"Because she was proud of herself," I said truthfully, "and defiant. Once she knew she was going to go down for this murder, she bragged about why she did it. Before her lawyer got hold of her, of course."

"And to think all I worried about was whether she still loved Win or had really gotten over him and was ready to turn to me."

If Geoff was going to move on, the truth seemed important, if somewhat brutal. I delivered it gently. "Keeping Win in the picture was a good way to keep you at bay, wasn't it? Your friendship was convenient, but she didn't want complications. She didn't need or want a lover who would try to control her gambling. You can be glad you're a take-charge guy, the kind who would never put up with losing all your money after you'd worked so hard for it, and she knew it."

He didn't look stricken. I think Geoff had figured that out on his own.

"Just one other thing," I said after we'd both nearly finished our coffee. "The one important element I haven't been able to figure out? It doesn't bother the police, since Marie has already confessed, but it does bother me. Why did she call the coroner and insist on an autopsy? She nearly got away with murder. If she hadn't demanded the autopsy, she might have. That was why she was never much of a suspect, at least not until everything else fell into place."

"Yeah, I can answer that. For the very reason you just said. She did it because she thought nobody would question her innocence if she was the one who insisted on an autopsy."

"Something's missing there."

"Me, I'm afraid. *I'm* missing. Because I'm the one who brought up the possibility Win had been murdered in the first place. I'm the one who mentioned it to her and told her I was tempted to talk to the coroner myself."

"Oh, wow."

"Win was doing so much better," Geoff explained. "He'd told me he was eating right, taking it easy the way he was supposed to. And his meds had finally been stabilized. I'm a pharmacist, remember, and he got his prescriptions from Emerald Eagle. I wondered if maybe somebody at our store had made an error. So after Win died, I asked Hildy to check his medication. She read me the dosage on the phone and described the pills. I was relieved we'd given him the right strength, but then she mentioned how many were left from his last refill. And the amount was a lot less than I'd expected. I wouldn't have been surprised to find more, because there might have been a few left over from another bottle that he took first, but I never expected so *many* to be gone."

"And you mentioned that to Marie?"

"I wondered out loud if I ought to tell the police or the coroner."

"So Marie told them first. That way there was a better chance no one would question her innocence."

Geoff nodded sadly. "At the time I thought she was just afraid I wouldn't come forward, and Win would be buried without an autopsy. All the time it was really just the opposite. She was afraid I would."

When we'd finally parted on the sidewalk in front of Give Me a Break, Geoff had looked forlorn. This afternoon, standing in the crowd listening to the final verse of "Walk a Mile in My Shoes," I was glad I didn't have to walk in Geoff's. Still, he had been duped by the woman he loved, but he would survive. Win Dorchester and Ellen Hardiger had not, and Hildy had nearly joined them. Even Daisy Dreyfus, whose generous bequest had ended up on roulette tables, was Marie's victim.

I noticed Hildy at the edge of the crowd and I waved. I figured the next moments would be historic. The two women who most loved to mother me, present in the same place at the same time. I was afraid to predict what might happen.

Junie is short, rounded, and blonde. So is Hildy. I wondered why I'd never before noted the similarities. They hugged like sisters. With a sinking heart, I wondered what was in store for my future.

From the podium Ida Bere motioned for Teddy. Junie said she'd escort her to the front, and I watched them go.

"She's so nice," Hildy said, "but I wouldn't have expected otherwise."

I slipped my arm around her waist. Hildy had been busy, and so had I. And maybe both of us had needed some space after the events at Lake Parsons. Whatever the reason, I hadn't seen her in a week.

"How are you?" I asked.

"Busy. I'm packing."

I drew back. "Really? You're going on a trip?"

"For now. John's asked me to visit him in Arizona."

"John Hammond?"

"He thinks I need to get away from Emerald Springs, and I think he's right. I'm not sure where I'll end up permanently, but it won't be here."

I was stunned, as much at my own sense of loss as at the revelation. "You don't want to stay here?"

"No, too many memories. I need a fresh start. John says I'll love the Southwest. Win never had a church there, so it will be exciting to be somewhere completely new. And closer to my girls."

I hoped her girls appreciated that.

Ed came over to join us. Maybe everybody was just grateful that the band had finished, because there was a lull just in time for Teddy to take the microphone. Ida announced that now someone with a huge stake in the future of Emerald Springs would speak to them, and she adjusted the mic.

Teddy looked darling in a peach-colored skirt and flowered knit shirt. She also looked as serene as a spring morning.

I listened to the familiar words. She was good, this daughter of ours. The lull actually continued, and I could hear her clearly.

I grabbed Ed's hand, and he squeezed in return. Deena poked me, but she was smiling.

We listened, then we applauded.

I knew my mother would be right there by the steps waiting, so I let Junie retrieve our star.

As they threaded their way toward us, people patted Teddy on the shoulder and smiled at her. That's when I realized that Fern Booth had stationed herself in Teddy's path. She wasn't smiling, and in the bright afternoon sunlight, she looked older and even more ominous than usual.

I wanted to protect my child, but it was too late. I watched as they exchanged a few words, then Teddy continued slowly toward us.

"I'll find her later and congratulate her," Hildy said. "When she's not swamped with people."

We moved away from the others a bit for privacy. "You'll come see us before you go? I have something to show you, and you don't want to miss it."

"I wouldn't dream of leaving without saying good-bye. We'll be friends forever. And I'll always think of you right here, doing a job that's so badly needed, and doing it well."

This was high praise indeed coming from Hildy. "Being the minister's wife?"

"Oh, that, too. Look how you took care of me? The way you reached out every way you

431

could after Win's death. I owe you so much, even my life, and who could ask for more from anyone? But what I meant? The job of being Aggie Sloan-Wilcox. No one could ever do that better."

I felt tears rising, and I figured when Hildy saw my new floor, she would realize how I felt about her, too. Because, after unsuccessfully attempting to order one floor, then another, I'd finally taken a look at the one Hildy had ordered for me. Black and white squares made from an easy-care laminate, and not yet returned to the manufacturer. I'd felt an emotional pull that could not be denied. The tiles were now nestled comfortably together in my kitchen. Right at home.

One hug later Hildy strolled off to talk to Sally and Yvonne, and Deena went to head off her sister and tell her how well she had done.

I rejoined Ed and cleared my throat. "John Hammond's asked Hildy to visit him. Did you know anything about that?"

"John's smitten with her, Aggie. You never picked up on that?"

"Hildy?"

"I'm sure some time will pass before anything comes of it, but they'd be perfect for each other. And then she can do what she loves most of all."

Be a minister's wife one more time. Better yet? Be Hildy.

I couldn't help but smile.

Teddy arrived, and Ed hugged her before I did. After a moment he was called off again, and Teddy and I were alone.

"Everybody loved your talk," I said.

"It was fun."

Teddy didn't seem unhappy. I thought it might be safe to pry. "I'm curious, what did Mrs. Booth say to you?" I asked, as nonchalantly as I could.

"The lady in blue?"

I looked up and saw that Fern was watching us. She was indeed wearing blue. "Uh-huh," I said, looking away.

"She said I was a very good speaker, and that if I worked really hard, someday I might even be as good as Daddy."

For once I had absolutely no idea how to reply. I looked up again, and Fern nodded at me, then she actually smiled before she turned away.

"Do you think it's true?" Teddy asked.

True? I really don't know. Truth is a slippery concept. After everything that had happened in the past weeks, that was the only thing I felt sure of.

"I think you can be anything you want to be," I told her. "And you have a lot of time

433

to decide."

"I might want to study gorillas."

I hugged my daughter all over again as the next speaker made his way to the podium. Like Teddy, the young man was here on our Oval to promote a hopeless cause. But what do any of us know about the future? Truth is, I'm wrong as often as I'm right.

I gave up predictions and settled in to enjoy our beautiful spring day.

ABOUT THE AUTHOR

Emilie Richards is the *USA Today* best-selling author of more than fifty novels. She has received a number of awards during her career, including the RITA from Romance Writers of America and several from *Romantic Times* magazine, including a career achievement award. She has been interviewed on both television and radio, including stints as a guest on the *Leeza* show and *Hard Copy.* Visit her website at www.ministryismurder.com.

The employees of Thorndike Press hope you have enjoyed this Large Print book. All our Thorndike, Wheeler, and Kennebec Large Print titles are designed for easy reading, and all our books are made to last. Other Thorndike Press Large Print books are available at your library, through selected bookstores, or directly from us.

For information about titles, please call:
 (800) 223-1244

or visit our Web site at:
 http://gale.cengage.com/thorndike

To share your comments, please write:
Publisher
Thorndike Press
295 Kennedy Memorial Drive
Waterville, ME 04901